The Jackson MacKenzie Chronicles

TORN HORIZONS

By
Angel Giacomo

1st Battalion
Publishing

Copyright ©

DISCLAIMER-FICTION

Other than actual historical events and public figures, all characters and incidents portrayed in this novel are fictitious. Any resemblance to actual persons, living or dead, is purely coincidental.

DEDICATION

This book is dedicated to all who have served in every branch of the military. I write it with extreme humility. It is to honor the veterans of the United States who fought in our conflicts, both past, present, and future.

 "The soldier above all others prays for peace, for it is the soldier who must suffer and bear the deepest wounds and scars of war." - General Douglas MacArthur

"Courage is not having the strength to go on; it is going on when you don't have the strength." -Theodore Roosevelt

"We make a living by what we get, but we make a life by what we give." - Winston Churchill

"If you want others to be happy, practice compassion. If you want to be happy, practice compassion." - Dalai Lama

"Wherever the art of Medicine is loved, there is also a love of Humanity." - Hippocrates

ACKNOWLEDGMENT

Thank you to those who have believed in me.

Thank you to Dr. Russell W. Ramsey – Lt. Colonel, U.S. Army (retired) USMA 1957 – 8th Regiment, 1st Cavalry Division –Vietnam – 1965-66, for being my friend. Hooah! Go Army! Beat Navy!

A special thank you goes to Dr. Gus Kappler, MD – Major, US Army – 85th Evacuation Hospital, Phu Bai, South Vietnam – 1970-71. Author of One Degree, An Historical Medical Mystery, and Welcome Home from Vietnam, Finally.

CHAPTER 1

February 10, 1971
2155 Hours
95th Evacuation Hospital
Da Nang, South Vietnam

"Doctor Howard, wake up." The loud female voice seemed to come from far away.

Franklin Howard, Frank to his friends, turned over on the bottom half of a blanket-covered twin bunk, sat up, swung his legs over the edge, pushed away the mosquito netting, and rubbed his tired eyes.

He'd just lain down after a long twenty-four-hour shift in surgery but couldn't sleep. Visions of bloody men, screaming in agony with missing limbs and grievous traumatic injuries, some fatal, some not, and some in-between, stacked like cordwood in the halls outside the operating room, kept him awake.

The medivac choppers were instructed to overfly them to alternative evacuation hospitals if the surgical backlog exceeded sixteen hours. Sometimes he wondered if that actually happened when the hallway became a maze of gurneys and blood.

"Yeah," Frank said, staring at the slender nurse standing in the open doorway. Her faded OD-green ripstop cotton jungle fatigues had dark spots from bloodstains that would never come out. Light filtered around her into the darkened room, shining down on him, making dancing spots appear before his eyes until they adjusted.

This room doubled as sleeping quarters and a supply closet. He felt like a first-year resident again, napping when he caught a short break. Around him sat stacks of boxes and sparsely loaded shelving. There wasn't much storage space inside these prefab corrugated steel Quonset-style buildings, so they had to make do.

Dust floated in the air above the damp stained concrete floor, stirred around by the overhead exhaust fans. The floor never completely dried, being hosed off constantly to remove the coating of blood from the wounded, dying, and the dead.

"Sorry to disturb you, Major," Nurse Cathy Alexander said, her red-haired ponytail flopping as she turned to point toward the ICU. "That

1

Special Forces officer you worked on earlier, Major Landry, the one with half his skull gone, opened his eyes."

Frank felt hope rise in his heart. Jake Landry was his undergraduate roommate at Pensacola State College. They had a lot of good times together, chasing girls, tanning on the beach, and surfing in the bay. While he pursued a medical degree at Florida State University, Jake, so much smarter than him, graduated with honors and a Master's degree in Physics from MIT.

Why Jake decided to join the Army or the Special Forces after graduation, Frank had no idea. The man had a bright future ahead of him as a scientist. Maybe even an astronaut. The only reason Frank could come up with, the same as his for joining the Army, to serve his country and pay off his student loans. Or maybe it was a stepping stone into NASA. They seemed to gravitate toward those in the military.

"Thanks, Cathy. Anything else?" Frank stood and stretched then grabbed his fatigue shirt hanging on a chair and put it on. His shirt looked like Cathy's, faded, tattered, and stained. Too much blood and too many washings. He covered it up with his somewhat white, wrinkled lab coat. The evidence of being in Vietnam too long - or being a "short-timer." For him, it was the former, even though he'd only been here a couple of months. But it already felt like years after the Army revoked his TDY status, ordering him to complete a year-long tour at the 95th Evacuation Hospital.

"No, sir." Cathy yawned, walking beside Frank down the hall. "Just wanted you to know. Did you get any sleep?"

Frank looked at his watch. 0300 hours. He'd been in bed for less than an hour. "No. As a captain, you've got seniority on most of the other nurses, Cathy, and you're a short-timer with three months left over here. Why do you work the night shift?"

Cathy smiled. "It's quiet and gives me a chance to study."

"For what?" Frank opened the door to the ICU and followed her inside.

"Medical school."

"Have you been accepted?"

Cathy pulled a medical chart from the holder at the central desk, handed it to Frank then smiled. "Yes, I start at Baylor in the fall. I was accepted last year, but when my transfer to the hospital at Fort Hood fell through, they put me in this year's class. Could you keep it under wraps? Please. I don't want special treatment." She looked around. "Or a party. I want to finish up my time here and go home without any fanfare."

"Well, congratulations. And I won't tell anyone."

2

"Thanks." Cathy nodded at the bed. "Go see your friend."

In the dingy sea green-walled, noisy, brightly lit Recovery Room/ICU, Frank looked at the chart. All of Jake's vital signs had stabilized. He sat in the chair next to the bed. Jake's face was barely visible under the large swath of white gauze bandages. They wouldn't put in a metal plate to replace the missing part of his skull until the brain swelling had subsided. Around the time he reached Tachikawa Army Hospital in Japan.

While Jake's glazed bloodshot brown eyes were open, they showed no sign of recognition. Nearby, the ventilator whooshed and thumped as it pushed air into Jake's lungs. All he did was breathe and look straight ahead. Right now, the only things keeping him alive were the endotracheal tube, blood transfusions, and IV lines.

Frank considered if Jake really should have been KIA instead. He knew from experience his friend, while alive, probably wouldn't have much of a life. All he would do was sit in a wheelchair in a nursing home, staring out a window with his meals going into his stomach through a tube in his nose. What was life without communication?

Frank removed his penlight from his lab coat pocket and checked Jake's pupil reaction. Sluggish at best. But there was some movement and maybe brain activity. He grabbed Jake's limp hand and squeezed, hoping for a return squeeze, something to say his friend was still there. "Hey, Jake." Nothing. The hand remained limp weight, cold and clammy, even in the humid warmth of the room. All he could do now was pray for a miracle. They did sometimes happen.

Frank lifted his head from next to Jake's when someone shook his shoulder. He looked up into Cathy's green eyes and beautiful smile. "Huh? What time is it?"

"It's 0555." Cathy tapped the face of her wristwatch.

Shift change. Frank straightened in his chair. "What happened?"

"You fell asleep, and I didn't want to disturb you. You're exhausted and needed the rest. He—" Cathy pointed at Jake. "Closed his eyes about the same time and seemed much more comfortable. Do you want to have breakfast with me before I hit the rack?" Cathy chuckled. "Such as it is…powdered eggs, watered-down coffee, and burned pancakes."

Frank thought about it for a few seconds. Like her, he was hungry and would grab a few more hours of sleep in his quarters. At least, according to the duty roster, he wasn't back on shift until tomorrow unless they got another influx of wounded. "Sure." And he wanted to know more about her plans. What kind of doctor she wanted to be. She was already one hell of a surgical nurse. Professional, kind, compassionate, and caring.

He'd heard about the young Special Forces Lt. Colonel, Jackson somebody, a man given a twenty percent chance of survival due to malnutrition and his severe injuries after escaping from a POW camp. Many of those still assigned here credited her with helping to save his life, both physically and mentally. He didn't know the particulars, but that opinion among so many said a lot. One day he knew she would be an exceptional physician. He pictured her as a pediatrician.

CHAPTER 2

The runny, rehydrated powdered eggs turned Frank's stomach. Applying a thick coating of ketchup didn't help. Only one thing tasted decent, the bowl of multicolored sliced fruit submerged in heavy sugary syrup. It was hard for the mess cooks to screw up opening a can, but he was sure they could find a way if possible.

Frank pushed his half-eaten meal aside, picked up his coffee cup, and leaned back in his chair, careful not to tip over backward. He didn't want to look like a klutz in front of Cathy, who sat across the table from him. That would give her pause in his abilities as a surgeon. Even though by this time, he'd surely proven himself.

The coffee was exactly like she described earlier…weak, probably brewed using two-day-old coffee grounds. Supplies sometimes were almost nonexistent. The few that arrived were picked over rejects by other units on their way up from the 14th Inventory Control Company.

"So, what are your plans?" Frank asked.

Cathy looked askance at him. "Could you clarify what you mean by that, please…Frank?"

Uh-oh, she thinks I mean something else. "Ahh…sure. Do you have a medical specialty in mind?"

"Yes, surgeon, maybe specializing in emergency medicine. I haven't decided yet. Why do you ask?"

Guess I'm wrong on the pediatrician part. She still has time to change her mind. I bet she wants kids, but I'm not going to ask and get my teeth knocked in. "Just curious."

"Okay, you've asked me questions, my turn."

"Shoot. Ask as many as you want. I'm an open book." Frank placed his chair back on the floor and set his empty ceramic mug on the yellowed plastic-covered folding table.

"Okay." Cathy imitated the Heisman Trophy pose, holding the salt shaker like a football. "Are you going to play on the flag football team?

We need a wide receiver. There's a hospital league. We have a running bet with the 85th about who provides the steaks for the victory party."

"Hell no. I've never played football. I'd look like a gangly ass fool tripping over my two left feet. But a good steak after the tough-as-shoe leather mystery meat of the day here sounds terrific. I'll root for us from the stands and take care of the abrasions, sprains, and strains afterward."

Cathy smiled. "What's your middle name?"

"Kevin, why?"

"You're an open book, remember."

Frank nodded. "I did say that. Keep going."

"Is there a reason why you have that old-fashioned pencil mustache and slicked-back short hair?"

Frank smoothed his mustache. "Old fashioned?"

"Yeah." Cathy ran her hand over the top of her head. "How do you keep it so nice?"

"Brylcreem. I like Clark Gable. Mom made me watch *Gone with the Wind* like a hundred times."

"Makes sense. And you do kind of look like him. Now for the serious one. Why did you become a doctor? With those good looks and fabulous smile, you could've given Hollywood a shot."

"Well, hmmm…acting isn't in my wheelhouse. I hated school plays. As for becoming a doctor, because of my father, I guess. He was a doctor at a Philadelphia hospital, and I used to go with him on his rounds during summer break. Kinda like a male candy striper without the uniform. I caught the bug from him. They were proud of me for continuing in Dad's footsteps. You?"

"I'll be the first in my family. My father works for King Ranch in Texas as a ranch hand breaking horses and working cattle. Mom teaches elementary school. I loved science class growing up, so I went to nursing school. The one thing I didn't want to do after college was become a teacher."

"What do they think of you being over here?"

"In Vietnam?" Cathy asked.

"Yes," Frank replied.

"They support me. My father and grandfather both served in the Army. My brother is in the Army now. He's currently stateside at Fort Benning after finishing his year in 'Nam. It's a family tradition to serve. Since you asked, Major, what does your family think?"

Frank shrugged. "Don't know. I'm not married and don't have any kids. Dad and Mom smoked a lot. They both died of lung cancer while I was in medical school. I'd like to think they would've supported my decision to volunteer instead of being drafted like the other surgical residents. I wanted to serve and save lives. But Mom was a pacifist at heart. She always thought the US should keep its nose out of other people's business. Even during World War II. She wanted us to stay neutral after Pearl Harbor. Dad loved her, so he kept his opinions to himself. Mom might've spit on me then locked the front door instead of welcoming me home with hugs and kisses. It seems to be the current trend among the war haters, flower children, peaceniks, and long-haired hippies."

Cathy cocked her head. "You're not getting out when your contract is up?"

"Nah, at least not at this time of my life. I'm an only child, so I've got nothing else. Where would I go? A big-city hospital patching up gunshot wounds? I can practice medicine in the Army and get that plus more. Who else will pay for my room and board?"

"Frank, you know, that's so sad."

Frank laughed, not because it was funny but because it was true. "I agree."

Cathy gripped his hand from across the table. "Then maybe you should change that...but not with me."

"My, my, Cathy. Do you have a boyfriend around here?"

"Here, no." Cathy smiled as if she had a secret. "And he's not my boyfriend. Not really even a friend. Just someone I admire. But you never know."

A corporal ran up to them and saluted. "Sir, ma'am."

Frank casually returned the salute. "Is there a problem?"

"We have incoming wounded, sir."

"Understood." Frank looked at Cathy. "You heard the man. Go get your people ready for another tumble in the washing machine."

Cathy saluted. "Yes, doctor." She hurried off toward the hospital.

Frank pushed himself out of his chair. So much for getting some sleep.

CHAPTER 3

1200 Hours
February 12, 1971
95th Evacuation Hospital
Da Nang, South Vietnam

Subdued and in a bit of a funk, Frank watched the OD-green, dust-covered ambulance leave the hospital compound carrying his severely wounded friend, Jake Landry. It was headed to the airfield and the C-130 en route to Tachikawa Army Hospital in Japan. He could picture in great detail what would happen next.

The surgeons would reopen the incision on Jake's scalp and substitute a metal plate for the bone removed from his skull. A surgical technique called a cranioplasty. After recuperating from that operation and stable, he'd be transferred back to the "world" and admitted to an Army hospital in the states. His recovery was still in doubt, up to the specialists to find out if Jake had any brain activity at all or was just a breathing vegetable.

Other than opening his eyes, Jake had no other reactions since that day.

Frank stood in the middle of the road until the ambulance disappeared from view, past the defensive perimeter made of concertina wire, bright lights, and manned guard towers. Now all he could do was hope and pray.

"Are you okay, Frank?" Cathy asked from behind him.

Frank wiped his eyes before facing her. He didn't want her thinking he was a wuss. "Yeah, I'm good."

Cathy smiled, tucking a thick manila folder under her arm. "You know men can cry, right?"

Frank rolled his eyes. "It's that obvious?"

"Yes."

He turned his attention to the folder she carried. "What's that?"

"Huh?"

Frank pointed at her. "Under your arm, that folder looks like it contains medical records."

Cathy held up the folder. "It does. We got a forwarding request from the Pentagon for these. I'm heading over to headquarters to put it in the outgoing mail."

"What patient?"

"Not one of yours. He was a patient of Dr. McKay's and released before you got here."

"Okay. Wonder why the Pentagon wants it." *Must be something big.*

Cathy shrugged. "Who knows? I'm just following orders. I'll catch you later." She headed toward the headquarters building.

Frank stuck his hands in his pockets. He trudged past the rarely hot communal showers building, six showerheads protruding from a white-painted plywood wall over a rough moldy concrete slab. It reminded him of his high school PE class, only with even less privacy.

Then came the two-or-three-holed partially-covered outdoor latrines. Crapping outside left something to be desired during the monsoon season. Frank hated peeing and getting drenched at the same time. The hovering flies were so big they could carry you off. Heaven help the poor guy on waste disposal duty, burning barrels of liquid shit with copious amounts of gasoline and diesel fuel, fouling the sky with a fetid, sticky, dense, black smoke.

The rest of the camp was made of small and large steel Quonset huts and elevated plywood buildings covered by corrugated metal roofs. The chapel, armory, motor pool, pathology lab, blood bank, mess hall, living quarters - separated by rank, station, and sex, all protected by sandbags and six-foot corrugated steel sand-filled abutments, there to stop rocket and mortar fragments. Not that they helped much.

The 95th Evacuation Hospital sat on a jetty of land near Da Nang, known as the Son Tra Peninsula. The hospital was a referral center for complex cases in the region. Neurology, dermatology, special radiologic procedures, oral surgery, psychiatric consultations, orthopedic surgery, neuro-surgery, and general surgery were all available here.

To the north of them, Monkey Mountain, and to the south, directly on the other side of the concertina wire and guard towers, the South China Sea, its waves lapping on a white sand beach. Other than the hospital, the most important buildings, the ones that provided everyone a needed diversion, were the enlisted and officers' clubs. Behind them, an improvised BBQ made from a 55-gallon fuel drum half with welded-on steel pipe legs. Next to it, an old C-130 rubber fuel bladder filled with water that doubled as a pool during their off-duty hours. The roof was their diving board.

He stopped at the officers' club. What he needed right now was a stiff drink, even the nasty local stuff, a rock gut concoction - Mekong Moonshine, otherwise known as Rượu đế, a usually clear, but sometimes cloudy distilled liquor made from rice. It was quite comparable in potency to American moonshine at forty percent alcohol by volume. Enough to knock you on your ass quickly.

Before he could open the door, the thump-thump-thump of incoming choppers sounded in the distance. Known as "dust offs," – UH-1s called "Hueys" were carrying inbound wounded.

"Shit!" He'd get the drink later. A swig or two from the whiskey bottle hidden in his worn-out footlocker while reclining in the chair he found in the trash. Well, after some sleep in his rusted cot frame and thin, ratty mattress covered with mosquito netting in what passed for his quarters – one of those plywood buildings – ten by ten feet. Not much larger than a jail cell. It sure felt like one. His metal roof leaked like a sieve when it rained. And it did that a lot during monsoon season.

Frank ran toward the hospital helipad, a large expanse of black square asphalt with two helicopter landing sites and emblazoned in the center with a red cross. The red cross told everyone this was a hospital. Not that Charlie cared. Next to the asphalt, an orange windsock on a pole fluttered in the light breeze. Parked next to the pad, several filthy OD-green box ambulances and one identically colored bus marked on both sides with a red cross on a white square.

Cathy joined Frank at the helipad a few seconds later with several other nurses, corpsmen, and hospital workers. As they waited for the chopper to land, Frank caught a whiff of decaying shit, driven by the wind. The local fertilizer for the area rice paddies and vegetable gardens. And he wanted to drink something made with rice. If it made him forget for a few minutes, so be it.

Above them, the chopper transitioned from forward flight into a hover and descended. Everyone braced themselves and covered their eyes with their arms to protect them from the dirt driven by the rotor wash.

Once the powered arc of the rotors slowed, Frank and the others moved to the open sliding doors in a smooth, practiced ballet, each performing their job and doing it with gentle compassion and care. Together, they rushed the four wounded men across the rutted ground to the hospital and onto improvised beds made of standard Army green canvas stretchers suspended across two wooden sawhorses.

Triage, the part Frank hated the most. He had to determine who lived or died via four categories. KIA – those were sent to the KIA shack. Expectant – Patients too close to death or with such extensive injuries they couldn't be saved with the limited resources available. Those were placed in a secluded space, given morphine, and allowed to die. Salvageable – They had the best chance of survival with the efficient use of resources.

And last, Delayed RX – Medically stable patients where treatment could be delayed.

He started at the first soldier laid out on a stretcher, moaning in pain. Someone had already cut off his clothing as they had with the other three men. This man had a few deep facial lacerations and a few to his arms and legs, but he was stable and could wait. Frank gave the word, and two orderlies moved him into a waiting area.

Frank moved to the next man. Cathy was there, inserting an IV in addition to the other two already hanging. She looked up at Frank. Her eyes held the deep inward gaze of sorrow. When Frank looked down, he knew why. This man, while alive now, wouldn't be for long. Wide, black tourniquets were strapped tightly around the soldier's thighs with both legs missing below the knees. So was his right arm, amputated at the shoulder. His abdomen was a cavernous hole with shredded intestines hanging out and a Swiss-cheesed liver.

"Cathy, what's his pressure?" Frank asked.

Cathy didn't say anything. She just kept looking down at the man in front of her.

Frank gripped her shoulder. "Cathy?"

She turned to him. "Sixty palp, but dropping quickly. Frank, what are we going to do?"

This decision ate at his soul. He had to deny treatment to a wounded soldier. "You know the drill. Take him into the other room and administer morphine."

"Yes, sir," Cathy said sadly. She motioned to the orderlies standing by. They moved the young man into the room reserved for the dying. Cathy followed behind them, her shoulders drooped and head down.

The other two men were being moved to the operating room, triaged by another doctor, Henry Buchannon, nicknamed Elvis because of his thick black, wavy hair with a curly lock that always hung over his right eye. Frank followed to scrub in to assist him.

Frank changed into his scrub shirt and pants. As he dried his hands at the sink, he heard, "Frank get your ass in here! Now!" in Elvis' frantic voice.

Confused as to the urgency since those men weren't critical, Frank ran into the operating room. "What?"

"Take a look." Standing next to the gurney, Elvis nodded at the x-ray hanging on the light board.

Even though he couldn't see Elvis' face behind the surgical mask, Frank could see his eyes. They were wide with what he could only

11

describe as...fear. He didn't understand. The naked soldier appeared unconscious while lying on his stomach with several IV lines running into his arms and an oxygen mask covering his face. Then Frank realized no one else was in the room. Only him, Elvis, and the patient. That really confused him. The OR, normally a hub of activity after an influx of wounded, seemed oddly quiet.

Moving over to the light board, Frank looked closely at the x-ray, and his heart cringed in fear. He'd heard about this happening on occasion but had never seen it. The soldier had what looked like the rounded business end of an unexploded 40mm grenade in his right butt cheek. *Shit!*

"Are you using anesthesia or a nerve block?" Frank asked, taking a position opposite Elvis on the other side of the gurney.

"Anesthesia. I don't want this guy moving...and I sent the anesthesiologist out of the room."

"Good point. Have you ever seen this before?"

"Once, when I first got here, and I wasn't the surgeon. I'm as much a newbie on this as you."

"Great. What now?" Frank asked.

The OR was now a lonely place.

Elvis picked up a scalpel from the stainless steel rolling table next to him. "We do this carefully. Once I expose...it, we'll use an en bloc resection to remove it. I don't want to touch the damn thing with anything metal. Make sure to keep it in the same orientation as the guy's body. Don't twist or push on it."

"Or what?" En bloc? They were going to excise healthy tissue with the grenade. This guy was going to have a hollow butt.

"We go boom with him."

"Don't want to do that." Frank gloved up. And doing it without assistance, he felt like all thumbs. Not good for removing an explosive-filled metal container. He clenched his hands to stop them from shaking.

Elvis had the elongated object exposed quickly. It had to be quick. Time was of the essence.

Frank placed a retractor on both sides of the object, keeping them against the cut-away tissue. The blood made it hard to lift the grenade as it slid around between the retractors. His heart thudded in his chest like a jackhammer.

"Here, sir," someone said behind him as a padded bucket was held up next to his right side.

Startled by the voice breaking the silence of his own breathing, Frank almost let go. He glanced over his shoulder at a man fully covered in an armored EOD suit. *He's got protection. I have surgical scrubs. Geez.*

Carefully inching around, Frank lowered the grenade into the bucket until it touched the extremely padded bottom then stepped back. The man put on the lid and exited the room in slow, precise steps, holding the bucket still.

Frank turned to Elvis, grabbing a sponge from the surgical tray at his side and wiping the sweat from his eyes. "Whew."

"Yeah." Elvis picked up a sterile scalpel from his tray as the surgical staff returned to the OR. "Let's see what we can do to save what's left of his ass."

Frank laughed. While sad they'd have to do that, it was funny at the same time.

Eight hours later, when Frank left the operating room, he couldn't find Cathy in the recovery room or ICU. He found her alone in the room with the now-deceased soldier who'd come in with no legs. She was sitting in a chair, holding his limp, pale hand.

"Cathy," Frank said softly. The sharp smell of iron filled the air as the concrete floor under the gurney looked like someone had painted it a deep crimson red.

"Huh?" Cathy looked up but didn't let go of the young man's hand. "Frank."

"Are you okay?"

Cathy placed the soldier's hand on his chest and stood. "Yes."

Frank wiped a tear from her cheek with his thumb. "You don't seem to be. What's wrong?" He'd never seen her this rattled. She was usually the rock of stability among the nurses.

"Nothing." She sniffed.

"Come on, Cathy. Tell me." He thought for a second. "Do you want a drink? I can sure use one." *After what just happened, I need one. Maybe she'll join me.*

It took her several seconds to respond. "Yeah, me too."

Frank led her to his quarters, known in-country as a hooch, noticing when they entered, it wasn't exactly up to Army spit-shine standards. His bunk was unmade with a pair of blood-covered combat boots under it. He hadn't had time to clean them.

A dirty, stained fatigue shirt and pants lay across the end of the bed frame. The air smelled of body odor and iron with a hint of shit from the nearby latrine.

Frank glanced at his green Class A dress uniform hung on a long nail pounded into the wall. The Meritorious Service, Joint Service Commendation, Army Commendation, Army Achievement, National Defense, Vietnam Service, and Vietnam Campaign ribbons looked out of place under the dim single fluorescent bulb. He vowed to put the uniform in a better storage spot, if one existed in this place. The plastic wrapper from the cleaners didn't stop anything. He needed to remove the ribbons from above the right jacket pocket and put them in his footlocker for protection. All around him, the oppressive humidity constantly worked to turn the omnipresent dust into mud.

Frank rummaged through the things on the table, trying to find a semi-clean glass or coffee mug. Unable to find anything, he checked one of the scavenged wooden rocket boxes stacked in the corner. The hinged lid made them perfect for storage.

He found two clear plastic party cups under an old copy of *Stars and Stripes*, got his bottle from his footlocker, and poured them both a large shot. Not two fingers, to the rim full. The alcohol would kill any germs. He handed her one then sat on his bunk with the other and indicated she should sit in the ratty chair he'd rescued from the trash and repaired. He'd nailed planks from a pallet to the broken chair legs, so it sat halfway level. A hospital pillow covered the protruding spring in the seat cushion.

Cathy sat, took a sip from her cup, and grimaced.

Frank gulped half of his drink in one swallow. "So, what's wrong," he asked, wiping his arm across his mouth. The warmth of the cheap whiskey spread down his throat into his stomach.

Instead of speaking, Cathy ran a finger around the rim of the cup.

Frank let her be. She needed to be the one willing to talk. All he would do by pushing was shut her down.

The silence of the room was deafening. Frank turned on his radio, set to American Forces Vietnam Network. He found it appropriate when *We Gotta Get Out of This Place* by the Animals started playing. While he sang along with the lyrics, Cathy laughed.

"Are you critiquing my musical talents?" Frank asked.

"What talents? You sound like a pig being strangled," Cathy replied.

"And that's the thanks I get," Frank said, trying and failing to sound put off.

"Frank...thanks."

"For what?"

"Getting my mind off what happened. It's not like I have never seen someone die. I've never frozen like that before."

"We all have bad days, Cathy. In the OR we only look at the wounds. It's postop when you finally see the faces and want to throw up at the inhumanity of it all. Do you know why this one hit so hard?"

Cathy drank a large gulp from her cup. "Ahh...he kinda looked like my older brother, Ryan. The same brown hair, cleft in the chin with little dimples in his cheeks. And his eyes were so sad...he knew he was about to die. He kept mumbling *I don't want to be alone* until he took his last breath. He even sounded like Ryan. All I could do was hold his hand, stroke his hair, and tell him God loves him."

Frank didn't know what to say, so he went from the heart. "And I'm sure he appreciated it. He wasn't alone. Cathy, we'll never be able to forget what happens here, just learn to live with it."

"Yeah." Cathy started crying.

Frank did the only thing he could, hold her tightly. Not a romantic hold. Only that of two people brought together by war, comforting each other in a place neither of them wanted. While she cried for the soldier, he did the same inside for his friend, Jake.

1015 Hours
March 15, 1971
95th Evacuation Hospital
Da Nang, South Vietnam

Over the roar of the generator on the other side of the thin wooden wall, Frank heard the ear-piercing scream of an ambulance siren. Casualties. Couldn't they wait until he was finished? He stood, tossed the toilet paper into the hole, buttoned his pants, and exited the latrine.

As he ran toward the emergency department, his boots slopping in the mud, the medivac helipad remained eerily silent. No medical personnel were staged and waiting in anticipation. Absent were the thumping rotor beats of inbound choppers loaded with wounded from some battle nearby that usually came with the ambulances. What was going on?

Once inside the ED, Frank entered a room of organized chaos. One soldier lay on the gurney as the medical staff worked around him. One person cut off his clothing while another inserted an IV and obtained vital signs.

Frank pushed between Cathy and a surgical corpsman. He didn't see any blood or wounds. "What have we got?"

"Looks like an OD." Cathy removed the stethoscope from her ears. "His buddies found him face down on the floor of his tent lying in a mound of vomit. Everything points to him sucking it into his lungs. The unit medic cleared his airway, and he started breathing shallowly. It took thirty minutes to get him here as the medic bagged him. No choppers were available."

"Shit! That's not good. Vitals!"

"Cyanotic upon arrival. Unconscious with labored respirations of 45 a minute. Blood pressure 40 palp. Pulse 50, weak and irregular. We've placed him head down on his right side to help drain the debris and administered fluids and oxygen."

Frank wanted to punch something. "That's the sixth guy this week. Fucking heroin. When will these kids learn a damn thing? This isn't the watered-down, cut-to-low-grade street junk like in the states. It's almost pure shit that will kill you quickly."

For the next hour, they tried everything – a nasal catheter – a red rubber tube "snaked" into the trachea to clear it with suction. While it did remove some of the thick milky putrid-smelling liquid, more remained. They inserted an endotracheal tube and used forced ventilation to prevent anoxia – brain death from the lack of oxygen.

As a last-ditch effort, Frank tried lung lavage, washing both lungs with a sterile saline solution followed by suction and oxygenation. If the young man lived, pneumonia was a real threat. Nothing worked as his patient went from a sluggish arrhythmic pace into full cardiac arrest.

Then came CPR until their arms became limp noodles, and Frank shocked him several times with the defibrillator. That failed too. Frank finally had to say the words he hated — "Time of death." He glanced at the wall clock, "1305 hours. What a fucking waste. You guys know what to do." He went outside and leaned against the wall, unable to get the freckle-faced nineteen-year-old blond-haired kid out of his mind. The name on the dog tags was Craig DeSoto. And he'd see it again — on the Army paperwork. The lab would have to do a toxicology screen first. But he was pretty positive about the actual cause of death. An overdose of heroin.

While he understood why these young soldiers took the drugs, to escape the horrors of war, it still didn't make sense to throw away your life. What it did to the body and mind was an absolute crime. And it wasn't limited to drugs like marijuana, LSD, and heroin bought on the black market. It flowed freely over the Cambodian border. The high-ranking brass prescribed pills to enhance their soldiers' performance, amphetamines for long missions – "go pills." Then the sedatives to relieve anxiety and prevent mental breakdown – "no go pills." That last part was laughable.

Well, it was all laughable in a horrible way. The destruction of an entire generation of young men.

Cathy joined him against the wall, shoulders slouched and head bowed. Her face told of her despair as tears streamed down her cheeks. "I hate this fucking place."

Frank gripped her hand. "So do I."

CHAPTER 4

1500 Hours
April 11, 1971
95th Evacuation Hospital
Da Nang, South Vietnam

Frank knocked on the doorframe of Cathy's quarters. She shared a hut similar to his with another nurse, 1st Lieutenant Peggy Sanders, a young, blond-haired woman from Brooklyn.

Cathy opened the screen door. "Hey, Frank. I'm packing. My flight leaves from the Da Nang airport tomorrow at eleven. To what do I owe the pleasure?"

"I know, but do you want to take a break and join me for coffee in the mess hall one last time?"

"Sure. I can finish this later." Cathy exited and let the door swing shut.

They walked together across the compound.

"Are you ready to go home?" Frank asked.

"Yes, I have a lot to do before I start medical school," Cathy replied.

"Do you have a place to stay?" Not that he knew anyone in Texas, but he could ask around. There had to be someone on the staff from Texas.

"Yeah, the Fort Hood bachelor officers quarters. It's less than fifty miles from Waco. I'm going to work at the hospital there until I start medical school. I'm going on the Army's dime."

"Oh. I didn't know. I thought you were leaving the Army."

Cathy shook her head. "Can't afford the tuition to attend Baylor on my own. This is the only way. It was good enough for you, Frank. It's good enough for me."

"I didn't know I made that much of an impression on you."

"I can read people pretty good. A trait I got from my father. You're a good and honest man, Frank."

Frank opened the mess hall door for her. "I'm glad you think so. After you."

Cathy entered with Frank following. Balloons and newspaper confetti floated down on them from the ceiling. Peggy, along with the off-duty doctors, nurses, and corpsmen, jumped from crouching on the floor behind the tables.

"Surprise," they yelled. Rock music from American Forces Vietnam Network started blasting from the rusty speakers in the corners.

Cathy turned to Frank. "I told you I didn't want a party."

"This is because you're going home, not medical school," he whispered to her. "I didn't tell anyone, and someone else planned this." But he did suggest the location. She hated the officers club as a non-smoker. The lingering, heavy cigarette smoke presence always gave her migraine headaches. She detested the odor of stale beer and vomit. Something to do with her father and Saturday nights. He couldn't get the rest out of her.

"Oh!" She kissed Frank's cheek. "Thanks anyway."

Peggy approached them with a plate loaded with delicious-looking, perfectly baked cookies. "Take one."

Frank grabbed two cookies and handed one to Cathy. "Here."

"Thanks." Cathy nibbled on the cookie. "Mmm. Chocolate chip with pecans. Where'd these come from? They're good. I'm sure they didn't come from the hospital kitchen."

"Got them from the PX in Saigon while I was on leave last week," Peggy said before presenting the plate to the other people in the room.

As everyone ate the cookies, and the assortment of bar snacks on the table, pretzels, peanuts, and popcorn, Elvis handed Cathy a gift nicely wrapped in shiny blue paper and red ribbon with a matching puffy bow.

Frank shook his head. While Elvis was a great surgeon, the time it took to wrap something that precise, sharp corners, feathered ribbons, and a hand-tied bow weren't on his list of specialties. One of the nurses must have done it for him.

Cathy tore off the paper. Inside the box, a framed 8 x 10 picture of the entrance sign of the 95th Evacuation Hospital, autographed by everyone serving at the hospital. She sniffed. "Thanks, guys."

"That's not it." Elvis held out a blue award box with the lid open. Inside, a red ribbon outlined by a gold frame – the Army Meritorious Unit Commendation Ribbon. "You helped us earn this."

Cathy took the box, looked at the ribbon for a moment, shut the lid, and placed it alongside the photograph on the table.

A mess cook in a dirty white apron placed a vanilla buttercream frosted sheet cake decorated with a red cross and a green plastic toy helicopter in the center on the table in front of Cathy. "Congrats on the Freedom Bird, ma'am." He returned to the kitchen.

After Peggy set the timer of her camera for a picture of everyone huddled up together near the American flag, Frank picked up a knife. "I guess this falls on me. I am the best surgeon here." *I want to see if I got*

19

my money's worth. This cake cost me a ton of favors to get it here on time from Saigon and all prettied up.

Cathy lightly slapped his shoulder. "Maybe in your wet dreams, Frank, but get to slicing. I'm hungry."

Everyone laughed at the joke.

Frank shook his head as he placed a slice of really moist four-layer chocolate cake on a paper plate. "I get no respect." *This looked delicious. Money and effort well spent on that chopper.*

CHAPTER 5

0700 Hours
June 9, 1971
95th Evacuation Hospital
Da Nang, South Vietnam

Elvis stopped at Frank's table in the mess hall, quickly halting his conversation with Peggy Sanders.

"Frank, I know you just got off duty on the night shift, but I have an assignment for you," Elvis said, pointing at the exit doors.

Frank set down his fork. He wasn't hungry anyway. The putrid smell of the mystery meat covered in brown gravy turned his stomach. Visually, it wasn't any better. It looked like a cross between a moldy shoe sole and spoiled fish oozing pond scum. "What?"

"Go out and meet an ambulance on its way here with a patient."

"Why not bring him in a dust off?"

"Grounded due to heavy fog in the area."

Frank looked through the mess hall window. In his short time inside the building, it had gone from sunny outside to gray. "Now?"

"Yeah. There's a jeep and driver waiting for you outside." Elvis held up Frank's green web belt with its attached magazine holder, combat knife, black holster, and .45 caliber M1911A1 Colt pistol. "You'll need this."

"Copy that." Frank put on the belt as he ran outside and jumped into the jeep beside the flak jacket clad driver. The fog wasn't that thick, at least to him. He could see for about half a mile.

As they sped out of the compound, Frank looked behind him at the two green canvas red-cross marked surgical packs, a cooler containing several units of O-negative blood, a flak jacket, and a green steel helmet on the rear bench seat.

An hour into the trip on a two-lane dirt road that felt more like a rutted donkey path, Frank heard something whiz by his head, then another and another. "Shit!" He pulled out his .45 caliber pistol, racked a round into the chamber, and looked around to see where it came from, but everything beside the road went by in a gray fog-shrouded blur.

"You can say that again, sir," the driver yelled over the wind noise. "Probably an NVA sniper beside the road, not expecting us out in this muck or a bad shot."

"Bad shot and sniper don't go together, Sergeant. We got lucky." Frank slid down as far as he could into the floorboard, reaching between the seats to grab the flak jacket and helmet lying with the surgical packs. The damn things were heavy but he would be better off uncomfortable than shot in the chest or head.

"You got a point, Major." The driver tightened the chin strap on his helmet then gripped the steering wheel, slowing down and zig-zagging back and forth across the road.

Frank hoped the NVA hadn't mined the crappy road. It might be safer to sit on the flak jacket than wear it. They went through several small villages with the outlines of people milling around in their daily activities. As they sped along, the fog got thicker, and the visibility narrowed to less than a few car lengths. When they came around a blind corner, Frank heard a siren over the wind noise. Then through the mist, two yellow-white headlights appeared less than one hundred yards away.

His driver stomped on the brakes with both feet, sending the jeep into a wheel-locked sliding stop in the middle of the road.

The two headlights got larger and larger with the high-pitched squeal of abused brakes. The headlights came to a stop a few inches from the jeep hood. Through the swirling fog, Frank could see the outline of an Army box ambulance.

Frank breathed a sigh of relief, grabbed the cooler, one surgical pack, and ran to the rear of the ambulance.

The double doors popped open, and a hand appeared then the rest of the medic, his green jungle uniform covered in dried and fresh blood. "Hey, Doc. You almost became a bug splattered on the windshield."

"Yeah, noticed." Frank gave the medic the surgical pack and cooler then climbed inside the ambulance. The jeep driver tossed in the second surgical pack and shut the ambulance doors with a bang. The ambulance took off suddenly, sending Frank sprawling on the floor next to the gurney.

Frank tried to stand, but with the ambulance rocking back and forth, he stayed on his knees for better stability while visually examining his patient. He unrolled a green canvas sleeve of medical instruments on the floor.

The soldier didn't look more than twenty with crew-cut dark brown hair and a five o'clock shadow under the sheen of sweat and dirt. Pain lines creased his face with his eyes squeezed closed. The right leg of his green fatigue pants was cut from the bottom cuff to the crotch with a wide black tourniquet strapped tightly around the thigh above a long, deep, ragged, gaped open slice. From what Frank could determine from a cursory examination, that cut was directly over the femoral artery, and while the tourniquet slowed the bleeding, it hadn't stopped it. The man kept leaking like a cracked water pipe.

The medic beside him hung a unit of O-negative blood and attached the IV line to it. He moved around the ambulance as if it were sitting still. He must have had long hours of unwanted practice.

Knowing time was of the essence and the ambulance unable to stop, Frank pulled off the helmet and flak jacket then tossed them aside. He used the only thing he could to stop the bleeding and not cause more damage. If he missed with the clamp or used too much force, he could crush what remained of the artery. And the young man would lose his leg. Quickly, he shoved his fingers into the wound, searching for his elusive, round, flexible, and slippery target.

The wounded soldier bucked and twisted, screaming, "Fuck…fuck…fuck…" All his extraneous motion pushed Frank over onto his butt.

"Hold him down, damn it," Frank ordered, kicking himself mentally for not warning the medic first.

The medic nodded, quickly laying his upper body across that of their patient.

Frank got back onto his knees and tried again, finding the artery quickly. He could feel the soldier's pulse under the clenched tips of his thumb and forefinger. "You can get up now," he told the medic.

The medic, who Frank finally noticed didn't appear any older than his patient, inclined his head once and moved around him.

The young soldier opened his eyes and lifted his head to look at Frank.

Unable to change positions with his fingers keeping the young man alive, Frank nodded to acknowledge him. "Please don't move around. What's your name, son?"

"Corporal Charlie Brighton, Major. Am I going to die?" he whispered, his upper lip quivering as a tear rolled down his cheek.

Frank gave the man his medical school rehearsed smile. "Not today if I have any say in it." And he did. From what he could see and feel, he knew he could save this man and his leg. He braced himself against the floor. This time he wouldn't let go, couldn't let go. Not with the soldier's life literally in his hand. He turned to look at the medic. "Give him a dose of morphine from my pack and tell that driver to stick his foot in it. Fuck the damn fog. Get us to the 95th in a hurry." He saw his flak jacket draped over a bench out of the corner of his eye. "Oh yeah, watch out for a sniper about forty miles from the hospital."

CHAPTER 6

0825 Hours
June 10, 1971
95th Evacuation Hospital
Da Nang, South Vietnam

Still dripping wet after rinsing clotted, sticky blood off his arms and legs with cold water from the hose, Frank leaned against the wall outside the OR, his legs ready to collapse. This was his first break in two days. An onslaught of wounded besieged the hospital after he returned with Corporal Brighton. The NVA decided to attack a firebase near Dai Loc. He saved Brighton's leg. One day in the future, the kid would walk again.

Frank looked up when he heard and felt the beating thump-thump-thump of chopper rotors and saw the silhouettes growing ever larger against the cerulean blue morning sky.

With a deep sigh, he trudged back inside to prepare for more casualties. Who knew how long he'd be in surgery this time. At least he wasn't on triage duty having to condemn unsalvageable men to a prolonged death in an attempt to save another life. Something that bothered him by challenging his ingrained moral code.

Twelve hours into this shift, two corpsmen placed another mangled soldier on his table. The man was already prepped by the expert emergency corpsmen and nurses. Multiple IV lines delivering fluids ran into the naked, dirty, blood-covered soldier from numerous cutdowns. His temperature, blood pressure, and heart function were all near normal.

Large caliber IV tubing ran under the soldier's right collarbone into the vein in his chest, delivering blood. Frank looked down at the face of a young man under the oxygen mask who couldn't be eighteen years old. More like fourteen with light-colored peach fuzz instead of facial or chest hair.

The anesthesiologist, Captain Kyle Varner, from Queens, NY, used his skills to place the moaning patient asleep quickly and efficiently.

Frank picked up a scalpel. Now he had to make sense of the injuries in front of him. Elvis assisted him on the other side. Amputations below both knees with wide black nylon tourniquets strapped near the groin, stopping the blood flow. A marble-sized hole on one side of the right thigh and a ragged exit wound the circumference of an orange on the other. On the abdominal wall, a small evisceration with a small loop of bowel protruding. The kid probably tripped a repositioned American Claymore mine or one of Charlie's homemade booby traps and, like the Claymore, full of quarter-inch steel balls. Somehow, he still had his testicles and penis with a capped Foley tube stuck in it.

Blood dripped continuously from the table onto Frank's scrub shirt, soaked into the pants, then his socks, running into his boots, pooling around his feet and between his toes. A horrible feeling as his feet stuck to the boot soles as he stood in one place while his upper body moved back and forth continuously. He'd have to pour water into his boots to soften the thick dried blood to get them off. That same blood coated his arms up to his elbows.

Sweat dripped from under his scrub cap into his eyes, blinding him, but he couldn't wipe it away. To do so would break the sterile field. He nodded at a nearby nurse, who blotted his forehead with a gauze patch. Now he could see again.

The corpsman at his side, functioning as a surgical nurse, handed him instruments before he asked for them like they'd done a hundred times before. Right now, he was resecting a piece of bowel and needed to concentrate on only that task.

"Scalpel, suction, retractor, sponge…" The words came from his mouth or Elvis' in a monotone, unending stream until it became "blah, blah, blah…" to Frank's subconscious. Action and reaction as he fileted open the right thigh to attempt an end-to-end repair of the femoral artery so the young man could keep his residual limb. He knew, once completed, he would save the remaining section of the young man's leg if he could find any viable muscle to cover the repair to allow it to heal. Only time would tell. Frank had to distance himself and do the work. His job. Tunnel vision. It happened automatically to save this one man's life.

Time stood still as unit after unit of blood was hung and pushed into the patient. Bottles of Ringers Lactate were emptied and replaced with fresh ones, only to empty again and again. Arteries clamped. Bleeding controlled. Removal of dead, unsalvageable tissue, bone, and pieces of metal going onto the floor or the trash bucket. Included in that waste, a large chunk of femur that didn't belong to this man. It probably came from his battle buddy standing next to him, blasted into his flesh by the force of the explosion.

"Frank, I'm not getting a pulse," yelled Kyle, sounding muffled through his surgical mask.

Frank looked at Kyle with his hands above the artery repair, dripping blood back into the open wound of obliterated muscle. "Get him back!"

"I can't. He's gone." Kyle's shoulders drooped as he turned off his machine.

"I said, get him back!"

Elvis gripped Frank's shoulder. "You tried. We need to move on."

"No!" Frank placed his bloody gloved hand on the carotid artery in the soldier's neck. Nothing. He moved to start CPR, but Elvis pulled him back.

"Stop, Frank. He's gone. In war, young men die. There's not a God damned thing we can do to change that. Let it go," Elvis yelled in Frank's face.

Frank stood there in a quandary. There was always hope. He tried to turn back to his patient, but Elvis pulled him away again, refusing to let go when Frank attempted to jerk his arm away.

"Frank, no! We can't save them all. You tried. We all tried. Let! It! Go!"

Frank looked over his shoulder as the corpsmen unhooked the young man from the various machines, removed the IV lines, and covered the young soldier's now cooling body.

"Is there anyone left in the hall?"

"No, we're done," Elvis said, releasing his grip on Frank's wrist.

Frank ripped off his bloody latex gloves, threw them on the floor, and left, stopping only long enough in the anteroom to rinse the blood off his legs and arms. After stripping out of the disgusting scrubs and blood-covered boots at his locker, he donned a t-shirt, his faded OD-green fatigues, socks, and a clean pair of combat boots then headed to the officers' club. He needed a drink or two or three.

After sitting on a stool at the bar, he leaned over the rail and slammed his hand on the scuffed, water-stained mahogany counter. "Give me a shot of whiskey...no, give me the entire bottle."

The bartender, Staff Sergeant Max Sharp, wearing green fatigues under a white apron, leaned across the bar. "Are you okay, Major?"

"Just give me the damn bottle," Frank responded, waving the noxious cigarette smoke away from his face.

Max nodded and turned to the shelf behind him which held alcohol bottles of every shape and kind. He took down a full bottle of Wild Turkey then set the bottle and an 8-ounce empty water glass in front of Frank.

Frank cracked the seal, filled the glass with the cheap whiskey, then downed it in a few gulps, feeling the brown liquid burn as it slid down his throat. He refilled the glass, drank it, and filled the glass again. The kid's face, transparent but in vivid color, green eyes open, pupils dilated in death, floated above his glass. He needed more whiskey to make it go away.

His shaky hand caused the neck of the bottle to clank against the rim of the glass. He was already feeling buzzed on an empty stomach and dehydrated on top of it.

Elvis sat on the stool beside him. "Frank, you've lost men before. What's wrong?"

"I don't know." Frank took another drink. "I've never felt like this before. Ever. I've hit a damn wall and don't know how to climb over it."

"You know this isn't the answer."

"I know." Frank slammed the glass harder than he intended on the counter, splashing whiskey on his hand. "But right now, it is for me. I can't explain it."

"You're stressed." Elvis tapped his head. "And your brain's trying to cope and escape from this horrible place."

Frank took a deep breath. "Yeah." He thought for a moment. "I guess seeing that man...kid, really, lying there, dead, blasted, chewed up by hunks of burning metal got to me. He looked about fourteen and should be home chasing girls and enjoying life, not here in this god damned jungle on a cold slab in the morgue and what's left of him going home in a flag-covered body bag." He felt sorry for this kid's now gold star mother.

"True. None of us should be here, but we chose to serve and save lives as best we can. That's all we can do."

"Uh-huh." Frank screwed the cap on the bottle and pushed it away. He felt woozy, drunk, and ashamed for falling into the trap of despair like a newbie. The alcohol hadn't helped at all. Nothing but a futile attempt that would result in a hangover. At least it wasn't heroin. The drug of choice for soldiers in Vietnam. He'd seen more overdoses here than a New York City street cop.

"Hey, Max, got any coffee?" Frank asked, turning his glass over.

Max took the bottle and glass then replaced them with a brown stained white ceramic mug full of black coffee. "Glad you came to your senses, Doc."

"Me too." Frank swallowed the bile in his throat. "But, boy, I'm going to regret it tomorrow when I have a headache the size of the Grand Canyon." He saw his face in the mirror on the wall behind the bar. The pale skin, broken vessels, and bloodshot eyes made him look as dead as the man in the OR. It gave him an involuntary shiver.

"I'll have a fistful of aspirin and an IV all ready for you," Elvis said, gripping Frank's shoulder.

"Uh-huh," Frank replied, sipping the robust, eat-the-spoon brew in his mug, feeling his stomach already rolling. It was time to go to his quarters before he wound up face down, puking his guts up on the nasty, no longer painted, sand-ground by their boots, rough plywood O-club floor. He'd rather be sick in private than out in front of his friends. Lesson learned. Don't drink cheap whiskey on an empty stomach. Or let grief consume you. Even if you didn't know why or where it came from.

CHAPTER 7

1000 Hours
June 11, 1971
95th Evacuation Hospital
Da Nang, South Vietnam

"Mail call! Mail call!" A loud male voice rang throughout the camp. Frank didn't get out of bed to check. Why? No one ever sent him anything. He had no living family, at least close family. An uncle and aunt or two, a few distant cousins, nieces, and nephews.

No one who cared about him being in Vietnam. He hadn't heard from anyone since he joined the Army. Besides, he had an IV catheter in his arm, rehydrating him after yesterday's stupidity, and his stomach hurt after dry heaving on his hands and knees into a trash can for most of the night. And he didn't remember the walk to his hooch last night. Elvis must have guided him, stripped him to his shorts and t-shirt, put him in bed, and inserted the IV.

Someone knocked on the door. "Are you still alive in there?" a familiar voice called out.

"I think so," Frank replied. You never entered someone's hooch without knocking to keep from getting shot. He, like most people in camp, kept a weapon nearby. His was a standard Army issue .45 caliber M1911A1 Colt pistol in a holster attached to an OD-green web belt hanging on a long nail over his bed. Everyone knew there were VC in camp. The so-called vetted "locals" worked for them by day and occasionally died as Viet Cong "sappers" by the concertina wire at night.

The screen door to his quarters opened, and Elvis came in. "Hey, Frank. How do you feel?"

Frank lifted his head from the pillow then dropped it back. "Awful. I have a headache the size of Texas and California combined."

Elvis checked the bottle of saline on the stand beside the bed. "This is almost empty. I'll remove the catheter in a few minutes." He poured water from a pitcher into a red plastic cup on the table then handed the cup to Frank. "You need to drink fluids instead of getting them through an IV."

"Yeah." Frank swung his legs off the bed, sat up, and gulped down the water. He knew that professionally, even if his stomach said *no*.

Elvis refilled the cup. "More."

30

Frank sipped the water this time as Elvis injected something into his IV line. "What's that?"

"Something for your headache. All you'd do with a couple of aspirin is throw up again."

"Ahhh…no. I don't want to do any more of that."

"I don't want to see it either. I've never seen anyone throw up that much, not having eaten in almost a day." Elvis set the half-full trash can outside the door then sat beside Frank. "Feel any better yet?"

Frank massaged his temples. His headache was fading. Whatever Elvis gave him worked. "A little."

"Do you want me to take you off the surgical rotation for a few days? Let you get your bearings back. I'm concerned about your—"

"Say it! My breakdown. No. I need to get back to work. If I stay in here moping, I'll lose a lot more." *Like all my marbles instead of a few.*

"Good attitude. There's a movie in the mess hall between lunch and dinner. Peggy managed to snag a bag of popcorn from the PX. She's going to pop it in one of the kitchen skillets right before the movie starts so we have fresh, hot, buttered popcorn."

Did he want to go to a movie? "What movie? Hope it's not as bad as the last ones…ahhh…*Monster a Go-Go* and *The Astro-Zombies*. Is it?" He couldn't take another movie about monsters or rampaging hideous creatures.

Elvis had an *I've got a secret* smile. "Not that I know of. And, yes, those were terrible."

"What's the movie?" Now Frank was curious.

"*MASH*," Elvis said with a flourish.

"Really? Here? Not that I'm disappointed. I saw it during basic training at Fort Sam Houston. I guess the instructors thought it was funny to show that movie to a bunch of Army doctors about to ship out to Vietnam."

"So you've seen it too?"

Frank laughed. "Yeah."

"If you had to compare us, who am I?" Elvis asked.

"Well…" Frank scratched his bristly chin. He needed to shower and shave before going out among the other professional but reluctant residents of the 95th Evac. They'd end up puking because he didn't smell good covered with whiskey-smelling sweat and vomit. "Do you really want me to compare you?"

"Yes." Elvis tapped his head. "Consider it a memory exercise to get rid of all those brain cells you destroyed last night and grow some new ones."

"Funny." He sure did kill a few brain cells and some of those who survived were still drunk. "Frank Burns."

Elvis stomped his foot. "I'm nothing like Frank Burns!" He paused for a few seconds. "You said that on purpose."

"Yes, because you insisted. You're more of a cross between Henry Blake and Father Mulcahy."

"Blake, I get, but the priest too?" Elvis exclaimed. "Why?"

Frank patted his friend on the back. "Because you've got a good heart, my friend. You're here trying to cheer me up."

Elvis nodded. "Okay. Who are you?"

"Hmmm…Trapper John."

"Not Hawkeye? You're the best surgeon here."

"No. While Hawkeye is funny and a good surgeon, I liked the Trapper John character better." Frank shrugged. "Don't ask me why. Just a feeling."

"Then take a lesson from him and don't let what happened get to you."

"Spoken like a true friend and commanding officer, Lieutenant Colonel Buchannon. Deal." *For now. I can't speak about the future. It could happen again. Who knows?*

Elvis removed the IV catheter from Frank's forearm, covering the small puncture with a Band-Aid. "How do you feel now?"

"A lot better. Thanks."

"Good." Elvis opened the door, leaned outside, and returned to Frank with a decent-sized cardboard box. "This came for you today. Since you didn't venture outside to check, I signed for it."

"Huh? From who?" Did one of his distant relatives finally give a damn? Or just feel sorry for him serving in Vietnam. He flipped the box around to look at the return address. It was even better than a relative. Captain Cathy Alexander – Ft. Hood, TX.

"What did she send you?" Elvis asked, sitting beside him.

"Let's see." Frank grabbed his folding buck knife off the table and slit the tape. He opened the flap and tossed the wadded-up newspaper packing material onto the floor. He'd pick it up later when he dumped, cleaned, and disinfected his trash can.

The delicious sweet smell hit him first. The box held a mountain of goodies. Chocolate bars, hard candy, gum, Ritz crackers, canned soup, potted meat, beef jerky, pre-packaged cookies, and a smaller cardboard box.

He pulled out the box and opened it. Inside was a folded piece of white paper, a Bundt cake wrapped in waxed paper, and aluminum foil with a store-bought can of vanilla frosting. He set the cake aside. He'd share it with everyone at the movie. The rest of the goodies were going into his personal stash.

Curious about how Cathy was doing, he removed her picture, paper clipped to the letter. It was taken at her going away party. He unfolded the paper while Elvis looked over his shoulder.

May 25, 1971

Frank,

I hope this package arrives intact and finds you well. Enjoy the cake. I made it myself. Sorry for the do-it-yourself portion. But knowing how the post office treats packages, I couldn't figure out a way to send an already frosted cake without it becoming a melted, gooey mess in the box.

Things are going great. I'm so glad to be back in the states, but I'm busy getting settled back into a normal life after leaving Vietnam. It's strange not to wake up to the sound of helicopter rotors or holding soldiers' hands as they die. After working in the ED at the 95th, the emergency room at Darnall Army Community Hospital is a much slower pace, but I miss my friends.

Now for the good news, I'm officially enrolled at Baylor for the fall semester. I got my books while I was on campus. Geez, how many books in anatomy does one instructor need? It felt like a ruck march during basic training getting them back to my car.

I need to get ready for my shift at the hospital and tape up this box so I can get it in the mail later. Tell everyone I miss them. Take care of yourself, old man. Call me when you get back stateside at the phone number written on the back of the picture.

Your friend,

Cathy Alexander

Frank carefully folded the letter and placed it in his footlocker. All his cherished items went into his footlocker. The picture he put on his table. He'd make a frame for it later with four tongue depressors glued together with a piece of cellophane over the photo to protect it.

Elvis gripped Frank's shoulder. "I'll tell everyone she's thinking of them."

"Thanks. What time does the movie start?"

"Fourteen hundred hours."

Frank glanced at his watch. 1135. He had plenty of time.

Elvis stood. "See you there." He opened the door and left.

Gotta get cleaned up. I stink. Frank grabbed a clean towel, fresh clothes, and his shaving kit from his footlocker. He would ice the cake when he wasn't a bacteria-laden science experiment gone bad.

CHAPTER 8

December 15, 1971
95th Evacuation Hospital
Da Nang, South Vietnam

Boom!

Boom!

Boom!

Frank tumbled out of bed, tangled up in his mosquito netting. He worked on getting free as the wooden plank floor rolled and bucked under him. The air vibrated like an electrically charged current, both positive and negative. His quarters rattled with each deafening explosion. Dust and splinters from the rotten wooden rafters rained down on him.

He ran outside, clad in nothing but his shorts, as the whistle of shells pierced the sky overhead.

The air, which normally held natural sounds, birds, leaves, and rain, was glowing with ash and embers and the moaning, screaming, and praying of those still alive. The smell of death was omnipresent.

Explosions continued to rock the compound. Billowing glowing orange clouds popped up everywhere. Smoke filled the air. The stink of nitroglycerin, sawdust, graphite, and burned flesh burst through on the hot blast-driven wind. Air pressure changes popped against his bare chest.

Frank's heart lurched. This was a hospital. But Charlie didn't care. A red cross sure wasn't Captain America's shield or even a deterrent. He ducked, covering his head with his arms as a shell hit nearby, sending dirt, rocks, flames, and shrapnel in every direction. A few pinpricks lanced his bare legs, but he couldn't let that stop him.

Running in a zig-zag pattern, Frank headed toward the hospital but slid to a stop when a man lying on the ground appeared through the smoke. He recognized him, one of the corpsmen, Sergeant Don Sadler. Frank knelt beside him and turned him over. Don had a large, heavily bleeding hole in his abdomen.

With shells landing around them, they couldn't stay here. They would both die. Frank lifted Don over his shoulder in a fireman's carry and ran in what he thought was the direction of the hospital. It was hard to tell through the smoke and mayhem.

A blast wave knocked one leg out from under him. Frank went sliding across the muddy ground on his belly with Don on his back. When they stopped, he stood, feeling his back and right ankle protest the movement. He ignored the pain, picked up Don, and proceeded forward as best he could.

The hospital door appeared out of the smoky haze, held open by a nurse. A light of partial sanctuary. With one last push, Frank launched himself and Don through the door, both of them falling into the arms of the waiting medical staff.

Frank tried to pull away, but strong hands gripped his arms, holding him in place. He didn't realize until that moment his legs were shaking like leaves in a strong wind. Even so, he had a job to do.

"Dr. Howard, easy, you're hurt," the corpsman holding him said.

"I'm okay. Just get me a surgical gown and boots so I can scrub up." He couldn't be mostly naked in dirty underwear in the OR.

"No, Frank. You're out for the count on this one," Nurse Peggy Sanders said.

Before he could do or say anything, two corpsmen lifted him onto a gurney.

Frank tried to roll off. They needed him. Again, he was held in place by several pairs of hands. A face appeared above his, Dr. Henry "Elvis" Buchannon.

"Frank, relax. We've got this," Elvis said.

Frank felt someone stick an IV catheter in his right forearm. Not in any real pain, he didn't understand why. His subconscious knew, the pre-programmed human response to injury, the morphine-like chemicals dumped into his brain. It just didn't register.

Peggy put an oxygen mask over his face then stroked his hair.

As his eyes got heavy, all Frank could think about was, *Is he Expectant or Salvageable?*

December 26, 1971
95th Evacuation Hospital
Da Nang, South Vietnam

Frank awoke to the sea-green, peace-sign-covered walls of the Recovery Room/ICU. He stared at the continually lit recessed fluorescent lighting of the dingy white ceiling above him. Without looking at the wall clock, you didn't know if it was night or day in the windowless room.

Someone shook his shoulder insistently. "Frank," said a female voice. "Can you look at me?"

Swallowing to soothe his dry throat, Frank turned his head to look at Peggy. "Hi," he croaked out. He could smell the dampness. The concrete floor had recently been rinsed of blood. Some of it was probably his, Don's, and whoever else was hit during the attack. And lived. The rest resided in the KIA shack inside a rubber body bag.

Peggy smiled. Her stethoscope hung around her neck over her faded fatigues. She looked bone-tired with shadows under her eyes. "Hi, yourself. Welcome back." She pulled a ballpoint pen from her shirt pocket and scribbled something on his chart. Probably the time he opened his eyes.

Frank looked down at his legs. Covered with a blanket, all he could see were two mounds of his feet sticking up. But that meant his legs were still there. He glanced at the stand next to the bed and the bottle hanging from it with a tube leading to his right forearm. Ringers Lactate. A salt solution to replace lost fluids. Next to it, a small bottle of antibiotics to prevent infection. Even though he couldn't see them, he knew his wounds were left open and dressed with antiseptic bandages to avoid infection several times a day. They would be sutured at the next hospital. Delayed closure. That was the Army's directive. And he had an oxygen cannula and a Foley. He knew the procedures well.

At the cluttered central desk, nurses and corpsmen went about their duties, checking charts and writing notes. A few looked his way and smiled, glad he was awake and alive.

"Am I...okay?" Frank asked. Drugged and in no pain, he had to know. What would he do if he wasn't?

Peggy nodded. "You're going to be fine."

"Tell me."

"You have shrapnel injuries to your legs. Mostly minor. A few of them were deep. One came close to an artery. Elvis removed everything without any problems. No fractures. You twisted your ankle. It looks like a swollen black baseball, and you sprained your back."

"Well, I guess it could've been worse." Frank motioned with his left hand at the blanket, feeling the dull ache in his lower back. If he felt the pain while on morphine, then it was more than a few muscle fibers stretched or torn. "Show me."

Peggy flipped the blanket down. His legs were covered with gauze bandages, just like he figured. He couldn't see his ankle, tightly wrapped in a tan ace bandage with only his toes visible. Another ace bandage was looped around his abdomen to support his back. A Foley tube ran from his penis to a bag hung on the bedframe. He studied it professionally. Partially full meant he was putting out a normal amount with the fluids they were pouring into him.

"Did I need any blood?" Frank asked.

She scribbled more on his chart. "A couple of units. You were covered in blood and still bleeding like a stuck pig when you ran into the hospital with Don."

"Oh." He didn't know, but he was probably going into shock by then.

"Did we lose anyone?"

Peggy nodded. "Yes, four of the perimeter guards died with seven wounded, including you," she said without emotion, which Frank knew was a façade that enabled her to stay positive in a world of misery and death. Just like everyone else here.

He hated whoever did this. The fucking NVA or Cong or both. Being in this God-forsaken country had changed him. Taken his morality learned from his caring parents away and turned it into us versus them. "And Don?"

"He's alive, thanks to you."

That made Frank feel better. Like he accomplished something other than causing them more work by getting wounded and leaving them short-handed.

Elvis joined Peggy, accepting the chart from her and flipping through the pages. "Hey, Frank, how do you feel?"

"Lucky." What else could he say? He ran through a fiery mortar attack in his underwear with a man on his back and lived to tell about it.

"I'd say."

"So, what's the plan?"

"You're going to Japan tomorrow to recover. We need to free up a bed so you can't stay here."

"What about my stuff?"

"Got a couple of guys packing it up now. It'll go with you on the C-130."

Frank held out his right hand, dragging the IV line with it. "Thanks."

Elvis took his hand in a tight grip. "You're welcome. Don't do it again."

"I don't intend to." Frank chuckled. "It sucks."

0800 Hours
December 27, 1971
95th Evacuation Hospital
Da Nang, South Vietnam

Frank lifted himself up on his elbow as the two orderlies carried him on the stretcher outside the hospital. He looked around at the small and large craters pockmarking the compound. Some of them looked big enough to swallow a man. All of them were filled with water from an overnight storm.

He fell asleep listening to the pitter-patter on the metal roof last night. It helped him relax. Well, that might have also been the sedative and pain meds the nurses injected into his IV line. Something, at least in his mind, he didn't need anymore. He was a doctor, after all.

Soldiers with shovels were in the process of filling the holes, splashing even more mud on their already drenched, muddy fatigues. Several buildings were blasted to pieces or burned-out hulks. Gone was one of the guard towers, the water tower, a latrine, a couple of their living quarters, a section of the perimeter fence, and the asphalt tennis courts. Several protective abutments were toppled over with sand spilling out in mounds on the wet ground.

Before the orderlies placed him inside the open doors of the waiting ambulance, Elvis and Peggy, waiting next to the doors, stopped them. Nearby sat the burned and shattered frames of three other ambulances.

"Frank, take it easy. Enjoy the vacation," Elvis said with a smile.

"Yeah, some vacation. I get to lie in a bed in a ward full of men like me," Frank said before plopping down flat on the stretcher, careful of the IV line still in his right forearm. He didn't want to jerk it out. At most, it would delay his departure by only a few minutes.

Peggy grabbed Frank's left hand in both of hers. "But you're alive. That's what counts."

"True," Frank responded. Now he knew how it felt to be on the other side of the lecture he'd given so often to his patients. At least this gave him an all-new perspective.

Elvis waggled his finger at Frank. "Follow your doctor's orders...or I'll come to Japan and kick your ass."

Frank nodded. With mostly everyone here on a first-name basis for unit cohesion, like a close-knit family, almost no one ever saluted, but today he did. "Yes, sir."

Somewhat reluctantly, Elvis returned the salute then shook his head. "Okay, guys, load him up and get going. You've got a plane to catch."

The orderlies lifted him into the ambulance, placed the stretcher into the holders then shut the doors.

Frank heard someone, probably Elvis, pound on the doors from the outside then a muffled, "Go." He leaned back for the bumpy ride to the airfield along a dirt road Charlie loved to shell or place landmines. Might be an exciting ride if he got there at all.

CHAPTER 9

0800 Hours
February 4, 1972
Yokota Air Force Base
Japan

Frank handed his Army-issue OD-green duffle bag to the aircrew and climbed the rear boarding ramp into the C-130. His first assignment since being released from the hospital two days ago. Tucked safely inside his gear were his newly-issued Purple Heart, Army Meritorious Unit Commendation Ribbon, and Soldier's Medal for saving Don. The one surprise that came with those awards was the Combat Medical Badge. Elvis thought he earned it.

Unfortunately, the muscles in his back took forever to heal then rehab to regain his mobility and some level of required fitness. Since his tour ended while recovering from his injuries, he was headed back to the "world." Except his "Freedom Bird" came with a job and responsibilities.

He looked around. His temporary staff was taking care of nine patients assigned to him for this trip. With the plane about to leave, he sat on the bench close to Sgt. Gonzalez. He wanted to keep an eye on him, having read the files of all his patients. A few days ago, Gonzalez lost his right leg at the knee and nearly died from blood loss. Only by the grace of God and a great medic, Gonzalez was going home on a blanket-covered standard Army stretcher, not on ice inside a flag-draped pine coffin or a rubber body bag.

The force of the takeoff roll pressed Frank sideways on his bench. Once the plane leveled out at its cruising altitude, Frank stood to check on his patients. The plane rocked back and forth after hitting an air pocket. He stumbled forward before catching his balance, sending a spasm from his back down his legs. To get out of the hospital, he hid his lingering minor pain from his orthopedic doctor. His back would heal eventually. He could tough it out for the ability to go home.

As Frank bent over to check Sgt. Gonzalez's pulse, he heard a male voice screaming at the front of the plane, "Stop ignoring me. Get a doctor over here before the colonel dies!"

Who's dying? All my patients are accounted for. What's going on over there? Frank looked over at Sgt. Peters, one of his medics. "Can you take care of this for me?" He had to find out what was going on.

Peters nodded, jumping up from his seated position on the bench a few feet away. "Yes, sir." He traded places with Frank.

Frank followed the unceasing noise, rising with intensity and volume with every word. Whoever was screaming sounded desperate. Frantic. Anxious. As he came around the cargo pallets separating the seating area from the cargo bay, he stopped, disturbed at the scene in front of him. A soldier slumped so far forward in his seat he looked like a pretzel. On his left wrist, a handcuff attached to the chair arm. His battered green field uniform was so dark, it looked like it had been dunked in water. Four other soldiers with a week's worth of facial hair and dressed in filthy, mud-encrusted green, black, brown, and olive drab tiger-striped jungle fatigues sat in the same row. All of them had handcuffs attached to their wrists and chair arms, keeping them seated with little to no movement. Army prisoners. For what, he had no idea.

Even from a distance over the pungent, putrid aroma emanating from the men, Frank could smell the iron in the air. A familiar odor from the OR at the 95th Evac hospital. Under the man's seat, a pool of black, crusted crimson blood with fresh red blood dribbling down the chair frame.

"Shit!" Frank ran to the MP with staff sergeant stripes on his sleeves. The man's OD-green ripstop cotton stiff-looking jungle fatigues had the name tag Reynolds over the right pocket. They still had that "new" smell. A sharp contrast to Frank's current jungle fatigues that were worn-out, faded, and stained. A badge of honor, of sorts, for his Vietnam service.

Frank pointed at the injured soldier. "Where are the medical personnel accompanying this man? He's almost dead already. Half his blood is on the deck under him."

Staff Sgt. Reynolds shrugged, his face hard and unfeeling. "MacKenzie's a prisoner. He doesn't have any."

"What! That's against the regulations!" Frank took a step to go around the man.

Reynolds sidestepped into his path. "You don't have clearance to be around those men."

"Get out of my way!" Frank pressed his height advantage over Reynolds. Six feet to five-ten. He breathed into the man's nose the remnants of last night's Italian dinner. *Hope he likes garlic and anchovies.*

"No, sir."

"I'll have you up on charges, Sergeant." Frank clenched his fists at his side. He wanted to bop the man on the head, but that went against his oath and ethics as an Army officer. Assaulting an enlisted man could get him court-martialed. But for this asshole, he might make an exception. Right now, he had a deep hatred of stupidity.

"Don't think so, Doc. My orders are quite clear. If you want to see the traitor, then do it, but I ain't moving."

Frank climbed over a small stack of empty cargo pallets to get to the wounded man, feeling another twinge in his back, but it quickly passed when he stood up straight. He picked up the dog tags hanging from the soldier's neck to check the blood type and name. *O positive, MacKenzie, Jackson J.*

In the next seat, a dark-haired young staff sergeant motioned for him to bend over.

"The MPs pulled him out of the hospital. Colonel MacKenzie received several nasty shrapnel wounds four days ago. Dr. Nicholson probably removed the big stuff to stabilize his condition. Most of it's still embedded," the staff sergeant said.

A colonel. Great. Why's he wearing Sergeant's stripes? Wonder what he did to wind up here. Doesn't matter. He's my patient now. Frank glanced at the young man's name tag. "How do you know that, Sergeant Roberts?"

"I'm a medic, sir. The colonel was under my care until we arrived back at base camp. I checked his vitals as best I could before we took off. His pulse is weak and rapid. I'd estimate it at around 150-160. He's in hypovolemic shock from blood loss. His eyes are rolled back into his head. The pupils are fixed and dilated. And his forehead is hot and dry to the touch." Worry lines creased his brow, and his brown eyes bore the look of a much older man. Deadly experience gained as a combat medic in the hazardous jungles of Vietnam.

"Thank you, Sergeant Roberts, for the excellent report." The young man needed the attaboy to hold up his spirit. And it was an excellent report, given, like MacKenzie, Roberts was handcuffed to his chair. Frank moved a few feet away to his next target. Back ramrod-straight, clenching and unclenching his fists, he stood in front of Reynolds. "Read my lips. This is a direct order. Take that cuff off now!"

Reynolds glanced at the gold oak leaves on Frank's collar and yanked the cuff keys from the clip on his belt. "Whatever, sir. MacKenzie can't go anywhere. We're over the Pacific Ocean." He bent and unlocked the handcuff.

Finally. This man hasn't got a lot of time left. Frank waved over his two best medics, Sgt. Peters and Cpl. Tanner. Once they arrived, he unlatched the seatbelt.

MacKenzie, unconscious and limp, pitched forward, slinging blood all over them as he fell. Frank and the medics caught him before he hit the floor.

Frank looped his elbows under MacKenzie's armpits while the medics grabbed his legs. Together, they carried the wounded man to the cargo area, leaving a blood trail behind them, and laid him on a cot.

Frank examined his patient while his medics cut off the blood-soaked clothing and bandages, rendering the man naked. He confirmed Sgt. Roberts' rundown then glared at Reynolds through narrowed eyes. His medics waited for orders beside him. "Sergeant Peters, start two wide-open IV lines of fluids and plasma to raise his blood pressure. It's too low. Add a round of heavy antibiotics to the bags. We need to curb the infection present in the open wounds. Corporal Tanner, get him on a full face mask with one-hundred-percent oxygen. Then cover him with blankets to keep him warm. He's in shock."

The two men rushed around in a coordinated ballet. Smooth and practiced, just like the medical staff at the 95th Evac. Frank grabbed a morphine vial, injected a dose into the port on one IV line, and sat next to his patient. He turned to his medics. "Tanner, Peters, go help my staff take care of the other wounded men. My duty is clear. I need to stay with Colonel MacKenzie and monitor his vital signs. He's walking a fine edge between life and death."

1800 Hours
February 4, 1972
Wheeler Air Force Base
Oahu, HI

The second the landing gear touched the runway, Reynolds and two MPs shoved Frank, Sgt. Peters and Cpl. Tanner away from MacKenzie's unconscious, prone body. The MPs stood there with their arms crossed. The two lower-ranking ones, standing on either side of Reynolds, removed their nightsticks from their belts and smacked their palms continuously, sounding like an uncoordinated and spastic junior high school drumline.

They're trying to intimidate me! Fucking assholes. "Get out of my way. That's an order. Medical protocol dictates I transfer Colonel MacKenzie to the hospital," Frank yelled at the men standing between him and his patient.

Staff Sgt. Reynolds chest bumped Frank, causing him to take a step backward to maintain his balance. "No! He stays on the plane. I'm not losing my stripes for a traitor."

Frank wiped spittle from his face. "Sergeant Peters, Corporal Tanner. Put Colonel MacKenzie on a stretcher and take him to the ambulance."

As the two men picked up MacKenzie from the cot to transfer him to a waiting stretcher, three MPs ran forward and pointed M16s at their heads.

Frank waved off his medics. "Sergeant Peters. Go to the hospital and grab as much O-positive blood, plasma, saline, and morphine you can cram into a transport container while they refuel the plane. Including the kitchen sink if you can swing it. I will not let a wounded soldier die on my watch." He turned to Staff Sgt. Reynolds. "Since the cargo deck of a C-130 isn't a proper medical facility, could you at least let Sergeant Roberts help me take care of Colonel MacKenzie?"

Reynolds shook his head. "No can do. These guys are Green Berets. I don't want a scalpel in my back. You'll have to keep him alive all by yourself."

"Sergeant Reynolds, you made a hard job for two people almost impossible for me." Frank pointed at the colonel's bloody shoulder bandage. "If I can't get the bleeding stopped, Colonel MacKenzie will die before this plane gets halfway across the Pacific Ocean. He won't have enough blood left in his body to keep his heart beating. I hope you can live with yourself. You're nothing but an ignorant redneck. A wad of gum on the shoe of civilized people."

"Whatever, sir. He still stays on the plane. Deal with it." Reynolds flipped Dr. Howard his right middle finger.

"Asshole!" Frank bent over his patient to check his pulse. *It's barely palpable. I don't think I can save him. God help me. And him. Geez, what did the colonel do to deserve this?*

Two hours into the flight to California, MacKenzie's breathing came in short, quick gasps. Frank pumped the blood pressure cuff around the colonel's left bicep. "Shit, I can't even get a reading." He put his stethoscope on MacKenzie's chest. "And he's tachycardic. His heart's racing over 210 beats a minute," he said to himself.

Frank grabbed a central line kit from the transport container and inserted the catheter under Colonel MacKenzie's left collarbone. He pulled a unit of blood from the cooler, attached it to the line, and squeezed the bag to force every drop into his patient. Pumping up the cuff, he rechecked the colonel's blood pressure. "Crap, no change."

The scene around Frank changed from the inside of a C-130 to the sea-green walled OR at the 95th Evac. Instead of Lt. Colonel MacKenzie on the cot, the body became that of the mutilated kid with the peach fuzz he lost back in June. He looked into the open abdominal cavity at the perforated stomach and bowels, smelling their putrid, bacteria-filled contents. In his bloody, latex glove-covered hands, a scalpel posed over the wound. He squeezed his eyes shut. This couldn't be real.

Slowly, Frank reopened his eyes to Lt. Colonel MacKenzie gasping for air, his skin taking on the blue tint of oxygen deprivation, his body jerking in muscle spasms. Shit! He kicked himself for freezing in a crisis. MacKenzie's life depended on him.

After squeezing three more units of blood into his patient, MacKenzie's breathing slowed, and a hint of color returned to his face. Frank checked the blood pressure again. "Finally, a reading, 90 systolic by palpation. Not good, but better. At least he's not as blue, and his heart slowed to 150." He inserted two more IV lines then hung a bag of plasma and saline wide open. Desperate, he went down on one knee next to the cot. "Colonel, keep fighting. It's taking every trick I know to keep you alive," he yelled in Colonel MacKenzie's ear.

The same routine continued for the next six hours. By the time they landed, the green plastic transport container was empty of every scrap of supplies save a couple of rolls of gauze and a few 4 x 4 bandages. The only thing in the green-painted metal Lasko cooler was a chunk of ice not even big enough to chill a small glass of water.

Frank was met by the same excuse in San Diego. Orders. As they refueled the plane for the final leg of the journey, he stood toe-to-toe with Reynolds. "Are you a robot? How can you let another soldier die? You're treating him like a piece of trash."

Reynolds walked over to MacKenzie, pulled a Colt service pistol from his holster, and racked a round into the chamber. He pressed the front sight between the colonel's closed eyes. "I can put him out of his misery if you want, Doc. That way, he doesn't suffer. It's what we do for dogs and horses. He's a traitor, and not even worth the price of a bullet, but I'm willing if you are. There are no deviations in our destination per orders from the Pentagon."

Frank pushed between Reynolds and his patient, the pistol muzzle against his chest. He glanced back at the colonel before returning his gaze to Reynolds. The muzzle had been pressed so hard into MacKenzie's forehead, a small circle impression remained. *He acts like a dictator. Must have little man syndrome. I bet his penis is the size of my pinkie. The colonel's defenseless.* "No, that's murder. If you do, I'll make sure you stand in front of a firing squad. You'll have to shoot me to get to him."

Reynolds holstered his pistol. "As you wish. I don't think you'll have to worry about it much longer." He turned and walked back to his post next to the other men.

"Dr. Howard," someone called from the front of the plane.

"Yes." Frank turned around.

The pilot stood in the cockpit doorway, waving a piece of paper. "There's a delivery for you at the main gate from the San Diego Naval Medical Center. The note from Sergeant Peters says he figured you would need more supplies. This is like the last one. Do you want it?"

Peters, I'll put you in for a commendation and promotion for your quick thinking when I get a chance. "Yes, get it here, stat. I'm out of everything."

Eight hours later, the plane landed at Simmons Army Airfield. Frank stood in front of Reynolds when he approached to take MacKenzie off the plane. "Don't touch him. He's barely alive as it is. Get me an ambulance. Now!"

"There's one waiting at the edge of the airstrip. Your CO pulled a few strings. Not that I care. MacKenzie's a traitor. He deserves to die." Reynolds picked dirt from under his fingernails.

Frank leaned into Reynolds' face until their noses touched. "If I had the time, you would be scraping yourself off the deck." He pushed past the soldier as two corpsmen carried MacKenzie off the plane on a stretcher.

As Frank went down the ramp, he glanced at the OD-green bus next to the plane. MacKenzie's men were climbing on board in handcuffs and leg irons. Their shoulders slumped forward, and heads hung low. They looked like walking question marks. The medic, Roberts, was last. He looked in Frank's direction.

"I'll do my best," Frank yelled. He'd heard the men screaming at him over the engine noise. Wanting to know about their CO. Robert's voice the loudest of all. He couldn't leave his patient to tell them anything. The other problem was the line of MPs standing in his way. If he tried to speak with the men, MacKenzie would not have anyone watching over him. Who knew what the MPs would do out of Frank's view? Yank out MacKenzie's IV lines? Introduce air into one of those lines to induce a heart attack or stroke? Remove the oxygen mask? Pull off the mound of blankets? Or all of it.

Roberts nodded and disappeared through the door.

Frank hopped into the ambulance. "Stick your foot in it, Sergeant. Colonel MacKenzie's barely breathing!" He squeezed blood into his patient. At his side, a medic bagged MacKenzie with a positive pressure mask attached to a green oxygen cylinder. Both men grabbed the gurney rails to keep from being dumped onto the floor as the ambulance slid sideways turning onto the asphalt road with lights and siren screaming.

Upon their arrival at the hospital, Frank rushed his patient into the surgical theater. Time was now the enemy. That golden hour slipped away hours ago. He had three possibilities. Death, brain damage, or a miracle.

CHAPTER 10

February 8, 1972
Womack Army Hospital
Ft. Bragg, NC
Room 611

Frank tuned the radio on the table to a local easy-listening station. The music would help him to think. He returned to his chair and picked up his *Time* magazine with Henry Kissinger's picture on the cover.

He still couldn't wrap his brain around what happened to MacKenzie. The man had severe injuries. Why was he on that plane? Treatment protocol dictated he be stabilized at the first medical facility, which was at Phước Vĩnh, then moved for further treatment once stable. That should have been either the 93rd Evacuation Hospital since it was close or Frank's old unit, the 95th Evacuation Hospital, with its ability to deal with complex cases. But that didn't happen. And MacKenzie barely survived. Probably out of sheer stubbornness and a tremendous will to live. Two personality traits whoever did this couldn't factor in. Thank God.

According to the report forwarded to him by Dr. Nicholson, four MPs burst into the recovery room, tore out all MacKenzie's IVs, and manhandled him into a uniform since he was naked after surgery. If that wasn't bad enough, they threw him into the open bed of a truck and left with him rolling around unsecured like a side of beef. Then he flew unconscious, strapped in a seat from there to Japan, where Frank came into contact with him.

Given what he knew, if MacKenzie had come in as anything but a single at Phước Vĩnh, they might have labeled him Expectant during triage, loaded him up on morphine, moved him to a private area, and let him die. Who knows? Everything depended on the number the rolling dice landed on that day. It could have easily been snake eyes instead of eleven.

Something else bothered him. Why would someone do this? It went against all humanity, morals, and decency. He didn't recognize the last name on the C-130, but now he knew his patient's identity and history. MacKenzie's medical records made for interesting reading. West Point graduate. Career officer. Service in Korea and Vietnam with six combat tours in total. One as a POW with an extended stay at the 95th Evacuation Hospital. Cathy's name popped up a few times in those records. The soldier, Jackson, he'd heard the hospital scuttlebutt about her helping to save. He wondered how well she knew him.

MacKenzie had numerous injuries in combat with awards for bravery attached to most of them. The one that opened Frank's eyes to MacKenzie's character. He was a recipient of The Medal of Honor for saving a SEAL team singlehandedly on a riverbank in 1968.

If the Army felt he earned that award, why treat him like shit? They didn't treat mangy stray camp dogs or enemy prisoners of war this badly. Surely just being charged with a crime wasn't the reason. Was it? If so, this stunk even more. He'd been convicted in absentia without a trial and sentenced to a slow, painful death without the chance of appeal. A permanence so wrong it was unfathomable to contemplate what human monster could be that cold-hearted.

They told him MacKenzie and his men stole paintings from the Vietnam National Museum of Fine Arts in Hanoi to sell to the highest bidder on the black market. But if MacKenzie wanted money, why venture into the enemy's capital city, even under cover of darkness, and take a chance of being captured? Again. He'd already been a POW once and barely survived. His escape from that camp made him a war criminal with a hefty price on his head to the North Vietnamese government. And a valuable propaganda tool for the communists as a Medal of Honor recipient.

With MacKenzie's background as an expert in small unit tactics and close-quarters combat, he could find a much easier target for a score. Being a common thief didn't fit MacKenzie's reputation. It was the exact opposite. From what Frank knew or heard about him, MacKenzie was the poster child for following the regulations, labeled by many as ruthless and hard-assed but fair, always willing to listen. He didn't seem the type to go somewhere without orders on a whim and a prayer.

As Frank scanned an article in his magazine, he heard a groan and looked up. Lt. Colonel MacKenzie moved around in his bed. He seemed restless. Suddenly he opened his eyes and immediately slammed them shut.

A few seconds passed, then the colonel reopened his eyes a millimeter at a time and looked around. He seemed confused as if wondering how he got there. Considering his probable last memory was the hospital at Phước Vĩnh, completely understandable.

Frank lowered his magazine. The melody *Tie a Yellow Ribbon Round the Old Oak Tree* came from the radio, which he thought was appropriate. "Good. You're awake. I'm Dr. Frank Howard." He checked Colonel

MacKenzie's pulse at his wrist then placed a stethoscope on MacKenzie's chest. "Don't talk." He adjusted the valve on the wall next to the green line leading to the oxygen cannula under MacKenzie's nose to give him additional oxygen. His face seemed a little bluish. "Okay, I'm finished."

"What happened? Where am I? Other than in a hospital, I mean. Where are my men? Are they okay?" MacKenzie gasped.

Dr. Howard looped the stethoscope around his neck. He pulled a clipboard from a hook on the wall and wrote notes on the first page. "They're fine. You're the only one in the hospital. As to where they are, I'll get into that later. Please don't move your right arm or leg. I removed a pound of shrapnel from your body. The wound in your thigh went all the way to the bone and took over 150 sutures to close. The one in your shoulder is only slightly better at 125. You're on pain meds to maintain your comfort level. The wounds are infected, and you developed a high fever. To counter that, you're on heavy antibiotics. You'll be in the hospital for at least two weeks. Probably more."

Colonel MacKenzie swallowed. "Okay. I know the hospital at my base camp, and this ain't it. You're not Dr. Nicholson, so where am I?"

Frank knew that well-rehearsed hard command tone. He'd heard it numerous times from the high-ranking brass visiting the troops at the 95th Evac. The colonel expected answers. Now. "Colonel MacKenzie, you've been in the ICU for three days with a tube down your throat to help you breathe. That's the reason for your sore throat. You need to take it easy and not move around so much."

Colonel MacKenzie reached up to scratch. His left arm stopped two inches above the bed rail with a sharp rattle of metal on metal. "Why the handcuff? Am I under arrest or something?"

"Yes, you're under arrest, and I can't tell you why." Frank's jaw muscles bunched out as he ground his teeth together. He complained ad nauseum about the handcuff when they moved the colonel into this room in the high-security wing a few hours ago after he fought the ventilator, attempting to breathe on his own. The man didn't have the strength to lift his head, let alone get out of bed. The cuff was completely unnecessary. "I'm merely your doctor. I don't understand it myself."

Colonel MacKenzie nodded. "I like honesty, Doc. I'm sure this has something to do with our last mission. Are my men in the stockade?"

"Yes, and I do believe it has to do with your last mission." *I hope he'll tell me what happened and why.*

"Then I wish I'd gone with my gut feeling. Now, where am I?"

"Home. Fort Bragg."

"Bragg, huh?" Colonel MacKenzie glanced at the window.

"Yes, they yanked you out of the hospital against medical advice and tossed you on a plane." Frank shoved his hands in his lab coat pockets. "You were at death's door when we arrived at the hospital." He wanted to use the head of the person who ordered it as a bowling ball on nailed-down pins and watch it go bounce and splat.

Colonel MacKenzie's face contorted into a serious expression. "You must have something to do with me surviving or you wouldn't be here."

"You're perceptive, even pumped full of morphine and cephalosporin. You have a lucky leprechaun on your shoulder. No one will tell me why it was so important to damn near kill you getting you here in a hurry." *And it doesn't make sense either.*

Colonel MacKenzie reached for the cup of water on his bedside table. The handcuff skipped across his wrist and jerked the IV line from under his skin. Ruby-red blood ran like a flooded river from his forearm, soaking the colonel's light blue hospital pajamas and his blanket.

Fuck! Frank grabbed the arm in a tight grip. He saw this coming. With the other hand, he hit the bed buzzer repeatedly. "Someone get in here and help me!"

Six members of the medical staff dressed in white scrubs ran into the room.

Colonel MacKenzie sat unmoving while Frank snugged a white gauze bandage around his forearm, ripped the end into two pieces, looped it around, and cinched it down with a double knot.

"Gee, Doc, can you loosen it up? I want to keep my fingers," Colonel MacKenzie grumbled.

"No." Frank laid Colonel MacKenzie's wrist across his chest. "Keep that where it is for a few minutes." *Or I'll tie it down.*

"Testy, aren't we." Colonel MacKenzie settled back in his pillows as everyone but Frank and a nurse left the room.

When it comes to my patients, yes. And you're a special case. Lucky to be alive. Frank turned to the nurse. "Insert the line a little higher this time. I have a call to make...and get him some clean pajamas and another blanket." He stomped to the door. On the way out, he propped the door open. As the guard started to close it, Frank yanked it from his grasp. *You fucking asshole!* "It stays open, Corporal. I want to keep an eye on my patient. You damn guards are nothing but idiots."

Frank picked up the phone at the nurses' station and called headquarters. This had to stop before their damn mistakes injured his patient further or killed him. He was ready to take this to the top.

Thirty minutes later

Dressed in his green Army class A dress uniform with a round blue, white, and red CONARC left shoulder patch and rows of ribbons, Colonel Salem approached Frank at the nurse's station.

"Doctor," Salem said with contempt in his deep voice.

Frank slammed his hand on the desk. He discussed this same issue with Salem this morning. "That stupid handcuff pulled out Colonel MacKenzie's IV line again. I poured over eight units of blood into the colonel during surgery to keep him alive. I don't need him losing more. That one small hole became a problem since he's on blood thinners to prevent blood clots due to his immobility. Are you trying to kill him? Sergeant Reynolds damn near succeeded."

"No. Let me make a call. I don't have the authority to remove the handcuff. Only General Kowalski can do that." The man reached for the phone next to the patient monitors. A few minutes later, he hung up. "Okay, the general agrees to remove the handcuff. But the guard stays."

"As long as he stays outside the room, I don't care. I don't need any additional stress to my patient since some numskull ordered him flown nine thousand miles around the world while unconscious and nearly dead."

Salem bowed up, back straight, teeth clenched, and shoulders thrown back. The man was clearly pissed off. "Are you calling one of your superiors a numskull, Major Howard?"

Frank flashed an annoyed smile. "Yes, because it's the truth. I've already had this conversation with my commanding officer last night when I explained to him why I'm at Bragg, not Tripler. I sent him my report this morning. He agrees with me that anyone who gives an order that almost kills one of our own is an idiot. What are you going to do about it?"

"At the moment, nothing. I have my orders. Good day." Colonel Salem turned and walked away.

Frank dragged the guard into Colonel MacKenzie's room by his shirtsleeve. "You heard him." He pointed at the cuff. "Take it off. Now!" *Or I'll do it for you.*

The corporal glanced at Colonel MacKenzie as he held the key over the lock.

Frank cleared his throat to make a point, ready to jerk the key from his grasp. The corporal removed the cuff from MacKenzie's wrist and the bed rail, tucked it in his back pocket, and exited the room. The door closed slowly behind him.

"Doc?" Colonel MacKenzie called out.

Frank lifted his head from writing notes on his clipboard. "Yes, Colonel MacKenzie."

"You've got some balls on you. Most staff corps officers I've run into don't push back like you do. From your reaction in the hall, my ride home wasn't pleasant, and the guys watched all of it."

That's quite a compliment coming from a Green Beret. "Yes, they did. You have a good medic in Roberts. He gave me an excellent rundown on your condition before I examined you."

Colonel MacKenzie nodded. "I agree. Mikey's a great medic. He kept me alive while we humped back to the base. Those guys are my friends. We escaped from a POW camp together."

"That explains why they wouldn't give up on getting my attention." *I thought Roberts was about to chew his arm off to get to me. I'm shocked he didn't lose his voice. Those MPs are lucky he never got free, or that scalpel prediction might have come true.*

"Is anyone going to explain to me what exactly is going on?" Colonel MacKenzie reached up to scratch his nose. "And do I need the feeding tube now that I'm awake?"

"I don't know the answer to your first question." Frank's lips twitched in annoyance. He knew about MacKenzie's history. "But in answer to the second one, yes. I know about your eating habits from Dr. Nicholson. Major Russell gave him a briefing once a week. If I were in Nicholson's shoes, I would've sent you home months ago. I'm surprised you didn't collapse from malnutrition in the field. Right now, all we're doing is maintaining your weight. Your body is burning off everything in the healing process. Since you need to gain over twenty-five pounds, it's in for the duration of your hospital stay unless I determine otherwise. With that huge gaping hole in your leg, at least you won't be jogging around the hospital."

Colonel MacKenzie rolled his eyes. "Doc, could you do me a favor?"

"Sure, what do you need?"

"My executive officer, Major Harrison Russell, was hit during a mortar attack the day before we left on the mission. Dr. Nicholson was positive the orthopedic surgeon would remove Harry's foot once he arrived at Da Nang. Could you find out how Harry's doing and if he's stateside yet? We've been together for years. He's my best friend. Many a night, he would meet me with a candy bar in his hand at our quarters to keep me going."

So his friend went to the 95th Evac for treatment. I wonder if Elvis worked on him. "Sounds like something a best friend would do." Frank leaned on the bed rail. "Sure, I'll check on him. Major Russell won't be able to make a trip to see you until his leg heals up enough for a prosthetic. I'll contact his doctor and swap information with him about your injuries. Since Major Russell's your XO, I'm sure the Army will talk to him shortly. I read in your records about one of your quirks."

Colonel MacKenzie cocked his head. "What's that, Doc?"

"Milkshakes. You drank gallons of them while recovering from the POW camp when you wouldn't eat anything else. If the staff brings you a milkshake every day, will you drink it?"

Colonel MacKenzie gave a couple of half-head nods. He seemed somewhat dizzy as his blue eyes darted haphazardly from side to side as if trying to fix on something.

Frank watched him cautiously, afraid he was about to pass out. *All the drugs in his system probably have him a bit confused.*

"Yep, I love ice cream," the colonel continued. "That was my mom's trick when I got sick and refused to eat. The guys surprised me with a milkshake two days before the mission. How Lieutenant Carter obtained a gallon of still-frozen ice cream at our base is a mystery. It's a rarity at a forward firebase since we don't have a lot of refrigeration capabilities." He chuckled softly. "If we did, Harry would've met me every night with one at our quarters, and I'd weigh a lot more."

"Good. I'll make sure the nurses bring one loaded with protein powder before you go to sleep." *And make sure you drink all of it.*

Colonel MacKenzie smacked his lips. "As long as it's also loaded with a lot of ice cream, I'll drink it."

The levity caught Frank by surprise. As his laughter joined the colonel's, the door opened, and two officers walked inside. Colonel Salem and his aide, a young second lieutenant. Their solemn looks changed the mood in the room to one of hostility and skepticism.

"Dr. Howard, could you leave the room for a few minutes? We need to speak with Lieutenant Colonel MacKenzie in private," the colonel stated, utterly professional, emphasizing MacKenzie's lower rank.

Frank pointed at the door. "Your call, sir." *Not that I would leave anyway. I don't trust them. The colonel shouldn't be alone with anyone after what happened on that plane.*

Colonel MacKenzie shook his head. "Stick right where you are, Doc. With all due respect, Colonel Salem, I would prefer Dr. Howard stays after how well I was treated on the flight home."

The two officers outwardly bristled. They looked at each other, then Colonel MacKenzie, and last at Frank, who crossed his arms, ready to observe the conversation. He wasn't going anywhere.

"As you wish," Colonel Salem said in a flat tone. "You want a witness, given everything that has happened. I will say you shouldn't have been shipped home medically unstable. The records I received said the command staff wasn't informed about your medical status. There is a JAG investigation into criminal conduct by the guards. But first things first, I'm sure you want to know why you and your men are under arrest."

Frank almost laughed. That was a load of bullshit. JAG investigation, his ass. Those guards said they were following orders. Whose orders?

Colonel MacKenzie nodded. "Yes, sir. If it's about the mission, those orders came from the Pentagon. I forwarded my doubts up the chain of command after Colonel Johnson briefed me. I never heard back from General Thomas, so when Colonel Johnson gave us the green light, we went as scheduled. I don't understand any of this."

Neither do I. Frank moved over to watch his patient when Salem stepped in front of him.

Colonel Salem waved the other officer behind him and stood beside the bed. "Understandable. Because you've been unconscious since you returned to the base, you don't know Colonel Johnson died during a mortar attack. The HQ took a direct hit. All they could find were body parts and his blackened, half-melted dog tags. His aide is also missing, presumed dead."

Colonel MacKenzie returned the man's glare. "I was awake when we went through the main gate and remember seeing the HQ burned down. After my men dropped me off at the hospital, I sent them to report in. I didn't know about Colonel Johnson. As I stated before, we were under orders from the Pentagon for the mission."

"Your men told us the same thing. No one can find any written confirmation the orders ever existed."

Colonel MacKenzie's eyes narrowed into crinkled slits as his face turned beet red. "But they came by special courier in a locked briefcase. Those don't appear on our doorstep out of thin air as if by magic. It takes all kinds of forms to send one. There's a record of it somewhere. I left certified copies of the orders at the supply office and flight ops. That's the place to start looking."

"We already have. The North Vietnamese government is raising all kinds of hell about the museum." Colonel Salem pulled a document out of his pocket and handed it to MacKenzie. "Here's the propaganda statement they issued. As you can see, they have your names. They threatened to pull out of the peace talks unless the Army arrested your unit for war crimes. That has the State Department running scared."

Colonel MacKenzie glanced at the paper then back at Colonel Salem. "How do they know we were in the building? We didn't come into contact with anyone. How do they know our names? Doesn't anyone wonder how Charlie has that information?"

"I'm not part of the investigation. My job is to inform you about your arrest and the charges against you. Nothing more. Since your unit was TDY with the 1st Cav, you're still under 5th Special Forces designation. The charges, however, are coming from a different command."

"If not the 5th or the 1st, then from where and who are they coming from, sir?"

"I don't have access to that information." Salem tapped the table with his finger. "All I have is you're being charged with Article 86, 106, 129, and 133 of the UCMJ. By who is classified above my clearance level."

Frank was taken aback by the number of charges. It didn't make any sense. *Why dump so many bricks on MacKenzie's head? It seems on the excessive side.*

"How can the convening authority be classified? Don't we have the right to confront our accusers?" Colonel MacKenzie asked.

"I'm not a lawyer, either. JAG will assign one for your defense," Salem said.

That doesn't sound right to me. Frank felt sorry for MacKenzie dealing with problems on two fronts. Legal and physical. Stress he didn't need.

Colonel MacKenzie slammed his hand on his bed table. "We don't need a defense. Someone needs to get off their butts at the Pentagon and confirm the orders. Do you want me to fill out an after-action report?"

Salem pointed at himself. "I'm not part of the investigation. Tell your lawyer. As for an after-action report, that's up to you. If you want to lock yourself into a statement, by all means, write one out. Rumor has it, you're a rogue and let your men do whatever they want. That's why so much equipment disappeared around your base."

"I'm a *what*!" Colonel MacKenzie pounded the bed with his left fist. "With all due respect, sir, I know about the missing equipment. Most of it was mine! As for my men, I expected military courtesy from the soldiers under my command at all times. I sure as hell enforced the regulations. It blows my mind why someone would call me a rogue! Except to sully my reputation and spotless record by suggesting I don't believe in military discipline. I went to West Point, not OCS."

The lieutenant stepped toward the bed. "You don't speak to a superior officer like that."

Frank wanted to slap the man silly. The numskull lieutenant yelled at one superior officer to defend another.

"OCS, right?" Colonel MacKenzie glared at the man. "Shut up, Lieutenant."

MacKenzie got him back good. Frank stifled a laugh. It wouldn't do to show his enjoyment of the lieutenant's dressing down in front of Colonel Salem.

Salem held up his hand. "Step back, Cramer. Go ahead, MacKenzie."

Colonel MacKenzie returned his gaze to Salem. "Locking myself into a statement. That's rich. It's the truth. That's easy to say when you're not in my position. I'm flat on my back. My arm's full of tubes. I damn near died, and now you're telling me I'm charged with a crime! Why? Is it because some dumb ass can't find the orders? Or wants to hide them since they're now a political hot potato. And no one can explain to me how the North Vietnamese government has our names. There's a leak somewhere. Doesn't anyone care who or where it might be?"

"Since you're extremely medicated, MacKenzie—" Salem's irritation showed in his animated body language and rigid upright posture. "—I'll let the way you said that slide. You have a valid point. I can't do anything about it. I'm here to inform you about the charges, nothing more."

Frank almost laughed at the statement. *Extremely medicated, hah! He's got enough morphine in him to sedate a horse. I've never seen anyone with a pain threshold or tolerance that high and still able to function.*

"Understood, sir," MacKenzie said in a non-apologetic tone.

The two men left, and Frank walked over to the bed to check on his patient. "Colonel?"

Colonel MacKenzie took a deep breath. "Yeah."

Frank leaned over the bed rail. "What was that all about?"

After shaking his head, Colonel MacKenzie met Frank's gaze. "I have no idea, a warning, I think. I get the funny feeling the sky is about to fall and smash us flat. Then we'll be thrown under the bus and run over a few times for political expediency." He waved the propaganda report in front of his face. "What bothers me the most is the North Vietnamese government has our names and ranks. Since Harry's on that list, it was before the shelling. No one is investigating how they obtained the information or where the leak is, and there's nothing I can do about it."

"Colonel MacKenzie, you just told me everything I need to know about your character."

"How did you come to that conclusion so quickly? You don't know anything about me."

But I do. More than you know. "Easy." Frank yanked the propaganda report from Colonel MacKenzie's grasp and held it up. "They're worried about what our declared enemy thinks. You're concerned about a security leak. It tells me a lot. The fact they'd do this to a Medal of Honor recipient worries me about the direction our government is taking."

Colonel MacKenzie choked back a snicker. "The fact I have that particular award will be conveniently forgotten. So will any mention of us being POWs, and neither one is a secret. Instead, the Army will throw us to the wolves."

"You genuinely think that'll happen? Do you really think the United States Army would stoop that low?" Frank wanted to believe MacKenzie was wrong, but his heart knew the colonel was correct. And that was a hard pill for him to swallow.

"Given what I just heard, yes. Those officers wouldn't give me any information on who brought the charges. The sixth amendment states we have the right to face our accusers. That's the convening authority. No one will tell me who it is. I've never heard of that happening before."

Frank picked up Colonel MacKenzie's wrist. "Well, your pulse is 120, and you need to sleep. I'll have the nurse give you a sedative. Don't try starting an argument with me that you won't win."

Colonel MacKenzie gave him a crooked half-smile. "Hey, Doc. Can I have some coffee?"

"After you wake up, sure. Black, or do you want cream and sugar?"

"Black. Make it really strong."

"So you like the corrosive kind."

"The more the better."

"I'll see what I can do." Frank knew this man, even stuck in a bed, would be a handful. No, downright the most challenging patient he'd ever had in his career. But, after what happened in the last few days, MacKenzie had every right to be that way. He didn't know who to trust. And Frank knew he had to earn it by his own actions. Getting him the coffee could help in that regard.

February 10, 1972
Womack Army Hospital
Ft. Bragg, NC

Frank looked up from writing notes on Colonel MacKenzie's chart at the nurses' station when the white bubble light snapped on next to the colonel's room number and buzzed on the wall panel. He strolled over to Colonel MacKenzie's room and went inside. "What do you need, Colonel?"

"Are you moonlighting as a nurse now?" Colonel MacKenzie picked up a full white ceramic coffee mug from his bedside table then held it up like a toast before taking a long drink of the steaming black liquid.

"Nah, I was on my way to your room when the light came on." Frank was glad to see his patient in such good spirits, considering what happened a couple of days ago.

Colonel MacKenzie pushed a piece of paper across his bed table to Frank. "Since you're here, can you help me with my after-action report? And take it by the main office?"

"Sure. What made you decide to file one?" *Interesting. Tells me a lot. And I gained his trust if he's okay with telling me what happened.*

"It could make a difference to have my side on paper if someone investigates the case. Sure can't hurt to have the truth out there and might keep us from turning into sacrificial lambs led to slaughter."

Good idea. His sarcasm sounds just like Jake's. Frank picked up the pen. "On one condition. You call me Frank, not Dr. Howard."

Colonel MacKenzie nodded. "Okay, if you insist. That goes both ways. Call me Jackson."

"Deal. Tell me what to say, and I'll write it out for you." *I want to know what got him into so much trouble. But whatever it is, it's not worth almost killing him.*

"Thanks, Frank." Jackson cleared his throat. "At the top, next to the subject line, write Vietnam National Museum of Fine Arts - Operation Memphis - 72002001…"

1530 Hours
Fort Bragg, NC

After finishing his shift at the hospital, Frank, dressed in his newly-issued OD-green fatigues and a lab coat with a stethoscope around his neck, delivered the document to the 5th Special Forces Group headquarters. He felt strange here. He was a doctor. Although he saved lives, these guys demonstrated a different kind of bravery at every turn. Honorable men to be respected for their dedication to doing a tough job only a select few could master.

A Sergeant First Class wearing pressed and starched OD-green fatigues walked up to the desk. "What can I do for you, doctor? Are you thinking about joining us?"

Frank shook his head as he slid a manila folder across the counter and checked the man's nametag. "No. I have an after-action report from Colonel MacKenzie for you to file, Sergeant Collum."

"Okay. Is this for the mission I've heard so much about?"

"Yeah, that's the one. He told me to get a receipt and make sure you put this report in his file."

"How's the colonel doing?" Collum pointed at Jackson's picture on the far wall under the Medal of Honor banner. "He's a legend around here for saving those Navy Seals in '68."

"He's upset about everything, but healing nicely and still bedridden." *And having to deal with too much external pressure.*

"Give it to me. I'll have Colonel Fox sign off on the receipt." Collum pointed at the door. "Can we go see him?"

"No." Frank jammed his hands in his lab coat pockets. "He's under a no-visitor hold. Only people cleared by the 525th Military Intelligence Group can go into Colonel MacKenzie's room. Why?"

"A bunch of us wanted to come by and give him our support. We ran into a brick wall named Colonel Hammond."

"Yeah, I know. The guy's an ass. He's the commanding officer of the 525th. I've already butted heads with him over Colonel MacKenzie's care." *I want to pound some fucking sense into the egotistical bastard. The guy is a moron.*

One general after another tramped into Jackson's room for the next week. One to three stars on their shoulders. Frank stopped counting at twelve. He was ready to ban anybody but medical staff from Jackson's room.

After each general, Jackson became more agitated when no one answered his questions. This impeded his recovery by causing anxiety and ongoing stress. That led to wild fluctuations in his pulse and blood pressure. And the need for more medication, which the colonel hated and complained about constantly. Not that Frank didn't understand. The colonel probably saw more men overdosed on heroin than he ever did at the 95th Evac hospital. But Frank needed his patient relaxed, not pressured into a heart attack or stroke.

Everything came to a head when a four-star general, the Army Chief of Staff, General Windom, wearing his class A uniform with rows of ribbons and awards, approached Frank at the nurses' station on day seven.

"Is he awake, Major?" the general asked.

"Yes, sir," Frank replied.

"Can I speak with him?"

Frank almost said *no*, but this might be good news with the general smiling pleasantly. Maybe the Army figured out its mistake, and Windom was here to apologize to Jackson for everything that happened to him. "Yes."

A few minutes later, Frank heard, "I'm a *what*? How am I a traitor? I nearly died for this country!" Jackson's raised voice came clearly through the open door.

"Shit!" Frank exclaimed, slamming his clipboard on the counter at the nurses' station, glancing at Jackson's heart monitor among the ones hanging on the wall. The blip bounced up and down in a blur with a digital reading of 160.

The general's aide ran from the room.

As Frank walked in to check on Jackson, he ducked a full water pitcher thrown in his direction.

"Sedate him, doctor! MacKenzie's gone off his rocker," Windom yelled from behind an overturned chair.

Not good. "He'd listen to you, general, if you'd answer his questions." Frank went to Jackson's bed and grabbed his left arm before he could cock it back to throw again. "Calm down, Colonel."

Jackson blinked. "What?" He looked at his hand and dropped the phone.

"I think it would be in your best interest, sir, if you didn't throw any more heavy objects at superior officers." *Or me and the staff.*

"Yeah, me too. But they won't listen, and it pissed me off. All they're concerned about is what the North Vietnamese government wants. Not about the security leak."

Both men looked up as the general disappeared around the doorjamb.

Fucking bastards. Frank yanked the blood pressure cuff off the wall, tightened it around Jackson's left bicep, and pumped air into the cuff. "Your blood pressure is 160/110, and your pulse is 150." *At least it slowed a little.* He hit Jackson's buzzer. When the nurse walked in, he turned to her. "Get me a sedative! Colonel MacKenzie's going to sleep for a while. I need his blood pressure and pulse to go down before he has a stroke."

After unloading the syringe into the IV line of his unhappy patient, Frank watched Jackson's eyelids droop lower and lower. "Stop fighting it. Go to sleep." *Geez, how high of a tolerance does he have? I can't give him more. Too risky.* He hit Jackson's buzzer.

A nurse came into the room. "Do you need something, Dr. Howard?"

"Yes." Frank finished writing notes on Jackson's chart. "No more visitors for Colonel MacKenzie without my permission. His medical condition is not stable. I don't care if it's the President of the United States. They see me first before coming into this room. Understood?"

"Yes, doctor. I will inform the staff."

"Good. I'm not about to have the colonel die of complications on my watch because the Army's full of stupid officers. If you need me, I'll be right here in the colonel's room on my version of guard duty."

CHAPTER 11

1200 Hours
February 18, 1972
Womack Army Hospital
Ft. Bragg, NC
Room 611

Frank entered Jackson's room and placed a cloth napkin-covered tray on the rolling bedside table.

Jackson pushed himself into a sitting position with his good arm and leaned back against the pillows. "What's that, Frank?"

"Lunch. I thought you'd like something other than the bland hospital food they've been feeding you." His patient needed the protein. He'd seen Dr. Nicholson's notes in Jackson's medical records from Phước Vĩnh base hospital in Vietnam. Jackson had stomach problems associated with the mess hall food. Not that Frank didn't as well. The food was usually rank and horrible. However, Jackson's seemed extreme and strange for someone who'd spent his entire adult life eating field rations and in different Army mess halls. That problem was a significant contributor to his weight loss while in-country.

"You got that right." Jackson leaned forward and took a big whiff. "Smells like Thanksgiving."

Frank removed the napkin with a flourish to reveal sliced turkey, stuffing, mashed potatoes with a dollop of melting butter in the center, a roll, and a slice of pumpkin pie. "Good guess. Your nose is working better than the rest of you."

"Aren't you the funny one." Jackson picked up his fork. "No gravy?"

"No, too rich. While I amended your food restrictions from—" Frank laughed— "almost pureed baby food to add lean protein and low salt to the mix, you still get the loaded milkshakes."

"Fine by me, as long as it tastes good." Jackson paused with a bite halfway to his mouth. "Have you been talking to Harry?"

"No, just reading your records." Frank chuckled at the disgusted look on Jackson's face. "And I have news about Major Russell."

Jackson dropped the fork back to the plate. His expression turned serious. "Has something happened?"

Frank realized he'd just dumped a bombshell on his patient without explaining first. "Nothing. I checked on him like you asked me. He did lose his left foot at the ankle and is healing well. Once he's ready, they'll fit him with a prosthesis. He's stateside at the Los Angeles VA hospital."

"The VA?" Jackson's eyes narrowed into crinkled slits. "Why not an Army hospital? That's not procedure."

"I know." Frank didn't understand it either.

"It's me, right?"

"I think so," Frank replied. "From what Dr. Baffert told me, Major Russell raised a big stink with the brass trying to find out what happened to you."

"That sounds like Harry."

Frank sat in a nearby chair. "Yeah, a hard-headed Special Forces Army officer like someone else I know."

"Uh-huh." Jackson stabbed another piece of turkey, stuck the forkful into his mouth, chewed a few times, and swallowed. "Is there a reason he couldn't find out anything?"

Please don't choke yourself. "You know the word."

Jackson rolled his eyes. "Classified?"

"That's the one." Frank held up a finger. "He did hear some pretty outlandish stories from Captain…ahh…I don't remember his name. He was Russell's XO in the 2nd Battalion."

"Huddleson?" Jackson suggested.

"Yeah, that's it. He said one intelligence report suggested your helicopter ran out of fuel and crashed in the ocean."

"Well, we did crash, but from an RPG hit to the tail rotor." Jackson wiped his plate clean with the roll and ate it. "If I know how Army scuttlebutt travels, that isn't the only rumor. What else?"

"The jump plane was shot down."

"Nope. HALO jump and too high. And?" Jackson inhaled the small sliver of pie in two bites.

"Ahh…" Frank almost couldn't say this. It was that outrageous knowing the character of the man in the bed. "You jumped ship to become highly paid communist agents."

Jackson choked while sipping his coffee. His face darkened into the deep red of anger as his lips turned downward. He smacked the bedside table with his hand. "That's an absolute truckload of bullshit. It goes right along with Colonel Salem's self-righteous load of crap. No wonder they're treating me like the plague. Sounds like that one got believed."

Frank nodded in agreement. "Yeah, it sure does."

"Forget about that nonsense for now. We can't do anything about it. That food was good. Thanks." Jackson patted his stomach. "Hey Frank, think you can scare up a deck of cards?"

"Sure." Frank saw a well-used deck at the nurses' station. He was relieved Jackson kept his emotions under control instead of throwing something angrily across the room. The last thing he wanted to do was sedate him…again. "Why?"

"Let's play poker or gin and get to know each other. Whoever wins the hand gets to ask a personal question."

"Sounds like fun." Frank stood. He wanted to know more about this man. Something told him Jackson was a pretty good poker player, and he might be the one doing all the talking. At least until Jackson fell asleep.

February 20, 1972
Womack Army Hospital
Ft. Bragg, NC
Room 611

A baby-faced young man wearing an Army class A uniform and carrying a briefcase hurried past Frank at the nurses' station and gripped the doorknob to Jackson's room.

Fed up with the intrusions disturbing his patient, Frank grabbed the man by the shoulder and spun him around. "Who in the hell are you?"

The man stepped back. Over his left jacket pocket was a single with a single ribbon, the red, blue, white, and yellow bar of National Defense. Standard issue. On his lapels, under the gold U.S. pins, the insignia of JAG, a gold quill crossed above a gold sword, superimposed over a laurel wreath. Attached to the outside edge of his shoulder epaulets, a single gold bar. His face flushed in what Frank could only describe as fear.

"Second Lieutenant Moretti, sir," the young man said shakily.

"That tells me who you are, not why you're here," Frank snarled.

Moretti swallowed. "I'm Colonel MacKenzie's assigned JAG lawyer, sir."

"Really? Where are your orders?"

"Here, sir." Moretti pulled a folded paper out of his coat pocket.

Frank unfolded it and looked at the JAG header, MacKenzie's name, and the signature of the Judge Advocate General at the bottom. "Okay. Here are your ground rules, Lieutenant. You do not piss off my patient. Is that perfectly clear?"

"Yes, sir."

"And if you do, expect my wrath. Understood."

"Yes, sir."

The man didn't look old enough to be a lawyer. He looked sixteen years old. "How old are you?"

"Twenty-four. I passed the bar and received my commission last month."

"Meaning you have no experience at all." *What a fucking bad joke.*

"Well," the man stuttered. "No, sir."

"Just what I'd expect from these moronic staff officers, a fucking green as grass attorney! They sold MacKenzie out, didn't they?" Frank thundered. He was pissed.

Moretti cringed. He appeared ready to run or wet his pants under Frank's stern gaze. "What do you want me to say, sir?"

"How about the truth? Is that hard?" Frank wanted to throttle the little weasel. He looked like a follower, not a leader, afraid of his own shadow. This guy couldn't win a court case without a paint-by-the-numbers checklist and an equally inept opposing attorney.

"All I know is what I've been told, sir."

"Which is?"

"It's classified, and I couldn't tell you anyway. Attorney/client privilege, sir."

"My ass." Frank leaned into Moretti's face until they were almost nose to nose. "Remember my warning. I don't give second chances. And I'm really skillful with a scalpel as a trauma surgeon. Remember that."

Moretti's eyes widened. He nodded and entered Jackson's room.

Frank sat at the nurses' station. He wanted to be close in case Jackson raised his voice or hit his buzzer. Then he'd toss that lawyer out of the hospital and request JAG assign another one. Someone with more experience and ethics. This guy had neither.

February 21, 1972
525th Military Intelligence Group Headquarters
Fort Bragg, NC

Frank stood in Colonel Hammond's outer office next to the desk of his clerk, Sgt. Ralston. He looked at his watch, 1500 hours. He'd been here an hour, listening to nothing but an occasional phone ringing and the clicking of an electric typewriter. Hammond, it seemed, wanted him to sweat. Not likely after everything he went through in Vietnam. The only thing waiting was doing, making him madder.

Ralston checked the wall clock then entered Hammond's office. He returned a minute or so later. "He's ready for you now, Major."

Frank nodded. "Thank you, Sergeant." He knocked on the door. When he heard a muffled "Enter," he went inside and stopped in front of the desk in a loose attention until acknowledged.

Hammond looked up. The man with his sweaty bald head, potbelly, and hooked red nose looked like one of Santa's elves except taller. "Major Howard." He put a stressed emphasis on Frank's rank—major.

"Colonel, I want to speak to you about Colonel MacKenzie. He isn't nearly ready to be released from the hospital yet. He's still recovering from his wounds. He needs to start rehab to gain a full range of motion in his arm and leg. Placing him into the stockade will only cause additional problems." *Especially since the man was a POW, all that will do is hurt him more. I can already tell he's trying to hide the issues stemming from it.*

"I have my orders, doctor, and so do you. Don't force my hand. It won't be pretty for either one of you. If you don't release MacKenzie tomorrow into my custody, I will take it to General Kowalski."

"You can take it all the way to the President of the United States for all I care, sir." Frank shook his finger at Hammond. "Neither you or General Kowalski can override my medical opinion or authority."

Hammond stood and slammed his hands on the desk. His eyes flashed with anger. "Watch me, Major."

"I'll fight you all the way."

"If you try, you're bucking with a court-martial for insubordination."

"Insubordination for following the Army's own regulations? That's rich, Colonel. Try that and see how far you get. I'll win, and you know it." Frank knew his contemptuous words could be construed as insubordination, but now all he cared about was his patient, medical oath, and ethics. *Primum non nocere*, Latin for *First, do no harm*. Right now, he wanted to do considerable harm to Hammond.

"Before you do something stupid, Major. Get out! Now!"

Frank considered doing something stupid, like slugging Hammond right in his huge-ass nose with a bop on the head with the business end of a stapler for good measure. But Jackson still needed his help. He couldn't do that if he wound up in the stockade for assaulting or disobeying the direct order of a superior officer.

"Did you hear me, Major?" Hammond thundered.

"Yes, sir!" Frank turned to leave then faced Hammond. "This isn't over...sir. Not by a long shot." He left, knowing he got nowhere, but at least he tried. Jackson was an honorable man who stood by his convictions and duty. So would he. Hammond was a paid-off moron. He probably bought those eagles in an auction. From the lack of a ring on his right hand, he wasn't a West Point graduate – a "ring knocker" like Jackson.

Frank paused at the exit door of the headquarters building. *What did Jackson call Hammond under his breath yesterday? Oh yeah, a friend of Dorothy. He might be right.* Knowing what Jackson meant, he laughed all the way to his temporary OD-green Army-issued sedan in the parking lot.

February 22, 1972
Womack Army Hospital
Ft. Bragg, NC
Room 611

Frank swallowed and opened Jackson's door. He didn't want to do this. Two members of the regular guard rotation, Cpl. Stevens and PFC Hanson followed him inside. Those two narcissistic pricks glared at Jackson with utter contempt.

Jackson's gaze changed from the TV program to Frank, looking him right in the eyes. "Hey, Doc. What's up?"

Frank placed his hands behind his back and frowned. "I'm sorry. I lost my battle with Colonel Hammond's authority on this base. General Kowalski overrode my medical orders. These men are here to take you to the stockade." *I'm still not giving up on this.*

"I knew that was coming. They think I'm a traitor. Let's get it over with." Jackson stood with his hands out in front of him, the right arm supported by a black nylon sling. He ground his teeth together as the handcuffs bit deep into his wrists. "Corporal Stevens, I'm not going to give you any problems."

Stevens bent down to snap on the leg irons.

Fuck no! Frank stepped between Jackson and Stevens. He resisted the urge to kick Stevens in the face or, even better, his balls. "That's where I draw the line, Corporal. His right leg is weak. Besides, he's leaving in a wheelchair." He stepped outside the room and returned with a wheelchair. "Sit."

Jackson eased himself into the chair.

Frank carefully placed Jackson's injured leg onto the elevated footrest then grabbed the wheelchair handles. He pushed Jackson through the hospital to the ambulance bay where an OD-green Army box van sat idling with the rear doors open.

Stevens and Hanson, each holding an arm, helped Jackson climb into the back of the van and sit on the bench. Hanson hopped in and sat across from him with his hand on his pistol grip.

What does that asshole think he's going to do? Run? Escape? He can barely walk. Frank banged on the door with his fist to get Jackson's attention. "Take care of yourself, Colonel MacKenzie."

Jackson peered around the doorframe to make eye contact with him. "I'll do my best. Thanks for everything, Frank. Where are you headed next?"

"Fort Campbell."

Corporal Stevens slammed the door shut and turned to Frank. "Get your ass out of here, Doc. Your stupid-ass worthless opinions are moot now. And you're in my way."

Frank balled up his fists. "Say that again, Corporal."

"Moot. No one cares what you think or say. Go, before I arrest you for loitering. It might not stick, but I'll sure have fun doing it, especially processing you and the strip search." Steven looked at his watch. "Don't you have a flight to catch?"

"I sure do, asshole." Frank flipped Stevens his middle finger then went into the hospital to grab his duffle bag from the staff lounge. The couch there had been his bed since the day he and Jackson arrived. He didn't want to leave his patient, or someone might try to kill him by making it look like an accident. Either removing needed medication and fluids or secretly juicing Jackson with too much.

1400 Hours
February 22, 1972
Fayetteville Regional Airport
Fayetteville, NC

Frank had only a few minutes before his flight boarded, but he needed to let Jackson's friend, Harry Russell, know what happened. He dialed the phone number of the Los Angeles VA hospital.

"Operator, Veterans Administration hospital, how may I direct your call," said a female voice.

"Can you transfer me to Harry Russell's room, number 107?"

"Please wait."

Frank listened to the hold music, a strange, almost hypnotic new age drumbeat with flutes, then it stopped.

"Hello," said a male, suspicious voice.

"Major Russell?" Frank asked, not knowing who was on the line.

"Not anymore, but yes, I'm Harry Russell. Who is this?"

"Dr. Frank Howard. I wanted to call before I get on a plane for Fort Campbell, Kentucky."

"You're JJ's doctor," Harry exclaimed.

"Who?"

"Lieutenant Colonel MacKenzie. I call him JJ."

"Oh…okay." It made sense. Jackson's middle name was Joseph. He saw it in the colonel's records.

"What happened?"

Frank stomped his foot. This made him mad. High blood pressure angry. "General Kowalski forced my hand this morning. Against my medical advice, he issued orders for Jackson to be moved to the stockade. They transported him an hour ago. He's going directly to maximum security."

"Not the infirmary? I was told his injuries were severe. He can't use his right arm or walk. What about rehab?" Harry asked.

"Won't happen. He's walking but barely. His leg is just strong enough to hold him up. His arm, about the same. He'll have to gut it out without rehab," Frank said, his voice reverberating in exasperation.

"In a six-by-eight cell, how's that going to happen?"

"Asked that question myself. Colonel Hammond of the 525th Military Intelligence Group made sure General Kowalski overrode my authority." *But I haven't given up.*

"They can't do that. It's against the regulations," Harry complained.

"Well, they did," Frank replied. "My superiors won't listen to me. Rest assured, I will be writing objection letters to everyone in my chain of command."

"Fat lot of good that will do for JJ. They've already made up their minds about his guilt. Do you know his lawyer's name?"

"Second Lieutenant Matteo Moretti. He's green as grass, and a wuss. Think cream-filled mushy cupcake." *And a fucking coward. He refused to do his job.*

"I'll call him. So he has the true story, not the Army's bullshit version of what happened?"

"I wouldn't make the effort. He'll only piss you off. He did me. I wanted to throttle the little weasel."

"Who's the infirmary doc? I'll call him to keep tabs on JJ."

Frank shook his head. "Don't bother. Dr. Wright's been told not to take your calls or give any information about Jackson's health status. You know the term."

"Yeah, *classified*. Geez. How can that be classified?"

"Have no idea. But that's their favorite term where he's concerned." Frank looked over his shoulder. The gate agent was frantically waving at him. "My plane is boarding. I have to go. Take care, Harry. I'll contact you if I get any news. If I can't, I'll send word through Dr. Baffert."

"Thanks, Doc."

Frank hung up the phone and picked up his carry-on bag. The rest of his gear was in the airplane baggage compartment. This situation really sucked.

CHAPTER 12

1800 Hours
February 25, 1972
Del Ray Apartments
Apartment 214
Oak Grove, KY

Frank unlocked the door to his new second-floor one-bedroom apartment. After two nights in a cheap motel room a few blocks from the base, he was ready to have his own space. He couldn't take kids running and screaming in the halls at all hours of the night after a day in surgery and rounds. His back hurt in the same spot he'd sprained it in Vietnam, courtesy of the lumpy old mattress. Guess it still hadn't fully healed. Thank goodness for aspirin and ice packs.

While he was on duty at the hospital, the movers left everything in his apartment that he placed in storage when he deployed to Vietnam. Now he had to unpack. He entered a room of absolute chaos and tossed his duffle bag on the floor. Cardboard boxes were stacked on his few pieces of well-used furniture. As a poor hospital resident before medical officer basic training at Fort Sam Houston, he didn't have much. A couch, cheap cloth recliner, two-chair kitchen dining table, console TV/stereo, a metal full-sized bed frame, his childhood wooden dresser, and a ten-year-old mattress were jammed into the small living room with only a narrow trail to the kitchen.

He removed his uniform and changed into a pair of sweatpants, sneakers, and a t-shirt. Time to get to work. First, he retrieved his footlocker from his car truck. That had his most cherished items inside.

By 2200 hours, he had his bed made, the couch, TV, and recliner in place, and his clothes placed in the dresser and hanging in the closet. Clearing out the rest of the boxes of his meager belongings could wait until tomorrow. Most of it was knick-knacks, pictures, kitchenware, and stuff from his childhood and college years, so no hurry.

For dinner, a box of cold C-rats from his duffle bag. Spaghetti. At least it wasn't the hated ham and motherfuckers, marked on the cardboard box as ham and lima beans. Those he had heard plenty of stories about, none of them good. It looked, tasted, and smelled so much like canned vomit, not even the VC would eat them.

He'd go to the store tomorrow to get a few groceries - beer, milk, cereal, lunch meat, frozen dinners, pretzels, peanut butter, mustard, mayo, and a loaf of bread. As a bachelor, he didn't cook much, reliant on pre-packaged meals and take-out food.

A few seconds after settling down with his dinner, he heard a single knock on his door. When he opened it, no one was there. Frank looked around the jamb into the empty hallway. The stairwell door across from him was slowly closing. Then he noticed a piece of torn-out spiral notebook paper taped to his door with a white envelope.

He yanked both items off, closed the door, and sat in his recliner to read the note. The handwriting on the paper was so barely legible, it looked like a child's, but a child would never address him as major or say this.

Major Howard,

Consider this a warning to stay out of any business involving Lt. Colonel MacKenzie and his men. You did your job, doctor. Now leave it alone. Stop writing letters on MacKenzie's behalf and remember, we know your every move. If any contact is made by someone involved with him, for example, Major Harrison Russell, report it to your superiors immediately. Failure to do so could result in you joining MacKenzie in federal prison at Leavenworth or six feet under at Arlington National Cemetery with no one mourning for your loss.

With a shaky hand, Frank opened the envelope and shook three Polaroid pictures out onto his end table. He picked up the top one. It was a picture of Jackson sitting on a bunk in a dingy six-by-eight cell, looking like a corpse, his eyes blank, glassy, and staring at something far away. His head was shaved, and his clothing consisted of worn-out, faded green fatigues and dull black combat boots.

Frank knew from Jackson's reputation as a squared away officer, he'd never look like that under normal circumstances. His OD-green ripstop cotton jungle fatigues would be straight, pressed, and starched with military creases, and his black jump boots shined to a high gloss.

And Jackson's scalp looked horrible, covered with inflamed, infected-looking scabbed over scrapes and cuts from a dull razor. When Frank last saw him, his dark blond hair was cut in a regulation high and tight, shaved on the sides and longer on top. The small tuft of hair that overlapped his forehead made him look like a teenage kid.

The second picture was of a white marble military headstone. On the front, under the Christian cross, *Jackson J. MacKenzie. Lt. Colonel U.S. Army. Korea – Vietnam. Medal of Honor. Distinguished Service Cross. 1934-1972.*

The third picture was also a military headstone and under the Christian cross, *Franklin K. Howard. Major U.S. Army. Vietnam. Purple Heart. Soldiers Medal. 1935-1972.*

Frank stared at the note and the pictures. Why was someone threatening him? No one was listening to his concerns anyway. He didn't understand any of this. Why would the Army and the United States government go after Jackson with such a vengeance? All Jackson did was follow orders like a good soldier. He wasn't a spy. Or a traitor. Only a man with problems.

Now, Frank would have to be really on his guard when he contacted Mangus or Harry. Any misstep could get Jackson dead and them right along beside him. Thank goodness they had already set up a system outside of normal channels. The one thing he wasn't about to do – stop sending letters or bucking the system. A normally unbreakable series of Army regulations were now shredded into tiny fragments. A friend needed his help, and he was sure going to give it.

0600 Hours
February 26, 1972
Del Ray Apartments
Apartment 214
Oak Grove, KY

Frank couldn't sleep, so he picked up his small address book from the kitchen table and ran his finger down the first page to Alexander, Cathy. He wanted to hear good news and dialed the number next to the name, curious about her first year of medical school.

The phone rang several times. Frank almost hung up before someone picked up on the line.

"Hello," said a sleepy, sweet female voice Frank instantly recognized as Cathy's.

"Cathy, is that you?" Frank asked, wanting to make sure first before making an ass of himself. He didn't know if she had a roommate. People always sounded different on the telephone.

"Yeah, who is this?"

Frank smiled. "Three guesses. But I'll give you a hint. I hate flag football."

"Frank! I mean, Major...ah...Dr. Howard."

"Frank's fine. We didn't stand on titles or ranks in 'Nam. Why start now?"

"Are you in Waco? If so, I'd love to see you. Take you out of an expensive steak dinner and a glass of wine to repay you for your help in Vietnam."

"No, Kentucky at Fort Campbell. I wanted to check on you. How are your classes?"

Cathy chuckled. "Hard. I'm doing lots of studying."

Frank was surprised, considering her experience in Vietnam. He thought her first year would be a breeze. "Which classes?"

"Huh?"

"What classes are giving you difficulty? It can't be all of them with your background as a surgical nurse."

"No, not all of them. Intro to Clinical Medicine and Anatomy I'm acing. Foundations of Disease isn't too bad. I've surprised the instructor a few times by knowing the answers to his pop questions. Epidemiology and Biostatistics are kicking my ass."

Frank could relate. Those classes weren't his favorites either, but they were necessary. "Just keep chugging along. I know you can do it."

"Thanks. What about you? Any excitement after I left."

"Yeah, the hospital and grounds got mortared."

"What! When? Anyone hurt?"

Frank didn't want to tell her about himself. And he'd never forget this date. "It happened on December 15th of last year. Don Sadler got hit in the abdomen. He's fine. Got the million-dollar wound. The Army sent him home."

"And?"

"Four perimeter guards died with seven wounded, including Don...several ambulances, part of the perimeter fence, a water tower, and the tennis courts were destroyed."

"Frank, I know you. What aren't you telling me? I can hear it in your voice."

Geez, I guess she knows me better than I realized from all those late-night talks while we worked our shift together. "Ahh...I was wounded."

"Are you okay? Aaa...it's okay if you don't want to tell me everything."

76

Frank was touched by her concern. After seeing all those men with so many missing pieces, she didn't want to ask if he was one of them now. "I'm totally fine. I had some shrapnel cuts to my legs, then sprained my ankle and back running to the hospital and saving Don. They gave me a Purple Heart and Soldier's Medal for it. It was right toward the end of my tour, so once I healed up, they sent me stateside." He didn't want to go into what happened next with MacKenzie and his ongoing problems with Hammond and his goons. It could involve her in this fiasco and get her kicked out of medical school through no fault of her own. And he didn't want that to occur.

"Thank God. That scared me."

I can tell. "Have you tagged up with that mysterious boyfriend of yours?"

"He's not my boyfriend, and no, I haven't. He's…tied up at the moment at Fort Bragg."

Bragg? Maybe he's involved with Hammond somehow. What am I thinking? Bragg's a massive base with thousands of soldiers. Whoever this guy is, he's probably a pilot or something. That's it. She tagged up with one of the dust off pilots in Vietnam, then kept it a secret, and now he's at Bragg. Better not to ask again. She might get mad at me. I don't need to lose a friend.

"Frank, are you there? Did you hear me?"

"Huh? No. Static on the line," he lied. "Sorry. What?"

"I'm in medical school. You know better than anyone I don't have time for any kind of relationship, let alone an intimate one."

Frank laughed. "I sure do. Anything else in your life I need to know about?"

"You already know everything. Did you have a life during medical school?"

Frank shook his head. She got him good. "No. I studied, slept when I could, went to class, and studied some more." And then he got the hint. "I'd better let you get back to it. Study hard and make me proud."

"Count on it. Goodbye."

The phone clicked as she hung up. Frank placed his handset on the cradle and looked at his watch. 0630. Time for him to head to the hospital. He had a hip replacement on a general in two hours. Then his sleep-deprived brain realized he called Cathy at 0500 hours since Texas was in the Central Time Zone. No wonder she sounded sleepy. Shit. He woke her up. The next time he called, he would make sure it was during normal hours. Not early on a Saturday morning. During medical school, that's catch-up on sleep day.

1900 Hours
March 3, 1972
Fort Campbell, KY

Frank tucked his red polo shirt into his blue jeans, took a deep breath, and opened the door. As he entered the Rakkasans Bar at the intersection of Fort Campbell Boulevard and Jackson Road, he had a flashback of the officers club at the 95th Evac. He shook it away. This time, he wouldn't end up on his hands and knees, drunk off his ass and puking on the floor.

The room smelled like a typical bar. Full of cigarette smoke, beer, and different types of booze with a hint of vomit. The walls were decorated with giant versions of the unit patches assigned to Fort Campbell. The 101st Airborne Division – The Screaming Eagles, the 506th Infantry Regiment – the Currahee, the 327th Infantry – the Bastogne Bulldogs, the 187th Airborne Infantry Regiment – The Rakkasans, which Frank learned was Japanese for parachute.

In the center of the white tile floor sat a mahogany bar with the regular shelf of every bottle of alcohol and spigot handles for draft beers in the kegs stationed somewhere under the countertop. Off to one side was a small hardwood dancefloor, but no one was dancing to the loud, hard beat of the disco music coming from the bubbling multi-colored neon jukebox.

Frank spotted Lt. Colonel Adam Gaston, his commanding officer, at a large table in the corner of the room. It was actually several tables pushed together. He recognized the people around him. Gaston wanted his staff to meet off duty to get to know each other. His version of bonding for unit cohesion. A bar wouldn't have been Frank's choice for that kind of activity. He thought dinner in a nice restaurant would be much better. But it wasn't his choice.

The senior shift surgical nurse, Major Shelia White, walked past him with a drink in each hand. He followed her to the table. Shelia handed one of the drinks to Gaston.

"Hi, Frank." Gaston raised his glass. "I'm glad you made it."

"Hey…Adam." Frank had a hard time calling his CO by his first name. This wasn't anything like the closeness of the 95th Evac. The staff at Blanchfield was way too formal with each other, preferring to use titles and ranks, not first names, falling back on military decorum, not the familiarity of family.

Another one of the nurses, 1st Lieutenant Liggett…he thought her first name was Patty…waved him over and pointed at an empty chair. "Please sit here, Dr. Howard. Can I buy you a drink?"

Frank wasn't sure about letting a maybe twenty-three-year-old beautiful woman who looked half-drunk already buy him a drink. He usually bought his own. But what the hell. He sat in the chair next to her. She was the only one talking to him. The other staff members were avoiding him, watching him across the table with an air of disdain. Using it as a barrier between them like he had contracted a highly contagious plague. "Yes, whatever beer they have on tap. I'm Frank. You're Patty, correct?"

"Yes!" Patty flipped her long shimming dark brown hair over her shoulder with her hand then leaned back as a waitress walked by. "Could you run me a tab and bring my friend a draft beer?"

The waitress nodded and went to the bar.

"Frank, how are you settling in?" Peggy gave him a huge smile, her white teeth flashing in the subdued lighting. She pushed out her ample chest, her cleavage plainly visible under the bright lime green halter top.

She's looking for something other than talk. He wasn't about to go there.

The waitress returned with a full glass of a dark-looking English stout with a frothy head.

Frank took a small sip before replying. It was strong but rich-tasting with hints of coffee, chocolate, licorice, and molasses, sliding down his throat easily. "Good. At the 95th, we had to choose who was worth saving because of the amount of supplies on hand. You know, Expectant, Salvageable, Delayed. Here you don't—"

Patty held up her hand. "We don't talk about that here."

"Huh?" Frank was confused. He thought this little get-together was for friendly bonding. "No shop talk?"

"I've heard you're a great surgeon and all. You saved a lot of men. Don't talk about Vietnam. As you said, we don't have those problems."

"But, you're in the Army. We have a few patients in the hospital recovering from battle wounds."

"True. Not on my floor. And they're here, not…there!" She pointed at a yellow and red South Vietnamese flag on the wall under the American flag. Her expression was one of disgust.

That statement was off-putting as it seemed more anti-war than someone who took an oath to serve their country in the US Army. She sounded kind of like a conscientious objector. Maybe her loose tongue was the alcohol talking without her brain engaging. He still didn't like it and stood to move somewhere else.

Patty grabbed his arm. "Where are you going?"

Frank drained his glass. "To get another beer." Really, he just wanted to get away from her. She wasn't his type, not that he had one, and he didn't want to hear her opinion of the war anyway. He sat on a barstool and ordered another beer. This one an American pilsner. He wanted to drink his beer, not eat it.

Gaston sat beside him. "Something wrong?"

Frank handed money to the bartender for the beer and gripped the condensation-covered cold glass full of amber liquid. "What's with everyone? They don't seem to like me. Is it Vietnam?"

"Yes, some of it. That's why I asked everyone here. I wanted you to feel like a part of the team. I guess it backfired."

"Big time. What's the problem?" Frank thought for a moment, remembering Patty's frown when he said *expectant*. "Is it how we judged who to save?"

Gaston fiddled with his half-full glass of brown liquid and ice. It smelled like bourbon. "Partly. Most of the staff here are young, either just out of residency or nursing school. They never made it to Vietnam. You know what that's like, don't you, Frank?"

"Yeah." Frank drank a long draw from his glass.

"It's hard for them to understand why those decisions are made without a reference." Gaston gripped Frank's shoulder. "You and I understand. We've been there. But until they experience how you change in a war zone due to what's happening around you, they'll never know how it feels. How sending someone behind a screen to die loaded up on morphine with their only solace someone holding their hand eats at your soul."

"True. What's the other reason?" Frank thought of a moment. "Hammond?"

"Yes. They were warned before your arrival about your dust-up with him and the command staff at Bragg. They know you're an excellent surgeon, but they don't want your problems invading their lives."

"And you?"

"I'm your commanding officer...but I know what you've been through. Let's take it one day at a time. They'll warm up to you eventually."

"Fine!" Frank downed his beer and plopped down the money for another one. And probably a few more after that. He could catch a cab home. But he'd rather drink alone here at the bar than with a bunch of people judging him for no reason other than their distaste of his morality and the fact he stood up for his patient. As Gaston said, they didn't understand. Now, Frank wished he'd gone home to whatever was on TV, a frozen dinner and a can of cheap beer instead. It would have been a lot more fun.

April 8, 1972
0800 Hours
Veterans Administration Hospital
Nashville, TN

Frank walked into the Nashville VA hospital. He discovered his friend, Jake Landry, was a patient here. After he got off duty at the hospital on Friday afternoon, he drove to Nashville and stayed the night in a nearby motel.

Since he was in civilian clothing, Frank set his brown paper sack on the white-tiled floor, pulled out his military ID card, and held it out to the nurse at the admissions desk. "Hello."

The young lady looked at the ID, then Frank, and handed back the ID. "How can I help you, Major Howard?"

Frank tucked the ID into his wallet. "I'm a surgeon at Fort Campbell. I'm looking for Jake Landry's room."

She turned to a wall with several hanging clipboards and chose one. "Let's see...Landry...Landry...yeah, here he is. Major Jacob Landry. Room 255. Go to the elevator, turn right on the second floor and follow the arrows on the wall."

"Thanks."

As Frank started to turn to leave with his sack, she called out to him. "Dr. Howard."

Frank faced her. "Yes."

"It says here he..."

"Has a head injury. I know. I'm the original surgeon in 'Na...Vietnam at the 95th Evac hospital."

"Okay, sir. I just didn't want you to be surprised."

"I won't be." While he wouldn't be surprised, he didn't know what to expect.

He followed her instructions to find Jake's room. After taking a deep breath, he opened the door and went inside. The room was a standard white hospital room with a bed, end table, closet, and bathroom. But what struck him was Jake, sitting in a wheelchair near the sunlit window. His shaved head had a thick, red scar running across his scalp from above the inside of his right eye, over the top of his head to underneath his right earlobe, exactly along Frank's original scalp closure.

Jake wore standard blue hospital pajamas with the left sleeve cut off. They hung like potato sacks on his thin frame. A peripherally inserted central catheter was embedded into the skin of that arm with a bag of saline and one of liquid nutrition hanging on the pole attached to the wheelchair. Hung on one wheelchair arm was a Foley bag half-full of yellowish-clear urine.

Frank crossed the room, knelt in front of the chair, and gripped Jake's hand. "Hey, Jake." He looked into Jake's sunken eyes, hoping for any indication of recognition. Any reaction. Jake stared straight ahead, unblinking, and his hand remained limp. While he was breathing without the aid of a ventilator, that was the extent of his improvement from the last time Frank saw him. And on the downside, he'd lost a great deal of weight, looking like a shriveled-up string bean.

"I know you can see me, buddy." With his free hand, Frank reached into the paper sack next to his feet, pulled out a framed picture of them on the beach with their surfboards, and held it up in Jake's field of vision. "Remember this day. That girl wanted to take you up into that vacant lifeguard shack for some afternoon fun."

Jake kept staring straight ahead without reaction.

Frank released Jake's hand and set the picture on the end table next to the bed. "I'll leave this here where you can look at it." He turned to wipe the moisture from under his eyes, not wanting Jake to see it.

The door opened, and a man in a white lab coat entered the room. "Hello, I didn't know Jake had a visitor." He held out his hand. "I'm Dr. Gary Zeigler."

Frank shook the doctor's hand. "Dr. Frank Howard. Jake and I went to college together."

"Howard, I've seen that name somewhere."

"Probably in Jake's records. I was the surgeon at the 95th Evac."

Zeigler snapped his fingers. "Yeah, that's where I saw it."

Frank nodded at Jake. "What's his prognosis?"

"I think you already know."

"I do, but I want to hear it." He needed to hear it but hoped he was wrong.

"He'll spend the rest of his life in a wheelchair under medical care in a nursing facility." Zeigler handed over Jake's chart. "Major Landry has had five surgeries since arriving stateside. As you have already seen, he has no awareness of his environment. He can't eat or drink, so all his nutrition is either through the PICC line or an NG tube. The blast destroyed the part of his brain that controls thinking, speaking, and voluntary movement. He's about eighty to ninety percent paralyzed but can breathe on his own and has occasional seizures which require medications to control. He gets nursing care twenty-four hours a day."

That's why he can't grip my hand. Frank flipped through the pages. They weren't optimistic. "Has he shown any reactions at all?" He hoped for something. Anything.

"Yes. Occasionally, he'll groan, smile, or laugh when the TV's on, but that's about it. He seems to like westerns and sci-fi shows."

Sounds like him. He wanted to be a cowboy as a child. He loved The Lone Ranger and John Wayne westerns. Frank would take hearing a laugh to know his friend was still in there somewhere enjoying a happy place of good memories he couldn't do physically. "How long will he remain here?"

"About another month to make sure he's stable. His parents have requested to have him moved to a nursing home in New York State to be closer to them. They're making the arrangements now."

Shit! He'll be thousands of miles away. Frank handed the clipboard back to Zeigler. "Can you keep me informed about his status? I'm assigned to Blanchfield hospital at Fort Campbell. Just call the switchboard, and they'll connect you. I have an answering machine. If that thing doesn't work, leave a message with the front desk."

"Sure." Zeigler wrote on the front page of the clipboard.

Frank turned on the TV, moved Jake's wheelchair in front of it, placed a chair beside him, and sat. He didn't care what program or the channel. They could watch together one more time like they did in college. Maybe a western would come on with lots of horses, cowboys, and cattle rustlers. He wanted to hear Jake laugh or see him smile, even if it took all weekend.

CHAPTER 13

May 12, 1972
Del Ray Apartments
Apartment 214
Oak Grove, KY

Frank looked around at the sea-green, peace sign-covered walls of the Recovery Room/ICU at the 95th Evacuation Hospital. The recessed lighting overhead in the dingy white ceiling was never turned off, bathing you in a perpetual yellowed daylight. He glanced at the half-full bottle of Ringers Lactate with a smaller one of antibiotics on the stand next to his bed. The bed was a torture device in itself. A thin foam mattress over a metal frame. It squeaked whenever he moved.

The nasal oxygen cannula tickled his nose, but the Foley catheter was downright uncomfortable. His legs hurt all the way from his groin to his feet. The shrapnel must have cut pretty deep. He tried to wiggle his toes. Pain. The morphine must have worn off. Then his gaze went down the length of his body to his feet under the blanket. But nothing was sticking up this time. They were yesterday.

He peeked under the blanket. White gauze bandages covered both of his thighs. The ends of his knees were rounded and slightly blood-stained. They had amputated his lower legs! Why? He wasn't hurt all that bad. Was he? Just a few cuts, a sprained back and ankle. He could've sworn his feet were there a few seconds ago.

"What! Fuck! No! No! No..." Frank kept repeating. His breath came in short gasps as his heart thundered in his chest.

Peggy ran over from the central desk and gripped his shoulder. "Take it easy, Frank. You developed an infection last night. Rapidly spreading gangrene sent you into septic shock. Elvis didn't have a choice. It was either your legs or your life. You're alive. That's what counts."

"Alive?" Frank pointed down at his missing feet. "How's this alive?"

"You still have the most important parts, your hands. Those and your brain are what make you a great surgeon. You can learn to walk again with two prosthetic legs."

"That's easy to say when you have all your parts. Fuck that." Frank flipped the green wool Army blanket over his head. He didn't want his friends to see him like this.

Frank opened his eyes to darkness. He removed the blanket from over his head, trying to slow his ragged breathing, and in turn, his rapid heartbeat. The room was dark with a beam of dust-filled light coming from the gap under the closed door. Door? Where were the lights? Did the generator fail? This bed was more comfortable than the hospital cot. Where was he?

Confused, he threw off the soft quilted blanket. Soft? Nothing in Vietnam was soft. He pushed himself into a sitting position and felt cold against the soles of his feet. Huh?

He reached over and turned on the lamp beside the bed. As his eyes adjusted to the sudden brightness, he looked at his bare feet next to an overturned empty beer can. He had feet! And wiggled his toes to make sure. What in the hell was going on?

Surrounding him, four white-painted textured walls. He wasn't in Vietnam or the ICU at the 95th Evac but home inside his apartment bedroom in Oak Grove, KY. It was a dream. A nightmare. Breathing a sigh of relief, he leaned back on his elbows.

A cold, clammy feeling entered his brain. He felt his pajama shirt. It was soaking wet. He didn't smell urine, so it had to be sweat and a lot of it. Stumbling to the bathroom, he peered at his reflection in the mirror. The bags under his eyes and bloodshot eyes told him so much. He needed to get some rest. Why did he have that particular nightmare?

Probably because he had to amputate the legs of a soldier the previous day after a motorcycle wreck on base. A few inches and seconds took this man's legs. If he'd managed to clear the intersection before the car blasted through it or waited until it passed by, he would have two legs and gone home to his wife and kids.

Those same few inches made the difference for Frank, as he discovered by reading his medical records. Elvis noted that one piece of metal missed the artery in Frank's left thigh by less than an inch. Fate allowed him to keep his leg and not die while taking two legs of someone else.

The one thing he did know, now he got a small taste of what Jackson was going through every night. If this one thing rattled him, there wasn't any way he could survive what his friend kept having to endure. It gave him a new respect for Jackson's toughness. The only thing he had going for him. Frank could only dream of being that brave.

Frank glanced at the wall clock on the way back to his bed, kicking the beer can out of his way. 0200 hours. He could still get three more hours of sleep. Maybe.

0900 Hours
June 1, 1972
VA Hospital – Room 107
Los Angeles, CA

Frank took a deep breath, straightened his OD-green pressed fatigue shirt, and knocked on the door. He wasn't sure if Harry Russell would trust him, slug him, or physically throw him out. The man was a Green Beret like Jackson – a trained commando, silent and deadly – a snake eater.

"Come in," yelled a muffled male voice.

It's now or never. Frank opened the door, went into the room, and stopped, staring at the man sitting on the bed, propped up on pillows.

"Something tells me you're Dr. Howard," Harry said, laying a folded newspaper on his bedside table.

How'd he know? The nametag, stupid. And I've got medical insignia on my collar. Frank smiled. "Yes. Nice to meet you, Major Russell." Harry looked just like he imagined him. A poster for a Special Forces soldier, tall, broad-shouldered, intelligent, and muscular, except missing his left foot and wearing standard blue hospital pajamas. The brown flattop haircut made him look like a 50s TV star. A new prosthesis wearing a sneaker was propped against the wall next to a pair of crutches and a wooden cane.

That gave Frank an involuntary shudder inside after that nightmare less than a month ago. That could easily have been his fate if things had gone south. And he'd be lying in a hospital bed like Harry instead of standing on two legs.

"Same here. Thanks for saving JJ's life." Harry held out his hand.

"I did my job. That's all." Frank pumped Harry's hand up and down. "Can't stay long, just on a layover. Headed to Hawaii. I'm escorting wounded back. Again."

"Again?"

"Yeah, I think it's punishment for being so vocal. The brass is trying to break me down with work. Won't happen. What about you? Dr. Baffert told me you're seeing a psychologist now."

Harry gave him a half-smile. "I'm okay. Talking helps. Still working through things. How's JJ?"

Frank sat in a nearby chair. "Not good. He needs help. Big time. But they won't give it to him. His nightmares are eating him alive. He can't sleep. Won't eat. Worst case of what some call post-Vietnam syndrome I've ever heard of as a medical doctor. I think a better term is one that's being bantered around in the medical circles, post-traumatic stress disorder or PTSD. It fits since this is a reaction to his torture in the POW camp. Dr. Wright is using drastic measures to keep him alive."

Harry's brow furrowed in concern. "How drastic?"

"Sedating him and sticking a feeding tube in his nose. He's walking a fine edge of life and about to fall off into the abyss. Malnutrition is a very real threat now. Combined with the PTSD, he may do something stupid. It's really messing with his mind." *From Sam's reports, Jackson's damn near psychotic.*

"Like what?"

"I think you know."

"You mean suicide, right?"

Frank glanced away. Unable to maintain eye contact. This thought hurt him deeply. "Correct."

Harry looked sick, almost green-in-the-face nausea. "Anything I can do?"

Frank snorted. "Not unless you know a way to transport him into another dimension or place in time."

"Not an engineer on a TV show. All I can do is write letters."

Frank laughed. "So you caught the reference."

"Yeah. Not a lot to do here besides watching TV and doing rehab."

"Good luck. Haven't had a lot of luck with mine. I'm going to keep writing and pray for a miracle."

"They do happen, Doc. Take comfort in that." Harry looked at the ceiling.

Frank knew what Harry meant. He crossed himself. While he usually wasn't that religious, right now, he was afraid for his friend. And it sure couldn't hurt. He'd take any luck sent his way.

1800 Hours
July 4, 1972
Del Ray Apartments
Apartment 214
Oak Grove, KY

Frank, dressed in black nylon shorts, sneakers, and a white tank top, leaned back in his lawn chair on his balcony with his feet propped on the rail. He downed the rest of his beer and popped open another can. It helped him to relax and think. He had the next two days off with no responsibilities, so why not enjoy it and get drunk. He wasn't planning on leaving his apartment. That's why he had four six-packs of beer cooling in an ice chest under his chair. People watching was more fun while drunk. When they tripped, it was downright hilarious.

Next to him, the folding TV tray held a plate with a mustard, relish, chili-covered hot dog, a handful of chips, a mound of packaged coleslaw, and a bowl of vanilla ice cream covered with chocolate syrup. Even on the nation's birthday, he had nothing to celebrate.

Yes, he was home. Back in the "world." But he was alone. While his younger peers at the hospital accepted him as a physician, a surgeon, he still felt alienated from them socially due to his Vietnam service and trying to protect a man who had no one in his corner. That's okay. He could tough it out and find friends his own age elsewhere. He learned how to cope with loneliness at a young age as an only child. However, his friend, Jackson, couldn't. Not in a prison cell, fighting for his life and locked in an internal struggle for his sanity.

Unlike Jackson, Frank could seek help if he needed it. Right now, he didn't. Somehow, he'd dodged that bullet the experts called post-Vietnam syndrome or like he told Harry, the new term, Post Traumatic Stress Disorder - PTSD. His nightmares were all work-related.

He ate his hotdog, chips, and somewhat melted ice cream. Putting aside his empty plate and bowl, he popped open a fresh beer. The bubbles slid down his throat into his stomach. He watched the orange-red sun grow lower on the western horizon as he finished one six-pack and started another.

Boom!

Frank opened his eyes as his balcony shook. He had fallen asleep. *What was that?* Must be a car backfire. The cloudless black sky lit up overhead with thousands of falling white sparkles, leaving streaks in their wake.

Boom!

"Attack! Take cover!" Frank toppled over in his lawn chair, smacking his head on the wooden floor planks, feeling them shake under him. The door glass vibrated in the frame. Above him, the blackness turned a glowing white/red/yellow/green as more sparkles fell, blocking the flickering stars of the Milky Way galaxy. The air felt electrically charged. He smelled smoke, burning gasoline, blood, and a distinctive acrid odor of cooked flesh.

Boom!

Frank covered his head, kneeling on crushed empty beer cans. His heart was beating so fast it wanted to explode from his chest. He felt cold, breaking out in a sweat. When the sky turned dark again, he crawled into a nearby room, knocking over his ice chest, spilling melted ice water and full beer cans across his balcony. Balcony? His hooch had two wooden steps. Where was he?

He shivered as he pulled himself up hand over hand using the gray blackout curtains. As he reached out to shut the door – Boom, another explosion shook the building, sending him back to his knees, arms covering his head.

Easing his eyes above his elbows, he saw more white streaks falling from the sky. Under his balcony, he heard kids screaming. He pushed himself to his feet and looked over the balcony railing at several children running on the street holding…sparklers in their hands.

Today was the 4th of July. *It's fireworks, stupid, not mortars. Not artillery. Not the NVA or Cong. I'm not in Vietnam anymore.* But it sure sounded like war. Frank straightened, feeling his heart still beating on overdrive. He felt nauseous, ran into the bathroom, dropped down onto his scraped knees and clammy hands, then threw up into the toilet.

What did that God-forsaken country of Vietnam do to him? Fucking gooks. Maybe he did need to talk to someone - off the record. Nah, he just needed to relax. He wiped his mouth with a towel and returned to his living room.

Boom!

Frank dropped to his knees then reminded himself it was only fireworks. Just people celebrating the holiday. As he started to stand, another burst went off, farther away, but enough to light up the sky outside, sending him back to the floor. He decided to stay there. His logical side knew they were fireworks, but his subconscious told him differently. It sounded like war. Exactly like the night he was wounded.

When silence reigned for ten minutes and the chirping crickets returned, he ventured back out onto the patio. After opening a new beer, he piled the rest back into the ice chest, moved the chest inside, then mopped up the standing water. The rest would dry overnight. He'd drink the rest of his beer from the safety of his recliner while watching TV with the patio door closed to muffle the sounds and concussion of any additional fireworks.

CHAPTER 14

```
1500 Hours
December 21, 1972
Blanchfield Army Hospital
Third Floor
Ft. Campbell, KY
```

Frank entered his office, 301, at the junction of the east and west wings. This office was a far cry from what he experienced in Vietnam or the one he was given his first few months here. That one was small with a window, a carpeted floor, and a standard metal desk like you would find in any office building.

Once he established himself within the hospital hierarchy and proved his surgical skills to the staff, they moved him to a larger office. This one had a picture window overlooking the base, nicely painted walls, a shiny white tile floor, and lighting easy on the eyes. Not harsh like at the 95th Evac hospital.

His military and civilian awards dotted the walls. He placed his Purple Heart and Soldier's Medal with their accompanying certificates inside shadow boxes. They were prominently displayed next to his medical school diploma and US Army commissioning certificate. He sat in the plush rolling chair behind his ornate wooden desk then noticed an envelope in his in-box with a return address for Dr. Samuel Wright, Womack Army Hospital, Ft. Bragg, NC 28307.

Quickly he pulled it out, opened the envelope, and removed the piece of standard white paper with US Army letterhead. The typewritten words made him cringe inside.

December 16, 1972

Dr. Franklin K. Howard
Major, US Army
Blanchfield Army Hospital
Fort Campbell, KY

Frank,

I'm out of options. Colonel Hammond keeps blocking me at every turn. I even went to a federal magistrate at the courthouse with the private lawyer you paid to file an injunction on MacKenzie's behalf with a request to have him transferred to a local civilian hospital for physical and psychiatric care. An Army lawyer got it thrown out within hours of filing as not within the court's jurisdiction, even though my lawyer says that is entirely false. He had no recourse but to withdraw his services.

Lt. Colonel MacKenzie admitted to me today he wants to die. That rock of a man is giving up. I don't blame him because he's in so much pain. The Army has driven every bit of hope out of him. If it weren't against my morals, I would help him along with something strong so he could find peace quickly. All I can do at this point is keep him alive for as long as possible via the feeding tube, IV fluids and control his pain with medication.

I placed him on suicide watch with the guards, but they seemed indifferent to it. They'll probably just watch him do the deed and laugh as he dies. Which, for him, would be a release. The guards need to go to hell.

After I pleaded again with Hammond to have MacKenzie admitted to Womack for psychiatric care, he went to MacKenzie's cell and proceeded to verbally mock him. First, he told MacKenzie that his superiors determined MacKenzie's problems were a smokescreen, and his court-martial is scheduled after the first of the year.

Hammond didn't stop there. He flat out told MacKenzie his request for psychological help was denied to his face, and he would be convicted no matter how much he tried to fake his way out of it. How do you fake being seventy-five pounds underweight, unable to keep food in your stomach, and having debilitating nightmares?

MacKenzie was extremely sick that night. I can't fathom what that did to him mentally. He is starting to show signs of liver failure. An almost imperceptible yellowing of his skin and eyes. You have to be close to notice. If it's not already too late to reverse it, in a few days, it won't matter. He'll die from neglect within the next two weeks.

I'll keep trying and hoping for a miracle.

Dr. Samuel Wright
Major, US Army
Womack Army Hospital
Ft. Bragg, NC

Frank placed the letter back into the envelope. What were they going to do now? Taking this to federal court backfired on them. They had to do something soon, or his friend would die an excruciatingly painful and prolonged death. The country would lose a hero but losing his friend was even worse.

1400 Hours
December 24, 1972
Blanchfield Army Hospital
Third floor
Ft. Campbell, KY

Frank slipped the patient's chart back into the holder at the nurses' station. As he turned to head to his office, his commanding officer, Dr. Adam Gaston, Lt. Colonel, US Army, ran up to him. The man looked flustered about something, nervously fiddling with the buttons on the front of his white lab coat.

"You got a minute?" Gaston asked.

"Sure," Frank replied, taking note of Gaston's flushed, sweaty face and rapid breathing. Something important was up. "Public or private?"

"Private." Gaston pointed down the hall. "Your office."

Frank led the way to his office. After they went inside, Frank pointed at a chair in front of his desk. "Please sit." He sat in his chair on the other side. "What's up?"

Gaston pulled a folded piece of paper from his lab coat pocket and handed it to Frank. "Have you seen the news or heard about this?"

"About what? I went on duty before the news came on, and I've been too busy on rounds to even eat lunch."

"Just read."

Frank unfolded the paper. A printed copy of an APB-All Points Bulletin sent out by the United States Army – 525th Military Intelligence Group – Ft. Bragg, NC.

12/24/72 – 0800 hours

To all law enforcement agencies - check medical facilities for a sick individual exhibiting symptoms of possible organ failure and jaundice within 500-1000 miles of Fort Bragg, NC.

Suspect #1: Lt. Colonel Jackson J. MacKenzie, United States Army - Race: White, Eyes: Blue, Height: 6'1", Weight: 125 pounds, Hair: Dark blond but currently shaved off. Identifying marks: Crisscrossing scars on his back, recent scar on right shoulder and thigh.

Four other individuals will possibly be with him. They are as follows:

Suspect #2: Captain William "Bill" L. Mason, United States Army - Race: White, Eyes: Brown, Height: 5'7", Weight: 160 pounds, Hair: Brown in a crew cut. Identifying marks: Dagger – "Death before Dishonor" tattoo on left forearm.

Suspect #3: 1st Lieutenant Tyler "Ty" M. Carter, United States Army - Race: White (can pass for ethnic with a dark, tanned complexion) Eyes: Brown, Height: 5' 10", Weight: 175 pounds, Hair: Dark brown, short and curly.

Suspect #4: Sergeant First Class Dakota "Chief" C. Blackwater, United States Army - Race: American Indian, Eyes: Brown, Height 6'2", Weight: 250 pounds, Hair: Black in a crew cut, Identifying marks: Bald Eagle tattoo on upper right shoulder.

Suspect #5: Staff Sergeant Michael "Mikey" P. Roberts, United States Army – Race: White, Eyes: Brown, Height: 5'9", Weight 150 pounds, Hair: Dark brown in a crew cut. Identifying marks: Scar on right calf.

These men escaped from the maximum-security area of the Fort Bragg stockade between 2000 hours on 12/23/72 and 0700 hours on 12/24/72. They are considered armed and extremely dangerous. Do not attempt to apprehend without backup. They are all trained United States Army Green Berets and experts in hand-to-hand combat, weapons, tactics and speak several different languages. SSGT Roberts is a medic, so also be on the lookout for break-ins or thefts from medical offices, pharmacies, and clinics. They may be driving a 1969 black 4-door AMC Ambassador with North Carolina license plate – CF-5856. If any of these men are spotted, contact the 525th Military Intelligence Group – Ft. Bragg, NC.

"Is this the man…umm…suspect number one, that you've been writing letters about to everyone the rank of Colonel and above in the Army medical department?"

Frank nodded. "Yes." *Jackson came up with a plan, and they escaped. Good for him. Probably saved his life. But from the first paragraph, the weight listed, and Dr. Wright's last report, Jackson was near death, so he wouldn't get far. It surprised Frank to see them looking for Jackson at a hospital or clinic since Colonel Hammond kept vehemently denying that Jackson was sick, saying he was trying to fake his way out of the court-martial.*

"I have to ask, Frank. Do you know anything?"

"No, I haven't seen or spoken to Jack…errr…Colonel MacKenzie since February 22nd, ten months ago." Frank thought for a second. "Do they think I'm involved?" *I wouldn't tell them even if I was, but I'm not.*

"I was instructed to ask by General Archer. Are you…off the record?" Gaston asked.

"No." *Why would I want to tell him anything off or on the record? They already know my stance about Jackson, and it's not about to change anytime soon.*

"You sure?"

"Absolutely. I haven't been in contact with Colonel MacKenzie or his men." Frank slammed his hand on the desk. "You can either believe me or not, Dr. Gaston, but you'll get the same answer if you ask me a thousand more times. A million."

"Understood, Major." Gaston stood and started for the door then turned to Frank. "I'd watch your back if I was you. And remember, the walls have ears. So be careful who you talk to. If you hear anything, come see me." He left the office.

Frank didn't trust Gaston any more than Hammond at this point. The man was career Army. Now he'd have to be on guard about everything. It wouldn't stop him from trying to bring Jackson's treatment into the light instead of the dark dinginess of United States Army secrets.

CHAPTER 15

December 25, 1972
Blanchfield Army Hospital
Office 301
Ft. Campbell, KY

Frank placed the newspaper on the desk. He'd been reading the article about Jackson and his men's escape. It was chock full of outright lies and complete fabricated bullshit. And the pictures. Chief, Ty, and Bill's were taken at the Ft. Bragg stockade. Jackson's photo wasn't current from the way his broad shoulders filled out the green class A award-laden dress uniform jacket, looking every bit of two hundred muscular pounds.

According to last week's report sent to him by Dr. Wright, Jackson weighed maybe 125 pounds with a face so gaunt and pasty he looked like a corpse. The APB, in a way, said the same thing by noting his weight and health.

He leaned over to pick up his desk phone when it rang. "Blanchfield Army Hospital, Dr. Howard speaking."

"Sir, this is Sergeant Jerry Rose. I'm a combat medic. You treated a shrapnel injury to my right shoulder. I lost a bunch of weight while I was in the hospital," said a tenor male voice Frank didn't recognize.

"Sorry, doesn't ring a bell, Sergeant." *Who is this guy?*

"I was in a helicopter crash about eleven months ago. An RPG hit the tail rotor."

I don't have a clue what he's talking about. I was in Japan recovering from the mortar attack in January. Wait! Jackson was in a helicopter crash around the same time with a shoulder injury. Is that what he's talking cryptically about? Frank dropped the receiver on his desk, ran to the open office door, shut it, returned to his chair, and picked up the handset. He still had to be careful. Unwanted ears might be listening. This might be a way to trick him into saying something incriminating. "Sorry about the delay. Yes, I remember you, Sergeant. I'll call you back after I check my records for the specifics. Do you mind waiting for a day or so?" *Have to play it safe and not say anything about this near anyone.*

"No, sir. I didn't expect to get you today. I was going to leave a message on your answering machine."

"Thank you, Sergeant Rose. Can you give me your phone number?"

"Sure. 769-555-0115. It's my dad's number. He's the town doctor. I'm staying with him until I can get my own place. I have to run some samples to the hospital lab. Dad might pick up if you call back today."

A doctor? That doesn't sound good. Maybe he's taking care of Jackson. "I understand. Does he know who I am?"

"Yes. Thank you, sir."

Frank heard the other end go dead and hung up his handset. Ever so curious but wary of a possible trap, he called Brooke Army Medical Center at Ft. Sam Houston where all the Army trained its combat medics. He wanted to confirm Jerry Rose's story and his identity.

"Brooke Army Medical Center. How may I direct your call?" the female operator asked.

"Records department for the combat medic program," Frank replied. He drummed his fingers on the desktop until the ringing stopped.

"Records, Sergeant King speaking," said a male voice.

"Sergeant, this is Dr. Howard at Blanchfield Army hospital. I need some information on one of your medics for my records. I think he was discharged a few days ago."

"Sure, sir. What's his name?"

"Jerry Rose."

"Hold on a minute."

Frank leaned back in his chair, listening to the humdrum hold music—bongos and bells.

"You still there, Doc?"

"Yeah, still here." *And bored out of my skull.*

"Sergeant Jerry Carson Rose. Served with the 1st Cavalry Division. Received the Bronze Star, a Purple Heart, and the Army Commendation Medal. He returned stateside on December 10th, assigned to Headquarters Company, and honorably discharged on December 22nd. Need anything else?"

Frank shook his head then realized the man couldn't see him. "No, that helps. Thank you."

"You're welcome, sir."

Frank placed his handset in the cradle, glad at that bit of good news. Jerry Rose was a real person. A combat medic. Not an Army spy. Now he had to be really careful. He felt like a spy from MI6 in a James Bond movie. Not double O quality, more like one O or just a sidekick.

1800 Hours

On the way to his apartment in Oak Grove, KY, Frank made several stops. First, the bank to use his plastic card with a magnetic strip in the new-fangled ATM. He needed some cash anyway. Next, he picked up a six-pack of beer, a pre-packaged sandwich, potato chips, and a brownie for dinner at the only convenience store he could find open on Christmas Day.

He wanted to make sure the FBI or Army CID wasn't tailing him, so he doubled back on his route several times. His home phone might be tapped too. And to make sure no one could overhear him, he entered a telephone booth out in the open a few blocks from home so he could watch the area. He dropped a handful of coins into the slot and dialed the number Jerry Rose had given him.

"Hello," said a winded male voice Frank didn't recognize. Had he dialed the wrong number?

"Is this Sergeant Rose?" Frank asked.

"No, I'm his father, Dr. Curtis Rose. Who's this?"

"Dr. Frank Howard. Your son called me. Did I catch his hint correctly? Is Jackson MacKenzie at your house?"

"Yes," said Dr. Rose in a skeptical and suspicious tone.

"How's Jackson doing?"

"Fighting for his life. Hold on a second."

The noise on the other end of the line became muffled, but Frank heard, "Jerry, go keep an eye on Jackson," then "Sure, Dad," in the same voice that called him earlier. Jerry Rose.

"I'm back," said Dr. Rose.

"What exactly is wrong with him? Sam was worried about organ failure."

"I don't know yet. Jerry took the blood and urine samples to the hospital two hours ago. It'll be a day or two before the test results come back. Upon his arrival at my clinic, the waste inside Jackson's bowels looked like black concrete. We gave him two enemas to remove the impaction. His liver and spleen are inflamed. He's dehydrated, malnourished, weak, has a 104-degree fever, and his blood pressure is erratic. I have him on a feeding tube, IV fluids, antibiotics, and pain medication."

"Sounds good. That's what I would do. What else? Jackson can be a difficult patient." *Like trying to herd a bunch of feral cats, impossible.*

"Tell me about it," Dr. Rose said with humor in his tone. "Earlier, your friend surprised me by drinking two pots of black coffee. It's amazing it didn't come back up. I wasn't going to let him have the second pot, but it's hard when he turns on the charm. I hope he has the strength of will to keep fighting."

"Jackson Joseph MacKenzie will fight until he doesn't have the strength left to fight anymore. I know how much he loves coffee. Give him all he wants. It can't hurt, and it helps with his attitude. He loves ice cream. It's second behind coffee. Give him vanilla or chocolate milkshakes. Take good care of him. Jackson's been through hell these last eleven months." *Something I wouldn't wish on my worst enemy. Well, except for fucking Hammond.*

"Yeah, Mikey and Bill told me about it. I want to clear up one question since Mikey and Jerry explained the medical regulations to me. How did he wind up on the plane?"

Frank released a long sigh. "Of all the things you could ask about, that one thing still bothers me. How? I have no idea. If I hadn't boarded that C-130, Jackson would've bled to death before the plane was halfway to Hawaii. He went into V-fib during surgery. It took two rounds of epinephrine and four hits with the defibrillator to stabilize his heart rhythm. I had to pump eight additional units of blood into his body to keep him alive. Since Colonel Hammond and I butted heads for days over his extended care, General Kowalski forced my hand by ordering his release to the stockade with no access to rehab."

"Anything else I should know?" Curtis asked.

"No." Frank leaned against the phone booth's glass wall. "I think that's it, medically. Wait, there's one more thing. It has nothing to do with his medical status. The Army wants this kept out of the press. It's not a secret, just forgotten about."

"What's that?"

He's in for a big shock. "Treat him with the respect due a man who's earned the Medal of Honor," Frank said.

"You're kidding?" Curtis sounded skeptical.

"The Army awarded it to him in '71."

"Do you know what for?"

"I do. But that's his story to tell, not mine. Jackson's tight-lipped about it. His response to me, he was only doing his job. Jackson's a certified master of understatement. He told me the wounds were minor. I believed him until I read his medical records. Minor, my ass. He was shot three times. One round collapsed his left lung, one went through his left bicep, and you could drive a golf ball through the one in his left thigh. He refuses to consider himself a hero and will not say anything about the POW camp. Period. If you want to know anything about that, ask his men. I'll tell Sam his star patient is in good hands. Call me when his test results come back. If you need anything special for him, let me know, and I'll get it." *Even if I have to sell my soul to the devil.*

"I'll take good care of him, Dr. Howard. Do you want to talk to him?"

Frank felt his heart explode in joy. He wanted to talk to his friend. To hear his voice as reassurance of life. "Is Jackson awake and coherent enough to talk to me?"

"I think so. Give me a minute to get him a phone. I removed it last night so it wouldn't wake him up."

Frank agreed. A ringing phone in a doctor's clinic wouldn't be good for a convalescing patient.

The ticking seconds seemed like hours.

"Hello," Jackson said, his voice strained and barely above a whisper. "Who is this?"

"Frank Howard. I'd say Merry Christmas, but it hasn't been much of a happy year for you."

Jackson sounded choked over the receiver before responding. "No, it hasn't, but at least I'm still alive. I guess Dr. Wright told you everything."

"Yeah, most of it. I'm glad you didn't get the chance to follow through with the idea. Sam did everything he could. Everyone took Hammond's word over Sam's, and no one I've spoken with can figure out why. He doesn't have any medical training."

"A rock has more medical training than Hammond. He reminds me of a tall, walking gnome with his bulbous pointed head, red Rudolph nose, and potbelly."

Frank howled in laughter so much his side hurt, and tears rolled down his cheeks. He wholeheartedly agreed. Hammond should be tending reindeer at the North Pole. "You say the darndest things. Sam told me about the big show."

"Yeah, Hammond acted like a pompous ass. It pissed him off when I didn't come to attention. It was all I could do to concentrate on what he was saying. I felt like a sick popsicle that night." The bitterness in Jackson's voice was palpable.

"That happened in December. The Army doesn't heat those cell blocks to save money. You're so thin, you don't have any extra padding to keep you warm. Hammond knows you're sick. It's impossible to ignore two doctors writing dozens of letters about your welfare. I think his instructions are coming from somewhere else." *They have to be. Hammond's too stupid to come up with this on his own.*

"Me too. I have an idea about it. Hammond's superiors were waiting for me to go crazy or kill myself, whichever came first. If I committed suicide, it would take care of the problem without the need to terminate me with extreme prejudice. I'm the only one, besides Colonel Johnson, who knew every detail of the mission plan."

Makes a lot of sense. "How long have you been thinking about this?" Frank asked.

"A little while now, when I've been thinking rationally, which hasn't been much lately. I'm the key to the whole thing. That's why they stuck us in maximum security. It gave Hammond more latitude. Moretti never made an appearance after the hospital, and my only visitor was Harry. Whoever's involved let Dr. Wright keep me barely alive to maintain appearances in case the press got involved." Jackson yawned over the phone. "Sorry, Frank."

He needs to rest. "Sounds like something right out of the CIA playbook. I'll stay in touch with Dr. Rose. Do everything he says while you're under his care. I agree with keeping you on a strict diet because of your stomach problems."

"I know. He explained it to me. I have to live with it because I don't have another choice, do I, Frank? Maybe next year, I can eat Christmas dinner at the table like everyone else."

"Sam told me about Captain Mason's little faux pas on Thanksgiving. The next time we meet, I don't want to see a rail-thin twig with skinny chicken legs." *I would've given Mason more than just a verbal warning. You don't feed a malnourished sick man a plateful of rich food. They're lucky Jackson only puked it up instead of going into a coma from an electrolyte imbalance.*

"Funny. I'll try my best. I promise to listen to Dr. Rose. He's been so good to us. I wish we could pay him for saving my life."

"Don't worry about that right now. I'll pay Dr. Rose for his services. You can pay me back someday. I know you'll be good for it. Get well, snake-eater." *I'll donate my entire bank account to Dr. Rose for saving Jackson.*

"Thanks, Frank. I'd better get off now. Dr. Rose might need his phone for a patient or something. Goodbye."

Frank returned the receiver to the payphone cradle with a metallic click. He checked the coin slot, pulled out a couple of dimes, pushed open the booth door, and went outside. Now it was time to go home. He climbed into his car. A cold roast beef sandwich, chips, packaged fudge brownie, and cheap beer sounded like a feast for his Christmas dinner tonight. Who needed a tree or presents? Just some semi-good news.

```
December 26, 1972
Del Ray Apartments
Apartment 214
Oak Grove, KY
```

Frank knew he had to let Harry Russell know about the phone call, but not by telephone. Surely the Army was watching both of them as possible co-conspirators with Jackson. To counter that, he used the code system he set up with Harry's doctor at the VA. Baseball.

He pulled an envelope from the stack on his kitchen table and wrote Harry Russell with the address of the Los Angeles VA hospital on the outside. For the return address, he wrote, Zip Dee Dooda, 25 Main Street, Cooperstown, NY 13326, New Baseball Stats.

Then he rolled a piece of blank white paper into his typewriter. And after carefully considering his words, he started typing.

12/26/72

Major Russell,

I'm sure you know about the escape. It's all over the news. I received a phone call last night from a doctor. I won't give a name or location for obvious reasons. Jackson's safe. So are your friends.

The bad news is Jackson's very sick. On top of the malnutrition, he had a complete blockage in his bowels. This caused a serious gastrointestinal infection and brought on a high fever. How his organs are doing is up in the air. Knowing him the way I do, he'll live. But it will be a long road to recovery.

If things turn for the worst, I'll contact you by phone, so you can get to him before…well, you know. I can't write it and won't. I will be there for him. He deserves to know people care about him. To show him the love he deserves before God takes him. The Army can go to hell for all I care.

Letters will have to do for now. Less chance of them being tracked. All further information will go through your doctor.

Hopes and prayers,

Dr. Frank Howard

After signing the letter and placing it inside the envelope, he sealed the flap then walked downstairs to the mailboxes. With a quick check of the area, he slipped the letter into the slot, looked around, and returned to his apartment. Only time would tell if he got away with all this. Or if he was going to wind up in federal prison for the next twenty years.

CHAPTER 16

1610 Hours
December 27, 1972
1615 hours
Fort Campbell, KY

Frank flipped his clipboard under his arm and stomped to his new office, 312. A small, what he could only describe as a former supply closet with cheap, already peeling white paint slapped haphazardly on the walls and a leaky, smudged window to the outside world. Overhead, exposed water piping dripped occasionally on the cracked black and white tile floor. The room didn't even qualify as a postage stamp.

It contained a worn-out scratched gray metal desk with sticky drawers, an ancient manual typewriter, two plastic bowl chairs, and a rusted file cabinet. To make it seem homier, Frank hung a few of his awards on rusty nails pushed into the decaying, water-stained sheetrock.

The brass in the offices upstairs booted him out of his larger one, saying it had mold growing inside the walls. No, it was punishment for being vocal about Jackson's treatment. Their suspicion of his possible involvement in the escape from the Ft. Bragg stockade didn't help matters. This room had more of a mold problem with it growing like weeds in the damp corners. Yuk. Maybe they wanted him to die from a lung infection.

He was pissed. His commanding officer had just grilled him again if he knew anything about the escape or Jackson's whereabouts. And again, he lied. While he would love to explain to his CO how deathly ill Jackson was, he couldn't. That would get Jackson and his friends captured and himself court-martialed. It was safer for everyone involved for him to lie and hope he kept getting away with it.

Right now, he wanted to change from his dress uniform shirt, tie, pants, black Corfam shoes, and lab coat into a comfortable shirt, blue jeans, and sneakers. What that United States Army uniform represented today disgusted him so much he wanted to puke.

Someone cleared his throat behind him. "Dr. Howard?" a deep voice asked.

Frank spun around. "Yes."

Standing in front of him, two strange men in casual civilian clothing so pressed and perfect, they had to have been in the military at some point in their lives. Frank's senses went on high alert. FBI, maybe? NSA? CID? CIA? One man bodily reminded him of a grizzly bear, around sixty to seventy years old, tall, stocky with broad shoulders and a white high and tight haircut. The other man was a bit younger, shorter, barrel-chested, and sporting the same silvered haircut. Their expressions were severe, gruff, and serious, with clenched jaws, squinted eyes, and lips thinned by pressing them tightly together.

"Is there any place we can talk in private?" the older man asked in a no-nonsense tone.

"First..." Frank looked them both up and down. "Who are you?" *Should I ask for IDs?*

"Lieutenant General Mangus Malone, Marine Corps, retired." Mangus pointed at his partner. "This is Sergeant Major Jason Nichols, Marine Corps, retired."

A retired general! Frank snapped to attention. "Sir." *Might better be safe than sorry.*

"At ease, Major. Now, where can we talk in private?"

"My office, General." Frank pointed at his name on a brass plaque next to 312. The only thing the hospital spent any money on. But all they did was unscrew it from the wall and move it down the hall.

"No! Not within Army ears." Mangus pulled a picture from his coat pocket, palming it where only Frank could see it.

Frank's eyes widened upon seeing a faded color picture of a grinning young Second Lieutenant Jackson MacKenzie. That was a personal picture, not an official Army one. From the darker lines around the edges, it was kept in either a frame or a photo album. *Who is this guy? One of Jackson's relatives? His father's dead. Uncle, maybe? He's trying hard to be discreet, so he's familiar with the situation.* "Are you hungry, sir? There's a nice restaurant nearby. It serves an excellent lunch and dinner menu." *I want to know more, but I still need to be careful. This might be an elaborate ruse to catch me in a lie to charge me with conspiracy.*

"Sounds good. The meal is my treat. I want to thank you for saving a good friend in Vietnam. Since I'm retired, it took me a long time to track you down."

He knows about what happened on the plane. "I accept your offer. Being a bachelor, I was going home to a frozen TV dinner and whatever's on television tonight. My car's in the parking lot if you need a ride?"

"Not necessary. We have a rental car." Mangus pointed at the elevators. "How about we follow you?"

"Yes, sir," Frank replied.

Fifteen minutes later, Frank pulled his OD-green US Army sedan into a restaurant parking lot two miles from the main gate. He got out, watched a 1972 gray Chevy Impala pull into the lot, went to the restaurant doors, and waited.

Jason and Mangus walked shoulder to shoulder up to him, in step with each other the entire way. They reminded Frank of two fearless sheepdogs ready to defend their flock.

Mangus pulled out the same picture and handed it to Frank. "That was taken at Fort Campbell. Before you ask, Jackson's my godson. Dr. Rose gave us your name."

He knows about Dr. Rose. So this isn't an Army trap. Frank glanced at the photograph and handed it back. *God, he was so young there. Looks like a damn teenager. Kinda resembles the one I lost...Shit! Why did I think about that again?* "I recognize the jump towers. How'd Dr. Rose know to call you?"

"He didn't. Colonel MacKenzie did." Jason pointed at the gold oak leaves on Dr. Howard's collar. "I will not disrespect his rank since the kid earned it. Jackson was the youngest and quite a bratty kid. His father called him little squirt."

"Interesting, but it fits what I've seen of his personality. Colonel MacKenzie felt betrayed by the Army when I saw him earlier this year. Let's go in, General Malone." Frank opened the door leading into the building. "We don't want to draw any unwanted attention by standing here."

"Right." As the senior officer present, Mangus took the lead to the waiting area. A hostess directed them to a table near the back. Mangus didn't look at the menu. "Give us three of the daily specials." He looked at Frank under hooded eyes. "Have you heard anything about Jackson's test results?"

Frank nodded. "Yes. Jerry Rose left a message on my answering machine this afternoon. Colonel MacKenzie's test results are normal. Now they're working on putting a few pounds on his skinny ass frame."

"That's good news. Dr. Rose said it would take a month."

"A month would be the bare minimum, in my opinion. Did Dr. Rose explain the issues about Jackson's diet?" Frank turned over his coffee mug when the waitress returned with the pot.

Jason spoke after taking a drink from his mug. "He mentioned something about getting him to eat, but nothing about that. Dr. Rose wanted off the phone. Jackson collapsed, trying to convince me he was telling the truth."

105

What! Frank's eyes narrowed. Now he was pissed. You don't do that to someone fighting for their life. "Makes sense. If Colonel MacKenzie felt you were questioning his honesty, he's so sick the stress probably sent him into shock."

"Yeah, that's what Dr. Rose said. Shock."

Mangus slapped his hand on the table to divert Frank's attention from Jason. "What's this about his diet?"

Frank stiffened. Even retired, as a general, this man expected immediate answers. "Okay, business first. I can do that. Excuse me if I get informal here. Colonel MacKenzie insisted I call him Jackson. It's better not to use his rank or last name in public around here. Because of the POW camp, Jackson's having a hard time tolerating some foods. His diet might be limited for the rest of his life. We'll see how it goes once he's on solid food. It's entirely up to him on what he can eat. He'll have to figure it out one step at a time."

"Okay, we'll wait to find out when he arrives in San Diego since it's an evolving process." Mangus' tone turned blunt as their meals arrived. "What happened to him, Dr. Howard? From the beginning."

Frank explained the last eleven months of Jackson's life as they ate. What happened on the plane from Vietnam to Ft. Bragg. Jackson's treatment at the hospital and the stockade. The physical assault by the guards on his first night in maximum security. Hammond's campaign of horror. His problems with confinement and the unending nightmares. Even though this took several minutes, one word summed it up. Horrible.

"Hammond! Why's someone from fracking intelligence involved in this?" Mangus latched onto the edge of his plate. "I sent a request via the Commandant of the Marine Corps to visit Jackson about seven months ago. It came back stamped *denied* in red block letters. There was a note attached on Army letterhead with Hammond's signature. It said, 'This is an internal Army matter. Therefore, assistance from the Marine Corps is not required. Request denied.' I stayed out of the matter for Jackson's sake. Do you know what I want to do to Hammond?"

"What, sir?" Frank grabbed Mangus' arm at the lowest part of the circle to stop the forward motion. It was like halting a moving freight train at full steam. The general was strong. "Please don't throw the plate across the restaurant."

Jason's fork hit the table with a metallic thwack. "Bet the same as me, sir. Turn him upside down by his ankles in front of the 1st Marines and let him suffer."

"Exactly. No one should treat a Medal of Honor recipient with such disrespect and lack of assistance when needed." Mangus leaned back in his chair. "Let me go, Major," he growled.

Frank released his grip. He could picture these two men doing precisely what Jason Nichols described with the 1st Marines, and he would stand there, applaud and whoop until his voice gave out. "General, I have to ask. How are you going to help Jackson with his nightmares?"

"I own a cattle ranch in Montana. We're going to take him to the wide-open spaces, far away from anything to remind him of the Army. There isn't a military base for five hundred miles in any direction. I'm going to work the crap out of him. He'll go to bed tired every night, and getting my hard-headed godson to talk will be easier when he's exhausted."

"Good plan. Now that I know more about Jackson, his eating habits make sense. It may have been the food in the chow hall making him sick rather than him refusing to eat. A field mess isn't known for having anything but grease, starch, or processed foods, and by the same token, neither is a prison mess. I don't think he can tolerate any of them." *And I can't believe it took this long to figure out. Those problems should've been corrected before he was ever allowed to return to full duty. He should've been evaluated by a psychiatrist too.*

Mangus tapped a finger on his empty plate. "I know how bad the food in the mess hall can be, doctor. Jason and I have eaten our fair share of K-rations, shit-on-a-shingle, lumpy gravy, burned mystery meat, and Jackson's favorite, powdered eggs."

"Me too, General." *From a year of nasty mess hall food in Vietnam.* Frank shoved his empty plate away. "I think Army cooks learn from the Marine Corps. I have to warn you, Jackson's mind may not return to normal, considering how long he's been under extreme stress. There lies the problem. Even if the Army does clear him, his career is over. They'll medically retire him. If that happens, you may need professional help if he tries something drastic. You'll have to watch him for the rest of his life."

Mangus stabbed his fork at Frank. "I'll do everything in my power to help him through this. Jackson Joseph MacKenzie is the embodiment of his father. Not only physically but also in leadership ability, bravery, guts, and sheer tenacity. He never gave up. That's his father to a T. Jackson's his mirror image. Every time I see him, I think about his father, our friendship, and my promise. Jackson adored his father and copied everything he did. James was his hero. They were inseparable before and after World War II. I've known the young man since the day he was born.

My godson will bounce back. I will get him the help he needs, no matter the cost. Anything else?"

"Yes. Dr. Rose is giving Jackson sedatives so he can sleep. Right now, rest is the most important thing. Once you get him into a controlled environment, he needs to stop. They're highly addictive. In his broken state, he could start depending on them and make things worse. He needs to talk about what's bothering him. It's the only way to put his demons behind him. Do you have any ideas?"

Mangus drummed his fingers on the table. "Yeah, I do. Several Marines who survived the Bataan death march are friends of mine. I've already asked one of them to give me a hand if I need more help. I figured if Jackson could talk to someone who went through the same thing, he might open up."

Inventive and unusual. "Good idea. It could work when and if he's willing to talk, but it'll take time to get him to that point. I have to ask about his men. They won't leave him, and he won't leave them." *They're probably the only reason he's still alive.*

"I have plenty of room, so no problem there. They are welcome to stay with Jackson, and he'll do more talking with them around."

Frank pulled a prescription pad out of his pocket, wrote Harry's phone number on it, then handed that page to Mangus. "You need to contact Major Russell. He's Jackson's best friend and the man who stayed on his ass in 'Nam. I don't know if you know this. Jackson volunteered to go home after the mission to help Harry through the loss of his foot. If anyone can get Jackson to talk, it's Harry Russell. Be discreet. Just like you were careful contacting me, the Army will be watching him."

"I know." Mangus patted his left leg. "Major Russell needs to visit the VA for his prosthesis fittings, right?"

"Yeah. Why?"

"Use his doctor at the VA to relay messages. They're government employees. Not military doctors. We'll use sealed envelopes with special markings."

Frank loved that plan. "Excellent idea. I call the VA all the time on consults. Please keep me informed about Jackson's progress. I'll call you instead of the other way around. That way, I can call from a different phone. Eventually, I'll want to examine him to make sure he's okay, health-wise." *That way, I can keep a running record for when the Army admits it's wrong.*

Mangus held up his empty mug when the waitress walked up with the coffee pot. "Jackson trusts you, or he wouldn't have mentioned your name.

If you hadn't suggested it first, I would have insisted you give him a physical once his head's on straight. You and Dr. Wright kept him alive, and I thank you for it."

"No need to thank me, sir. I did my job. Jackson's gone through too much pain and suffering for one lifetime. He deserves peace and happiness. I know his Army career meant everything to him. He needs to find something else to hold on to. I hope your ranch will give him the stability he needs. Maybe soon the Army will figure out its mistake."

"My thoughts exactly." Mangus held out his hand across the table.

Frank took it in a tight grip. He wanted to show them he was every bit of a man as them.

"I like your spunk. Jackson found a good friend," Mangus said.

I think he's impressed. Frank dropped his hand and cleared his throat. "If that's the case, call me Frank."

"Okay."

Frank poured sugar and cream into his coffee mug. He couldn't drink black coffee anymore. Just the taste ever since he got drunk in the O-club at the 95th Evac sent him down on his knees in dry heaves. He knew it was an unconscious reaction to the trauma of that day. A tiny manifestation of what Jackson was dealing with internally.

"General, you said Jackson acts like his dad. Did his father drink a lot of strong black coffee?" Frank asked.

"Yes. James always had a coffee cup in his hand. The mess at Pendleton kept a special pot just for him." Mangus picked up his mug. "Jackson followed his father's example when he was twelve years old. James gave him a pony before we left for the Pacific campaign. That damn kid spent every waking moment with Scout when he wasn't in school until James returned to the states. Kimberly told me it was all she could do to get him to come home, eat dinner, and do his chores. Then Jackson would jump on his bike and go back to the barn to do his homework. I think Scout helped him deal with his father's absence."

Frank stirred his coffee. "Now everything makes sense."

Mangus glanced at the inside of Frank's mug. "Typical Army guy. Looks like sweet milk. Not Marine coffee."

"You mean mud." Frank took a sip from his mug. Tasted great to him. The sugar covered the bitterness. "You're probably right about why Jackson spent so much time with his pony. He was afraid his dad wouldn't return from the war. As a seven-year-old kid, it was his way of dealing with the pressure. It's a good thing his mother didn't make him come home. Now that I know more of Jackson's history, your ranch is the best place for him. It will give him a stable platform to get his life back in order."

"I agree." Mangus tapped the table. "And he will. You can bet on it."

"Knowing how hard-headed he is, I have no doubt, sir." Frank was glad Jackson had men like Mangus Malone and Jason Nichols in his corner. Jackson needed a stable support system to guide him through his problems.

CHAPTER 17

January 13, 1973
Del Ray Apartments
Apartment 214
Oak Grove, KY

Frank looked from his console TV to the wall clock when someone knocked on his door. 2100 hours. At least they didn't disturb his new favorite program, *Emergency!* A drama series about doctors and paramedics saving lives. Although it was benign and sterile with simple and straightforward decisions by the doctors, unlike those he made in Vietnam, he enjoyed the show. It was a nice escape from the reality of life.

Who was at his door this late at night? He didn't have any friends here, so he wasn't expecting anyone. *Hope they don't mind tie-dyed pajamas.* He put aside his bowl of Jiffy Pop popcorn and beer then padded to the door in his bare feet, turned the deadbolt, and opened the door.

Standing at the threshold, Colonel Hammond, in his class A uniform and cover, two armed enlisted men wearing black MP armbands with matching helmets and two uniformed police officers. Did someone discover he knew Jackson's location? No. They'd already be storming their way into his apartment and slapping handcuffs on him.

"Can we come in?" Hammond asked brusquely. A vein on his sweaty forehead throbbed with his pulse. The mottled pale skin around his squinted eyes had tiny, broken surface blood vessels.

Frank wanted to laugh at the one row of ribbons on Hammond's chest. The National Defense Medal, everyone gets that, Legion of Merit, probably for hurting Jackson, the Army Commendation Medal, that was for keeping his paperclip supply fully stocked or yelling at his clerk. Why did he have a pistol marksmanship medal as an officer? *I bet someone else shot the course for him. That jerk couldn't hit the target from two feet away. Or he got it for pouring coffee into a cup.* No overseas service bars, no achievements, and no awards for bravery. The only colorful thing he had on that uniform was the black/yellow checkerboard, gray and blue lightning bolt patch of the 525th Military Intelligence Group on his left shoulder. Again, rolling on the floor laughable. He had no intelligence at all. The man was an out-of-shape, overbearing, paper-pushing moron.

"Well?" Hammond bellowed, tapping his foot with an annoyed air.

"Got a warrant?" Frank looked over at the two police officers, who shook their heads *no*. They were there because Hammond had no authority outside of a military base. Thank goodness for the Constitution and the Posse Comitatus Act. Now, Hammond might try the heavy-handed superiority routine without the police backup to harass someone not in the military into falling for his bombastic act of feigned authority. He wouldn't want official, knowledgeable witnesses to his illegal activity.

"Do I need one?"

"To come into my apartment, yes! You can say what you came to say right here." Frank pointed at Hammond's shoes. Even though he had nothing incriminating in view, he didn't want the asshole invading his personal sanctum. "What do you want?"

"Where's MacKenzie?" Hammond spat, stomping his foot.

Frank shrugged. "I have no idea. Haven't seen him since you forced him out of the hospital against my medical orders. Is this because of my letter-writing campaign to everyone about your little horror crusade against him in the stockade? You and I both know he needed to be in the hospital under the care of a doctor and a psychiatrist, not in a God-damned cell. The man was tortured as a POW. It had a lasting effect on him psychologically, and he needed a lot of counseling to live with the horrendous things they did to him. He almost died for this country. He's got the Medal of Honor for crying out loud!" He saw shocked expressions on the two enlisted men and police officers. They all looked at each other. *I guess they didn't know. Well, now they do. Maybe they'll tell Hammond to go take a hike.*

"That may go away. He's a war criminal. A menace to society. A crazed lunatic. A cold-blooded killer," Hammond yelled so forcefully that spittle flew from his mouth. "Major Howard, you're nothing but a two-bit, naïve doctor with a flair for the dramatic. MacKenzie had you snowed like a five-year-old child wanting his favorite toy. He faked everything."

Frank bowed up, clenching his fists. How in the world do you fake serious shrapnel wounds, almost bleeding out, and his heart stopping in surgery? Jackson deserved so much better than this. "He's a broken man, a soldier who needed…needs our help, not your load of mother fucking bullshit."

Hammond stepped up until his black Corfam dress shoes touched Frank's bare toes. "I could call that insubordination."

Today, Frank wished he owned a gun. Or just a baseball bat so he could beat this egotistical bastard senseless. "This isn't an Army base. You're at my door on civilian property inside the city limits of Oak Grove. Try it."

Frank knew he was rolling the dice, hoping he didn't end up with snake eyes, but he didn't think Hammond had the audacity to take it that far. He was at home, off duty, on his own time. And he had witnesses, the two police officers. The aggressor was Hammond. He didn't trust the two soldiers. They would stick up for the asshole as their superior officer.

Hammond shook his fist in Frank's face. "We'll see, Major Howard." He stormed off toward the stairwell with his entourage in tow, trying to keep up with him.

Frank shut the door, ran to the sliding patio door, opened it, and went out on his 2nd-floor balcony. Below him in the street, he saw a green Army sedan and a marked police car. Hammond stomped to the Army sedan, got in the passenger side, and slammed the door. One enlisted man got in the driver's side as the other one climbed into the back seat. The headlights snapped on. The Army sedan accelerated so fast from the curb the tires squealed and smoked as the back end slid sideways halfway across the two-lane asphalt road.

The police officers watched this happen, shook their heads, entered their car, and drove away at a normal speed.

Frank went back inside his apartment and shut the sliding door. "This isn't over." He grabbed a cold beer from the refrigerator, unwilling to drink the now warm one, returned to his chair, retrieved his popcorn, and started watching TV. Whatever was on the idiot box had to be a lot better and more interesting than dealing with Hammond. Even if it was only the station sign-off screen with a monotone, obnoxious noise coming from the speakers.

0600 Hours
January 16, 1973
Oak Grove, KY

As Frank drove his Army-issued 1970 green Plymouth Fury sedan on Thompsonville Lane toward Ft. Campbell in the early morning darkness, the wop-wop-wop of a siren overrode the jazz music coming from the radio. He looked over his shoulder at flashing red lights. Thinking an ambulance or fire truck needed to get by him, he pulled over to the right shoulder and stopped.

Instead of passing his car, the flashing lights stopped behind him. The headlights snapped to bright, blinding him in the glare from the rearview mirror, so he flipped it up, seeing spots floating in front of his eyes as he threw the gearshift into park.

A few seconds later came a hard rapping knock-knock against his window. He rolled it down, looking up at a uniformed police officer with a flashlight in his left hand, shining it into the front seat then the back seat of Frank's car.

Frank shaded his eyes, then saw the officer's other hand on his revolver grip inside an unsnapped holster. He placed his hands on the steering wheel where the officer could see them. The last thing he wanted to do was get shot. "Hello, officer. Is something wrong?" *I wasn't speeding. Why's he on his guard?*

"Your car matches an APB put out about a convenience store robbery in Clarksville two hours ago."

That's strange. "Huh? Officer, is the suspect driving a marked green Army sedan and wearing a uniform? Because I am."

The officer shined his flashlight on the driver's door, which Frank knew had U.S. Army – PF109179 – For Official Use Only printed in yellow, and the car had government tags. Something the officer saw walking up behind him.

"No, sir. May I ask where you're headed?" the officer asked.

"Fort Campbell. I go on duty in an hour."

"Where?"

"The hospital." Frank pointed at the gold medical caduceus on his class A uniform jacket lapel. The winged staff of Hermes with two snakes winding around it. "I'm a doctor."

"So I see. Can I see your driver's license and reg…uh, military ID card?"

"Sure." Frank pulled his brown leather wallet out of his back pocket, took out both cards and handed them to the officer.

The officer walked back to his black and white police cruiser.

Frank watched the officer busy inside his car in the outside rearview mirror. *This has Hammond written all over it. Why pull over an obvious Army car?*

The officer returned a few minutes later and handed both cards to Frank. "Your license checks out, Major." He shined his flashlight on Frank's briefcase beside him on the bench seat. "Can I look in your briefcase, sir?"

He knows I'm not the robbery suspect. That means he's looking for something. And there's nothing but work stuff in there. "No. I have patient files in it, and they are none of your business." Frank leaned out the open window. "Officer, tell me the truth. Who put you up to this? Is it an asshole Army colonel named Hammond from the 525th Military Intelligence

Group? Did he tell you I'm dirty or something like that?" *That fucking asshole is trying to ruin me.*

The officer looked away as if caught in something he shouldn't be doing. "Ahhh...yeah. He said you were dealing some pretty potent smack...uhh...heroin in Vietnam, and I'd make a great arrest. Get my picture in the newspaper and maybe a TV interview or two."

So, he wants to be famous. Frank grabbed his briefcase and opened it. "See, just papers. You just got conned by a royal class asshole. What's your badge number, name, and supervisor?"

"My badge is 105, my name is Tim Hopkins, and my supervisor is Sergeant Holland. He doesn't know about this. Hammond gave me the tip when I stopped for coffee at the 7/11 after I came on duty. Why?"

"To file a complaint of harassment with your department. And maybe a federal lawsuit. The thing about my car matching the suspect vehicle in a robbery is obviously a bald-faced lie. Don't ever stop me again. The same goes for all your fellow officers. Goodbye." He put his car in gear and drove away. *What a crock of shit.*

March 29, 1973
1300 Hours
Blanchfield Army Hospital
Office 301
Ft. Campbell, KY

Frank was glad they moved him back to his larger office. Hammond overextended his power more than once. He got caught trying to frame Frank with the bogus traffic stop, which brought his formal sustained complaint against the Oak Grove Police. He filed one with JAG on Hammond. That one was still under JAGMAN investigation, meaning, with Hammond's connections, it wasn't going anywhere.

Then Harry Russell's pending federal court case against Hammond for tapping his phones and breaking into his house without a warrant came along. The brass running the hospital finally believed he had nothing to do with Jackson's escape from Ft. Bragg.

He looked up from his paperwork when a shadow fell across his desk. Standing in front of him was Dr. Henry "Elvis" Buchannon, looking all fit, tan, and dapper in his green class A dress uniform.

Elvis had two rows of ribbons pinned above his left jacket pocket - Meritorious Service, Army Commendation, Army Achievement, National Defense, Vietnam Service, and Vietnam Campaign Medal. Over the right pocket flap and nametag, the Army Meritorious Unit Commendation Ribbon. He still had the same curly lock of dark hair on his forehead.

"Hey, Frank. How are things going?" Elvis asked, placing a tri-folded flag inside a glass-fronted cherry wood shadow box with a brass plaque on the desktop.

Frank stood and extended his hand across the desk. "Great. Who's the flag for?"

"You. It flew over the 95th on the day of the...shelling." Elvis shook Frank's hand then sat in a chair. "I was passing through and wanted to check on you. How's your back?"

"Good. It gave me some problems at first but finally healed. That can't be the only reason you're here."

"I heard about what happened with Colonel...ahh...what's his name?"

"Hammond," Frank suggested.

"Yeah, that's him and the guy that escaped, Colonel MacKenzie."

"Elvis, there's more to this situation than you know. Much more."

"Like what?"

Frank got up, shut his office door then returned to his chair, wondering if this was some kind of test. He trusted Elvis enough to tell him about what happened on his way home, but nothing more. "What have you heard?"

"MacKenzie faked everything."

Frank couldn't withhold the amused half-snicker that left his mouth. "You worked with me for almost a year. Am I that incompetent?"

Elvis shook his head. "No. You're a better surgeon than I'll ever be, saving men I didn't think would make it. That's what threw me for a loop when I heard the story. What's the real scoop?"

Frank explained what happened on the C-130 when he escorted the medical transport home from Japan and his extreme measures to keep Jackson alive. He spoke about the incidents with the generals and Jackson's physical and mental problems when General Kowalski forced his release from the hospital. Because he hadn't seen Jackson since that day, only spoken with him, he pulled copies of Dr. Wright's official medical reports from his desk drawer and handed them to Elvis.

Elvis read page after page of those reports for five minutes then placed them in his lap. "Holy crap!"

"That's a good way to put it. MacKenzie was a ticking mental time bomb waiting to go off after what happened to him in that POW camp. Being locked up in the maximum security section of the stockade only exacerbated the problem."

"Why do you think they escaped?"

"To save MacKenzie's life. Not because they're guilty. He was going downhill fast, both physically and mentally. You read Sam's reports. MacKenzie was jaundiced and probably teetering on the edge of complete organ failure. Not surprising after barely surviving the extensive malnutrition, malaria, and intestinal parasites from the POW camp. He should've been in a hospital under medical care, observation, and counseling."

"After reading all of this." Elvis patted the stack of papers in this lap. "I agree. Have you heard from him?"

Frank shook his head. "No." Which was the truth…well, a partial truth. Jackson never called him, but he was in contact with Jackson's godfather, Mangus Malone, and Jackson's best friend, Harry Russell. "I hope he's somewhere safe getting the help he so desperately needs. If that case had gone to trial, there's no way he could've aided in his own defense, and that's a violation of his civil rights. If he were even by chance still alive, he probably would've collapsed in the courtroom. Not that anyone seems to care. I don't know what the Army was thinking, treating him as an escape risk. All they did was make his trauma worse. Sam put him on suicide watch when he admitted he wanted to die."

"Again, I agree. But enough about that. MacKenzie's not my problem or yours anymore. How are you doing?"

"Fine." Frank was confused by the question. "Why do you ask?"

"You do know what today is?" Elvis pointed at the wall calendar.

"March 29th." *Where's he going with this?*

Elvis placed a folded newspaper in front of Frank.

Frank opened it to the headline - The last U.S. soldier leaves Vietnam. "The peace treaty? The pullout? Is that what you're asking about?"

"Yeah. Have you talked to anyone about…Vietnam?"

"You mean like a shrink? No. As for anyone else. Again, no. Most of the doctors and nurses here didn't go overseas. They shut you down if you even say the word Vietnam in casual conversation. And it's taboo to talk about it in public. You're liable to get spit on…or worse."

"Do you have any friends here?"

"Not really. I tried a couple of times to hang out with the staff, but we didn't have much in common. It's not like when we were at the 95th and all in the same boat. Doing a hard job and covering each other's backs. We were family."

Elvis loosened his tie. "I know the feeling. Got a lot of these younger guys on my staff too."

"The people I work with now don't understand what we went through. They only know peace, watching TV, going to movies, dancing, and listening to rock music. Not rockets and mortars hitting around you. Not how we played God. How our moral code changed in a war zone because it had to for us to survive and save lives. Deciding who lived and who died based on supplies and resources. The horrible things we saw. Did. The suffering. The never-ending sadness. The deaths with blood everywhere." Frank remembered his thoughts as he lay in that ICU bed after the attack on the hospital. "How we hated the fucking gooks. What about you?"

Elvis gave him a sad smile. "Pretty much the same at first. I got lucky enough to meet a young lady at a bar who was a psychologist. She helped me vent in a good way before I got hooked on booze trying to forget."

"A bar? Well, that's a lucky break. I've been so busy here, and with Hammond's recent crap, I mostly drink in my apartment. Bar hopping isn't my style."

"But you drink."

"Mostly a couple of beers in the evening to relax. I keep to myself, watch TV, and read a lot. That's how I cope." *I'm more concerned about Jackson. He's the one in real trouble. Me, I can work my way through it.* Frank decided to change the subject. "You do know MacKenzie was one of our saves at the 95th after they escaped from a POW camp?"

"No! When? Who was the doctor?" Elvis asked excitedly.

That got his attention. "August to December 1970. Dr. McKay was the primary. The entire staff, however, was protective of him until his discharge. Guess who his night nurse was?"

Elvis raised an eyebrow. "Who?"

"Cathy," Frank said proudly. One of these days, he'd have to ask her in private about Jackson's recovery at the hospital. He read the records, but he was sure there was more to it than written on paper.

"Really?" Elvis tapped his lips. "Now that I think about it, I do remember hearing something about MacKenzie before Dr. McKay shipped out. I just didn't know his name. Have you talked to Cathy recently?"

"About a year ago. She was busy in her first year of medical school. The second year is even harder, so I didn't want to disturb her by calling. I check with her advisor every few months. She's doing really good."

"Excellent. I'll make some inquiries through my contacts to keep tabs on her."

Frank saw the framed picture on his desk of him and Jake together at the beach. It reminded him of something he wanted to ask Elvis. "Do you remember Major Harry Russell? He would've been at the 95th around January of last year."

"Russell...Russell..." Elvis tapped his lips. "Hmmm...yeah. Came in from Phước Vĩnh. Blast injury. Disarticulation at the left ankle. Even with the foot still partially attached, the damage was too severe to salvage anything, and I had to remove it." He scratched his head. "Why do you ask?"

"Harry Russell was Colonel MacKenzie's unit XO and a survivor of the same POW camp. That makes him another one of our saves. He didn't go on that mission with MacKenzie because of the mortar attack. You're tied into this mess by association just like me."

"Uh-huh. I guess so." Elvis stood, placed the reports on Frank's desk, and straightened his jacket. "I need to head out." He held up his left hand with a gold wedding band on his ring finger. "I married that psychologist last week. She's expecting me back at the hotel. We're flying out tomorrow for our honeymoon in Hawaii tomorrow morning. Take it easy, Frank. He tilted his head quickly at the door and lowered his voice. "Be careful who you talk to about MacKenzie. It could come back to haunt you."

Hmmm. His CO said the same thing. Frank picked up his pen. "Thanks, Elvis." He wrote *Is someone listening outside?* on a prescription notepad and held it up. "Have fun."

Elvis nodded with a slight smile. "I will." He motioned for Frank to hand him the pad, picked up the pen, wrote on the pad, and flipped it around for Frank to read. *I had no choice or I'm toast at the next promotion board. I won't sell you out either. Be careful.* Then he handed the pen to Frank, turned, and exited the office.

Frank cracked open the door and watched Elvis speak with a man in a class A uniform that he didn't recognize. On the man's left shoulder was the patch of the 525th Intelligence Group. Now Frank understood. He was still being watched, and they asked Elvis to come by and see if he would confide in him.

Well, the Army spook got nothing that wasn't already documented. But it was sad the United States Army would stoop so low to use his friend from Vietnam in that manner. Just like they did with Jackson. Despicable. The staff of the 95th Evac was a tightly knit group of people brought together in the bond of saving lives. They would always go to bat for each other. That's why he brought up Jackson's stay at the 95th. To show they had a connection to him.

Was Elvis concerned about his well-being after Vietnam and all the crazy stuff that happened since, or was it a ruse too? Knowing Elvis, his concern was genuine. He was dealing with the same inner morality issues that clashed with their Hippocratic Oath from having to decide which wounded men lived or died in Vietnam.

Frank went back to his paperwork. His case reports were due before he left for the day. He didn't want his commanding officer on his back. This incident might send him back to the little mold-filled, leaky pipe supply closet office.

CHAPTER 18

1300 Hours
April 14, 1973
Blanchfield Army Hospital
Ft. Campbell, KY

As Frank exited operating room one in his sweaty green, blood-stained surgical scrubs, Dr. Gaston approached him with another man Frank didn't recognize. He removed his scrub cap and wiped his forehead with it. "Dr. Gaston."

"Major," Dr. Gaston replied.

Frank wanted to shake his head. Gaston loved to use rank to show who was in charge. It was so unlike their closeness with each other on a first-name basis at the 95th Evac. "What can I do for you…sir?"

The unknown man, older, bald, and overweight, wearing a wrinkled gray lightweight linen suit, stepped forward. "Dr. Howard, I'm Stuart Cain, CIA attaché to the Army. Could you give me a few minutes of your time?"

CIA? There's a contradiction in terms. He tensed at those three well-known, ominous letters. *Bet this is about Jackson.* "Sure." *I can tell him lies too.* Frank pointed at the locker room next to the OR. "Mind if I duck out for a couple of minutes to change first?"

"No problem," Cain said.

Frank went into the locker room, opened his locker, and stopped. His uniform shirt and tie were askew on the hanger. When he left, they were straight. His lab coat was missing a pen from the pocket. *Cain's been here. Nothing to find. He probably searched my office. Nothing there either.* He changed clothes, dumped his scrubs into the laundry bin, picked up his pen from the locker floor, and tucked it in his lab coat pocket. Taking a deep breath, he exited the locker room into the hallway. Gaston was gone, but Cain stood in the same location.

"Thanks. Come with me." Frank led Cain to his office, 312, after being moved again last week. He was tired of yo-yoing between 301 and 312. From the doorway, he visually examined his desk. Instead of the light coating of dust always floating in this small room, the desktop had been recently wiped down. One way to prevent any incriminating fingerprints. He pointed at the chair in front of his desk. "Please sit."

Cain sat in the unadorned white plastic bowl chair then glanced around the room.

Frank sat in his chair behind his desk. "What can I do for you, Mr. Cain?"

Cain placed a piece of folded white paper on the desk. "Take a look at this?"

"What is it?" Frank unfolded the paper.

"A message to Army CID from Interpol."

Frank looked at the printing on the paper.

To: US Army Criminal Investigations Command

From: INTERPOL General Secretariat – Red Notice

We have received information that two AWOL members of the United States Army were possibly involved in a murder on French soil on 05 April 1973. The shooter (suspect 1) was possibly Lt. Colonel MacKenzie, Jackson J. The spotter (suspect 2) was possibly Captain Mason, William L. Killed was the Mayor of Saint-Jean-de-Luz. We believe they were paid a half million US dollars for the hit by an opposition candidate.

Description as follows:
Suspect 1 – 5'10" – 6'0", Weight: 225 pounds, Hair: Brown/crew cut
Suspect 2 – 5'09 – 5'10". Weight: 190 pounds, Hair: Brown/crew cut

What? That doesn't match Jackson's current description at all. He's in Montana working through his problems and weighs about 145 now. He doesn't keep his hair in a crew cut. And he's not a for-hire cold-blooded killer. "Why are you showing me this?" Frank asked.

Cain leaned forward in the chair. "Do you know where Lieutenant Colonel MacKenzie is hiding?"

Frank shook his head. "No, I don't," he lied.

"Are you sure?"

"Yes." Frank slammed both hands on the desk. "If you have something that says otherwise, arrest me. I'm sick of this load of bullshit. First, Hammond, then the hospital brass boots me out of my office because of his ongoing accusations, my commanding officer, the bogus police traffic stop, and now you!"

"I was wondering why such a decorated trauma surgeon with your reputation for excellence was in a closet."

"Yeah, right, since you've already been in here and my locker." Frank pulled his pen from his pocket. "Next time, make sure you don't drop something." He waved at the desk. "And don't clean up after yourself. With those rusted air conditioning ducts overhead, you can't keep the dust off anything."

Cain smiled. "Not bad, Doc. You'd make a pretty good spook with some training."

"Don't want any. Just want to do my job in peace. I don't know where MacKenzie has gone. I'll tell you what I've told everyone else. I haven't seen him since February 22nd of last year when General Kowalski forced him out of the hospital against my medical orders."

"And your visit to Major Russell at the Los Angeles VA hospital?"

"Fulfilling a promise. Colonel MacKenzie asked me to check on him." Frank crossed his arms. "Got a problem with it? And why are you following me? I was on an Army assignment."

"No problem, and I understand a promise between soldiers." Cain leaned back in his chair. "We weren't following you," he said casually.

Then it dawned on Frank. "You were watching Harry Russell. But that was last year before the escape. Harry was still a patient at the VA hospital learning how to walk with a prosthesis since he lost his left foot. There was no way for him to be involved."

"True. He was causing problems for my boss by writing letters and calling every politician in the state of California trying to get the details on the charges against MacKenzie. Mr. Russell is off-limits now due to a federal court order. All thanks to that dipshit Hammond and his bumbling CID fools trying to tap Russell's phone without a warrant."

"So why bother me?" Frank asked.

"Because for someone who hasn't seen MacKenzie in over a year, you can't keep your nose out of it."

Frank pointed at his medical diploma hanging on the wall beside him. "That's why. I've been called an incompetent doctor. Stupid. Naïve. MacKenzie needed help and the Army refused to follow its own regulations. I want to know why. I want the Army to admit it's wrong. If they could do it to a West Point graduate with the Medal of Honor and the rank of Lieutenant Colonel, how would some poor slick sleeve private survive under that amount of pressure? I don't want it to happen to someone else."

Cain nodded with a sickly sweet smile on his face. Frank wanted to throw up.

"Spoken like a man who believes in *Do no harm*." Cain stood and leaned across the desk so only Frank could hear him. "Dr. Howard, we have been watching you. But you're a boring stick in the mud who has no life other than what happens in this hospital. I suggest you get a counselor for your own problems. You drink a lot of beer. A six-pack a night, doctor? Do you know what that does to your liver? It won't be long until you're an alcoholic in need of a transplant. I've heard the local VFW has an AA meeting once a week." He turned and left the office.

Frank watched the door close slowly. He didn't drink that much. Two or three beers with dinner, maybe. Four every once in a while. A six-pack on a special occasion. He always gave what he had left over to one of his neighbors, a wheelchair-bound WWII veteran. So, Cain only watched him from the outside. Not inside his apartment. No hidden bugs or surveillance cameras. Which was a good thing. His secret remained safe.

When the door opened again, Frank expected Cain's return. He glanced up from his paperwork at Dr. Gaston in the doorway.

"Sir." Frank placed his pen on the desk, expecting bad news. Were the MPs here to arrest him?

Dr. Gaston tossed Frank a set of keys. "Move your stuff back to 301."

Frank breathed a sigh of relief that he bluffed his way past Cain. "Is this over now? You finally believe me?"

"Yes. Cain said you don't know MacKenzie's whereabouts. You're just doing your duty as a doctor." Gaston opened the door, peeked outside, and shut the door. "I agree with you that MacKenzie was not treated properly while wounded or in the stockade," he said in a lowered voice. "That's apparent in the medical records written by you and Dr. Wright." He must have seen the shocked look on Frank's face. "Yes, I read them. While I might feel the same way if he were my patient, please tone it down until he's caught or the charges against him are dropped. I want you to continue to work here as a surgeon, not as a permanent resident of Leavenworth, taking care of jock itch and STDs."

Frank nodded, a bit surprised at the revelation. "Yes, sir." Not that he intended to stop shaking the trees trying to find the truth. He would just do it more discreetly for a while.

CHAPTER 19

1800 Hours
June 15, 1973
Del Ray Apartment
Apt. 214
Oak Grove, KY

Bang-bang-bang. Someone heavy-handed was knocking on his front door. Frank pulled his hands out of the soapy dishwater in his sink, dried his hands, and went to the door. He opened it expecting to see Colonel Hammond and his MPs, the police, or both, not a United States Marine captain wearing the standard white cover, pressed khaki shirt, blue pants with blood stripe, and shiny black Corfam shoes.

The captain had an impressive salad bowl of ribbons - Vietnam Campaign Medal, Vietnam Cross of Gallantry Medal, Vietnam Service, National Defense, Purple Heart, Bronze Star, Navy and Marine Corps Medal, and Silver Star. Under the ribbons, two silver expert marksmanship medals - pistol and rifle.

The Marine held out a sealed white envelope. "Major Howard, I bring a message."

Frank took the envelope cautiously. It had his address on the front but no return address. He had a good idea who sent the message, but he wanted confirmation. "From who?"

The major smiled. "General Malone, sir."

That was the answer Frank expected and relieved to hear. "Thank you. Where'd you come from? There are no bases around here."

"Fort Knox. There's a Marine detachment there."

"Didn't know. How long have you been home?" Frank pointed at the Vietnam Service ribbon.

"Six months." The captain saluted even though Frank wasn't wearing a uniform but a t-shirt and jeans. Good day, sir." He turned, opened the stairwell door, and left.

Frank shut and locked his door then sat in his recliner with the envelope. He carefully opened it and unfolded the expensive, thick, watermarked paper.

11 June 1973

Dr. Frank Howard
6221 Pembroke Oak Grove Road
Apt. 214
Oak Grove, KY 42262

Frank,

Harry Russell's wife, Gabby, gave birth to a son on June 5th. He's busy taking care of the baby, so he asked me to let you know. The baby's name is Jackson Joseph Russell. Harry plans to appoint my godson, Jackson, as the godfather of his child. Harry calls the baby Little JJ because he calls Jackson, JJ. The pet name was started by Jackson's mother when he turned five years old. They called his brother James, Jim, so Jackson wanted a shorter name, and it stuck. Kids and their strange ideas.

Since you want to check on Jackson, let's make it a family affair on June 30th. I will forward Space-A reserved flight information and a rental car reservation to you on June 20th via the same courier who delivered this letter. Rank does have its privileges. My wife Sara wants to thank you personally for saving Jackson's life.

In the last few weeks, Jackson has, for lack of a better word, blossomed. He is sleeping through the night. His nightmares have all but disappeared. Just a few bad dreams that he shakes off by talking to us or the horse I gave him. A huge chestnut Quarter Horse named Bandit. Oh, chestnut is horse talk for red.

Jackson has gained so much weight and muscle, he looks like a bodybuilder. Another thing, and it brings elation to my spirit, he is happy. Which I'm sure you will notice, having met him in his darkest days when he had little to comfort his wounded spirit.

Please join us to surprise Jackson and enjoy a week of country hospitality. I'm sure the new baby will bring joy to his heart. You'll enjoy seeing how he reacts, as will I. He talks about how you saved his life and wants to see you again. Instead of him taking a chance near Fort Campbell, I want you to come to him and give me that promised update on his health. Oorah!

Semper Fi
Mangus Malone
Double M Ranch
Beaver Creek, MT

Frank carefully folded the letter and placed it back inside the envelope. This he had to put in a safe place, so if Hammond showed up with a search warrant, Jackson would remain safe in Montana even if he went to prison. Feeling behind the refrigerator, he grabbed the lockbox magnetically stuck to the back, placed the letter inside, and put the box back in place.

He wanted to whoop with joy at the top of his lungs. The only thing stopping him was his neighbors. The Watkins, an older, prim, and proper couple from England, might not appreciate the noise. But who cares? Frank jumped up from his chair, bouncing around his apartment like a balloon, pounding the floor with his feet with each hard landing. "Yay!" he yelled.

Someone, probably Mr. Watkins, banged on the wall. "Quiet in there," came through the sheetrock in a male British accent.

Frank didn't care. He kept celebrating then stopped to take a breath and pulled out his duffle bag. Why wait to pack and forget something? At seeing U.S. Army stenciled in black on the green cloth, he had to do something before packing. He sat in his recliner, picked up the phone on his end table, and dialed the home number of his commanding officer at Blanchfield – Lt. Colonel Adam Gaston.

When the ringing stopped, "Hello, Gaston residence," said a female voice.

"Mrs. Gaston, it's Dr. Frank Howard. Can I speak with your husband, please?"

"Sure, Dr. Howard. Is there an emergency at the hospital?"

"Not that I know of, ma'am. I'm off duty. It's a personal matter."

"Okay, hold on."

Frank leaned back. What would he tell Gaston? The man knew his parents were dead.

"Frank, what's up? My wife said it's personal."

"Yeah, something's come up. I need to take some leave."

"When?"

"June 29th through July 8th. I need to visit my...brother in the hospital."

"You don't have a brother, Frank. Is this about your friend, Jake Landry?"

"No." But he needed to make plans to visit him soon. "My brother...Charlie lived with us growing up when his parents died suddenly. His father worked with my Dad. Mom considered him her son. I grew so close to him, I considered him my brother," Frank lied. "He may not be blood, but he is my brother." That part was about Jackson and true.

"Good enough. I'm glad you have someone. Put in the paperwork tomorrow and I'll get it in the books. Is he really sick?"

Frank anticipated this question. "Car wreck. Broken leg with some lacerations, a couple of broken ribs, and internal bruising. His doctor says he should be fine. They're waiting a couple of weeks for the swelling to subside before deciding if he needs surgery to place a rod in his tibia. He wants me there to ask questions when that happens."

"Understandable. And I know why you're not leaving now. It wouldn't do any good. If I had an experienced surgeon like you as a brother, I'd want his opinion too. I'll see you tomorrow. Good night."

Frank placed his handset on the cradle when he heard the click. Gaston was a trusting and naïve man. Not really Army officer material. While Frank hated lying to him, it was for a good cause.

CHAPTER 20

Frank pulled his rental car, a 1972 white and red two-door Mercury Cougar, into a driveway with a large overhead shiny brown square wooden sign - *Double M Ranch*. Engraved on the front, two crossed sabers with MM between them with horseshoes, the USMC Eagle, Globe and Anchor, and a bulldog in the corners. He parked in front of the main house and climbed out.

The ranch looked exactly like he pictured it. A two-story white farmhouse with a wraparound porch and a huge red barn surrounded by a three-railed white fenced pasture. Running parallel to the main house with a path leading to the door, a bunkhouse made of rough-hewn logs. It looked ancient. Something out of an old western movie or TV show. Jutting up from the wooden shake-covered roof, a cast-iron fluted chimney. All it needed was a saddled horse tied to a hitching post outside to complete the picture.

A twenty-foot flagpole surrounded by whitewashed rocks stood in the center of the neatly mown yard in front of the house. Two flags flapped in the breeze: The American flag, and under it, a red Marine Corps flag.

Frank saluted the American flag. He was an officer of the United States Army. After retrieving his duffle bag from the trunk, he rang the doorbell.

An older woman wearing a tucked-in white blouse, blue jeans, and black slip-on shoes with her silver hair in a bun answered the door. "Hi, are you Dr. Howard?"

"Yes, ma'am. Please call me Frank. Are you Sara Malone?"

"I sure am, and it's Sara, not Mrs. Malone. We've been expecting you. Come in, please." Sara stepped aside, allowing Frank to enter. She led him into the living room. The vast room contained a brown leather couch, matching loveseat, two recliners, a bookshelf packed with books and magazines, a fireplace, and a railed staircase. It had several connecting doors, all propped open. He looked through one door at the kitchen. Another was the dining room with a large table surrounded by six chairs and a china cabinet against the wall.

Mangus came up behind him and placed a hand on his shoulder. He looked exactly like the last time Frank saw him. Neatly dressed in a pressed tan short-sleeve button-up collared shirt, blue jeans, and brown leather cowboy boots.

"Welcome to the Double M," Mangus said.

"Thanks. Where's Jackson?" Frank asked.

"Working in the fields somewhere taking care of the herd. He'll be in later. He doesn't know you're here."

"So, it's a surprise." *I like that even better. His reaction will be natural and telling of his attitude.*

"Yes." Mangus' smile was infectious.

Frank looked up when the doorbell rang. Did someone follow him? Mangus didn't seem concerned at all. Instead, he leaned on the fireplace mantel and sipped the steaming liquid in his coffee mug.

Sara went to the door and opened it.

A few seconds later, Harry, dressed in a gray polo shirt and black slacks, appeared holding a baby wearing a onesie - green fatigues with gold second lieutenants' bars silk-screened on it. With him, a woman in a pink summer dress carrying a light blue diaper bag over her shoulder, his wife, Gabby.

Frank pointed at the baby. "Does Jackson know?"

Harry shook his head. "Nope."

Mangus stepped forward. "I'm Mangus Malone. Manny to my friends. It's nice to meet you and put a face with the name."

Harry nodded since his hands were busy. "Yes, sir."

"You're as pig-headed as Jackson. Manny, not sir."

"Yes...Manny." Harry sat next to Gabby on the couch.

Frank moved over to get a closer look at the baby. He had chubby cheeks full of color, brown eyes, a button nose, and an open toothless mouth. "He's beautiful, Harry. Got your nose."

"Ha-ha. And Gabby's hair."

Sara hip-checked Frank aside and held out her arms. "My turn."

"Yes...mmm...Sara." Harry handed his son to her.

Sara babbled baby talk to little JJ, cuddling him, kissing him, singing to him. *Three Blind Mice. Old McDonald's Farm. This Little Piggy.* Grandma stuff. Time kept marching along, and no Jackson.

Sara handed his son back to Harry and disappeared into the kitchen.

Mangus looked at his watch. "Jackson's never late on Saturdays. He always stops by the house to give me the weekly report."

Frank looked at the clock. 1601 hours. It wasn't all that late. But he didn't know their schedule either.

Harry handed the baby to his wife. "Do you think something's wrong?"

"Don't know. Other than an occasional nightmare, he's been doing good." Mangus pointed at the door. "Let's go." His voice resonated in the command style Frank heard so many times in 'Nam from visiting division commanders or higher. The general expected obedience. No way would he do anything but follow orders. So would Harry.

Their first stop, the bunkhouse. Inside the main room, they found ten made-up bunks, each one covered with a colorful quilt but no people. Against one wall stood a dresser with a small TV on top. In front of it, a worn-out green sofa. Six folding chairs sat around a collapsible table. Each corner was stacked high with cardboard storage boxes.

One bunk had a large framed picture on the wall above it—a color photo of two men in uniform in front of the Marine Corps and American flags. Frank recognized Jackson wearing the Army uniform with corporal stripes on the sleeves. He was the younger version of the other man. In fact, Jackson looked almost like his exact double. Frank realized the older man was Jackson's Marine Corps father, Colonel James MacKenzie.

Frank and Harry turned when the door slammed shut. They ran after Mangus as he double-timed to the barn.

Frank panted along beside Harry. "Guess he's in a hurry?"

"I can see that." Harry tripped on a rock, stumbled a couple of steps, regained his footing, and continued jogging. They caught up to Mangus as he opened the barn door.

In the wide expanse of the barn were two rows of stalls. Each one had a horse eating hay from a manger. Including a big red one with four white socks and a blaze Mangus had described in his letters. Bandit. Jackson's horse. The horse eyed them for a few seconds as if sizing them up and returned to munching on his hay.

"Well, he's around here somewhere." Mangus headed to the workshop – a large prefab-looking white metal building with a roll-up garage door.

It was empty, except for tools, a work table, and parts of different sizes and shapes. Out front sat a white beat-up Ford F-150 truck.

"Where in the hell is he?" Mangus stopped a ranch hand walking toward the barn. "Have you seen Jackson?"

The man pointed over Mangus' shoulder. "Yes, sir. He's in the foaling barn with Lady."

Mangus rolled his eyes. "I'm an idiot." Not breaking stride, he led the way to a small red barn set away from the others. Next to it, a three-rail white fenced pasture. Before Mangus walked through the wide-open door, he turned, put a finger to his lips, and entered the building.

Jackson stood twenty feet away, draped over the closed stall door on crossed arms. Due to the heat, he was wearing a white t-shirt. Tucked into the back pocket of his blue jeans, a long white towel.

Walking up behind him, Mangus leaned on the rail. "How are things going?"

"Take a look for yourself." Jackson pointed at the chestnut mare on the stall floor. "The front feet are showing, so it should be soon. I came to check on her before I headed to the house. Lady was restless when I walked in, so I stayed. Sorry if I worried you."

Mangus patted Jackson's shoulder. "No, it's okay. You made the right call. I'm letting you run the stock operation. It was my mistake. I didn't think about Lady foaling today. By the way, you have some long overdue visitors who've traveled over a thousand miles to see you."

"Who? Where?"

"Behind you, JJ," Harry drawled.

Jackson spun around so fast the air seemed to whoosh.

Harry remained in place, unmoving and staring.

Jackson closed the distance in three long strides and grabbed him in a bear hug.

Harry stood there for a long moment. When Jackson almost knocked him over, he kicked him in the shin.

Frank bit his tongue not to laugh. These two hadn't seen each other in over a year. And he knew they were best friends with the closeness of brothers. Their service together in Vietnam made them blood brothers.

Jackson turned to Frank with his right hand extended.

Frank brushed the hand aside. He enveloped Jackson with his arms like a vise. Patting him on the back and swaying back and forth. He could feel the muscle under Jackson's t-shirt. The man wasn't skin and bones any longer. His posture had straightened, no longer stooped over like an arthritic old man. He looked taller.

"It's good to see you too." Jackson raised his elbows to pry himself from Frank's tight grasp.

Frank backed up. "You look terrific, Jackson."

"Thanks. I could take on the world right now. It's much nicer than when we met."

"What's going on over there?" Frank pointed at the stall.

"Come take a look." Jackson waved them over to the stall door. "Lady's about to drop her foal."

Mangus, Frank, and Harry crowded around him.

Frank stared as the foal's feet came out, the nose, then the head and neck. He'd never seen anything like that before, at least in an animal, now in a human, many times.

Jackson went into the stall. He pulled the towel from his pocket and wiped the membrane off the foal's muzzle.

The mare grunted. A low, pained grunt. Not agony, but not comfort either. Her nostrils were flared out, red around the rims. A sign of straining—pushing hard.

Frank gripped the top rail, not knowing what to do. Those symptoms were not a good thing for an animal or human.

Jackson grabbed the front feet and gently pulled with each contraction. He rotated the foal from side to side until it slid out onto the ground. The foal plopped onto its side. A small whinny escaped his mouth.

Frank released a breath he didn't realize he was holding. Beside him, Harry did the same thing.

Jackson placed his hand on the foal's muzzle then levered him onto his belly. "It's a colt, Uncle Manny." He exited the stall, drying his hands on the towel.

"Good. With Lucky Cheyenne as his father, he'll bring a good price when we sell him."

Lady scrambled to her feet and began licking her foal clean, starting at the head and working her way down his neck and back.

Jackson leaned against the stall door as his friends stood next to him.

Harry pointed at the colt. "How long until he stands?"

"Say, thirty minutes or so."

The barn went silent as the colt stuck out his front legs and pushed up with his hind legs. His legs splayed out from under him, stuck out like an octopus. He fell into the straw with a faint plop.

"Come on, boy, one more time. I know how it feels." Jackson knocked on the stall door with his knuckles.

The colt stumbled to his feet. He swayed like a drunk at last call but stayed up on wobbly legs. Lady sidled up next to him. He pushed his nose under her belly and latched onto a teat.

"He's eating. Let's give them some peace and quiet." Jackson grabbed his shirt from a wall hook and exited the barn.

Harry, Frank, and Mangus followed him outside.

"That was incredible," Harry blurted out.

"A new life always is. I've delivered a few babies but never seen a horse give birth before." Frank pointed at Jackson. "I guess you have since you knew what to do."

"Yep, not my first time." Jackson flipped the shirt over his shoulder then glanced at his watch. "The guys are probably here by now. I need to shower and change clothes. Are you guys going to join us?"

Harry wondered what that meant. "For what?"

"Remember our little get-togethers before a mission?"

"Great. Dare I ask who's bringing the food?"

"Ty and Bill drew the short straw for the food." Jackson winked at Harry. "Chief bought the beer…of course. Mikey chose the dessert, and since I'm a little tied up, I hope someone started the fire."

Mangus grinned. "I'm sure one of them did."

Harry held up his wedding ring. "JJ, you do remember I'm married now?"

Jackson paused for a few seconds. "Yeah, I vaguely remember you telling me that. Her name's Gabby, right?"

"Correct."

"Go grab your wife while I take a shower. I won't make a good impression on her covered in the blood and afterbirth from a mare."

"Roger." Harry gave him a thumbs up then headed to the house with Mangus.

Jackson pulled on Frank's sleeve. "Come on."

As they came around the corner of the bunkhouse, Frank saw a large man with short black hair and Native American features tending a fire inside a stone-ringed fire pit. He recognized the man from that day on the C-130. *That must be Chief. Jackson said he's an Osage Indian from Texas.* Another thing Frank noticed. Chief was dressed like Jackson in a white t-shirt and blue jeans. Except he wore black high-top Converse Chuck Taylor All-Star basketball shoes instead of cowboy boots.

Jackson placed his foot on the wooden A-frame picnic table bench as Chief threw logs onto the fire. "Thanks for starting the fire. Lady decided today's the day."

Chief turned after covering the orange glowing coals with a fire-blackened steel grate. "Colt or filly?"

"Colt."

"I'll have to go by later and check him out. Red like mom or brown like dad?"

"Red, with a blaze and socks on the two back feet."

Chief let out a boisterous laugh. "He'll be spoiled with you around."

"Funny. Be back in a few." Jackson went into the bunkhouse.

Frank cocked his head. "Socks?" That was a new term to him when it came to horses.

Chief pointed at his shoes. "The two back feet are white like a pair of socks. It's nice to see you again, Dr. Howard. Come to check on your wayward patient?"

He already liked Chief. The man had a great sense of humor. "Yes, I did. Call me Frank. How're his nightmares?"

"Gone for the most part, along with the depression. Just an occasional bad dream. Since he talks about it right after they happen, including to his horse when no one else is around, they don't bother him anymore. The colonel is happy and loves it here, so he's doing great."

Frank scratched his chin. "I can see that. I almost didn't recognize him from the back since his upper body has bulked up so much. He still has skinny legs, but they have gotten larger. His waist looks like a man's, not an anorexic teenager."

Chief's face relaxed. His eyes sparkled in pride. "Yep, the colonel's worked hard to build up his legs since he lost so much muscle mass in his thighs. As for his waist, until a few weeks ago, I could yank off his jeans with them buttoned. Now they fit perfectly. He uses the belt to hold his knife. Why don't we sit and talk until everyone gets here?"

"Sure." Frank sat next to Chief on the bench. "Since Harry mentioned it, how did this tradition of having a party before a mission start?"

Chief leaned back, pressing his back against the table. "It was kinda by accident. Our first mission together after the POW camp, the colonel surprised us with a feast. Well, one for Vietnam. He cooked hot dogs over a fire on a grill made of a fuel drum lid with holes punched in it. The meal came with chips, canned chili, pre-made potato salad, and baked beans. For dessert, we had Twinkies and Ding Dongs. We had so much fun shooting the shit with each other, knowing what could happen the next day. The idea took off from there. I say it's along the same lines as one of the SEAL traditions."

"Which is?" Frank asked. That piqued his curiosity.

"They write a letter before each mission to give to their families in case they don't come back."

Frank thought about it for a moment. "I agree. How'd you start choosing who does what?"

Chief patted his chest. "That was my idea. We draw straws. Why lump it all on the colonel. He had to plan the missions. It became our job to take care of all the details of the pre-mission bull session and get the food."

"Nice. I love it. Got one more question."

"Go ahead, Doc."

"Why don't you wear boots like everyone else here?"

"I'm a mechanic. It's easier to climb in and around the equipment in sneakers." Chief brushed some wood ash off his shirt. "I do have a pair of nice boots. I use them on the weekends. The bingo hall has dancing on Friday nights. I love the Texas two-step."

"I see. Got a steady girl?"

Chief's face turned red. "Ahh..."

Ty, Bill, and Mikey walked up with full brown paper sacks in their arms, stopping Chief's reply. Bill, a stocky man who reminded Frank of a bull terrier ready to fight, and Mikey, the young medic from the plane. Both men wore the standard ranch wear of t-shirts, boots, and jeans. Ty, however, was dressed in gray shorts, red Puma Clyde sneakers, and a white tank top. His tanned skin, dark curly hair, relatively tall, slim frame, and handsome features made him look like a movie star on vacation.

Mikey glanced at the open bunkhouse door. "Is the colonel okay?"

"He's taking a shower." Frank stood from the table. "One of the mares gave birth today. Jackson wound up on the icky side since he was in the stall with her. General Malone invited me here to check on Jackson. Harry's here too. He went to get his wife."

Jackson walked out of the bunkhouse with his short hair still damp. "Hey, guys. Heard Frank tell you about Harry. They should be here soon. Who has grill duty? I did it last week."

"Me." Mikey's tone turned sheepish. "I'll try not to burn yours up like the last time."

"Yeah." Jackson scrunched his nose as he smacked his lips. "My burger looked like a charcoal briquette and was about as edible."

Bet Mikey keeps a close watch this time. Frank pointed at the fire. "What're you guys having?"

Ty pulled everything out of the sacks on the table. "Steak and baked potatoes. Ribeyes for us. A sirloin for the colonel. The potatoes are cowboy-style on the outside coals. I wish we'd known so we could've bought more food."

"Don't worry. I brought enough for the rest of us. My wife's joining us tonight," said Mangus' deep bass voice behind them. Everyone turned as Mangus set a large red ice chest next to the table.

Jackson pulled six collapsible blue canvas camp chairs out of the bunkhouse closet and set them around the fire.

Harry walked up, carrying four similar red chairs. Beside him, Gabby, holding the baby wrapped in a light blue fleece blanket. Ty, Chief, Bill, and Mikey's mouths dropped open. Frank smiled like a man who had won the lottery. He knew the secret about to be revealed.

Harry placed his chairs with the others in the circle around the fire.

Jackson walked up to Gabby. "Hi, I'm Jackson."

Gabby smiled. "I know who you are, JJ. Harry's told me all about you. I'm Gabby."

"It's nice to meet you." Jackson pointed at one of the chairs. "Please sit."

Gabby sat with the baby against her chest. "Thank you." She pulled the blanket back. A small brown-haired head appeared.

Jackson cocked his head one way then another as if flabbergasted, unable to understand why Gabby had a baby in her arms. He'd completely forgotten how long Harry and Gabby had been married. And what can happen in nine months.

Harry flipped a St. John's medal on a silver chain around Jackson's neck. "Surprise. Meet Jackson Joseph Russell. Your godson."

Jackson wiped a tear from his eyes. Humility, hope, and love lined his face. "The honor is mine. I hope to do as good a job as my godfather."

"I know you will." Harry took the child from Gabby and faced Jackson. "Your turn."

Jackson held out his arms. "Thank you." He cradled the infant against his chest and walked around the fire, softly cooing to him.

Frank couldn't keep the smile off his face. He loved seeing Jackson so happy.

"JJ, look this way. I want to try out my new Polaroid camera." Harry held up the white camera.

"Come on, Harry. Give me a few minutes."

"No. Smile." Harry put the camera to his eye.

"Whatever." Jackson gave such a cheesy smile Frank burst out laughing. Lips pulled back with his teeth showing and chin jutted out.

"You'll thank me when JJ's bigger." Harry pulled the photo from the camera and waved it back and forth.

Frank wondered if that action did anything or was an urban myth. As a man of science, it seemed counterintuitive to him for anyone to shake a developing picture.

Jackson handed little JJ to Gabby when he cried. "I think he's hungry?"

"Probably." Gabby unbuttoned her shirt, draped a large towel over her shoulder, and tucked her son underneath. Sucking noises came from under the towel.

Jackson's jaw dropped. He couldn't take his eyes off Gabby. He stood like a marble Greek statue as if his mind was utterly vapor-locked.

Harry poked him in the shoulder. "You look like a tomato. It's called breastfeeding. The same as your little boy in the barn."

"Too much information." Jackson went into the bunkhouse, shaking his head the entire way.

Frank followed him inside. He needed a few minutes alone with him to ask a few personal questions out of the earshot of everyone else.

Jackson set a coffee can on the countertop. "Hey, Frank, I know it's you. Only a doctor would wear Corfams on a ranch. I hope you brought a pair of boots, or those shoes will need some serious cleaning before you wear them with your uniform."

Frank leaned against the cabinet beside Jackson. *It can't hold a candle to your feet blood-glued inside your boots for sixteen hours in the OR.* "Cute. I brought my combat boots, but these are broken in and comfortable. How are you doing?"

"Good. I haven't fully recovered. I'd put myself at about eighty percent. I'll probably never get back to one hundred and will deal with this for the rest of my life." Jackson tapped the side of his head. "I'll have my good days, and, unfortunately, a few bad ones when my demons pop up."

"I agree with your assessment. Where were you the last time I saw you?"

Jackson filled the empty pot with water. "That's easy, zero."

"I agree with that too. You're totally honest with me, and that's good. Did General Malone tell you I asked a psychiatrist friend about his treatment plan if you were in his care?" *I asked him professional questions over an expensive steak dinner.*

"Yeah, he did." Jackson spooned four large scoops of fresh coffee into the basket. "The doctor was surprised I was doing it without drugs."

"Yes. What made the difference?" *I really want to know.*

"In my uneducated opinion, being out here with no constraints and the horse Uncle Manny gave me."

Frank's eyes widened. "The horse?" Interesting.

After starting the brew cycle, Jackson turned to him. "Yeah, the horse. He gave me a reason to get out of bed in the mornings. I had to take care of Bandit. He's my responsibility. I fixated on him and beat the crap out of a heavy bag every morning. I could talk to Bandit when I couldn't talk to anyone else. I'm not sure I'd be here without him."

"It was that bad?" Frank cocked his head. "And the horse made that much of a difference?"

"Yes, it was that bad, and he made all the difference. Horses, like most animals, are nonjudgmental. Bandit knew I was in pain and stuck his head in my chest to comfort me."

"Wow. I can't believe an animal made such a difference. It's unique." *I'll have to put that in my notes.*

"Well, I can't speak for anyone else, but it worked for me."

Frank looked his friend up and down. "I can tell. Mangus said they can't keep you out of the refrigerator. He told me about your reaction during the Belmont. That's so out of character for you."

"True, but that was history." Jackson spread out his hands with a slight shrug. "I love horses. What else can I say? And, yes, I eat a lot now. That's why we bought a refrigerator for the bunkhouse and installed a cupboard. Sometimes we get hungry at night. No one cares if we go to the house for midnight snacks. We've startled Aunt Sara a few times in her bathrobe when she wasn't expecting us. We keep stuff here instead."

Poor Sara. I bet she gave them an earful afterward. "Glad to hear it. Your huge appetite shows how far you've come in the last six months."

"Thanks. Where are you going to stay tonight? I'm sure Harry will hot bunk in the guesthouse with his wife. Do you want to sleep here or the main house?"

"My plan was to stick with you and Chief unless you don't want me to."

Jackson didn't stop to take a breath. The words poured out non-stop. "We'd love to have you stay with us. Do you want a tour of the ranch? If you do, I hope you can ride. I get up at 0500 to work out and take care of my horse. Breakfast is at 0800 hours. Be ready for a long day. I have a lot of ground to cover tomorrow."

Frank held both hands up, palms out. "Slow down, Mighty Mouth. I can hardly understand you. Yes, I can ride, and I'd love a tour. I'm in the Army, so I get up early. Medically speaking, I want to see how well you move around during your workout. What about Harry?"

"Sorry. It's nice to have company for a change. Harry's never ridden a day in his life. He's a city boy. I'm not about to put him on a horse for the first time to have him fall off and need your services now that he has a family. I'll take him around in the truck after I finish my chores. In 'Nam, he told me that he always wanted a big covered porch. The main house has a nice one. He and Gabby can kick back and enjoy the ranch. Besides, Harry will be here all next week. We have plenty of time to talk. He may be on vacation, but I have to work." Jackson pointed at the door with his full coffee cup. "Let's go join the party."

Even before they walked through the open door, they heard Chief singing with *Born to be Wild.* Next, he belted out, *Desperado,* making like he was riding a horse.

Frank stopped mid-step. "What's going on with Chief?"

"He says the song reminds him of me since my ranch duties include maintaining the fences and being AWOL makes I'm a desperado. When he heard the song on the radio last month, he pointed it out." Jackson chuckled. "He's right. The lyrics do sound like me."

"I agree with him."

"He's been practicing that song, using me as his audience and critic all month."

In full rapture, Chief had everyone's attention over the sounds of the crickets. At the end of the song, everyone stood and applauded.

Sara patted Chief on the shoulder. "You have a beautiful singing voice, honey. We need to get you on a stage somewhere and make a lot of money."

Chief kissed her cheek. "Thank you." He looked at Mikey. "See, someone thinks I sound like a real singer."

Mikey shook his head. "Guess I'm outvoted."

Jackson sat in an empty chair, relaxed with his feet out, ankles crossed, watching the white, puffy clouds float by overhead.

Frank pulled up a chair next to him, an open beer bottle in his hand. "No beer?"

"Nope. My stomach doesn't do alcohol very well now. Did Dr. Rose tell you what happened?"

Frank nodded. "About the bottle of Jack Daniels, yeah, he told me." *I know how hard it is to walk away from it too. Getting drunk is the wrong way to try to escape the pain.*

"There's another reason. My first day in 'Nam after being stateside for the Medal of Honor ceremony, General Thomas ordered me to report to the 6th Convalescent Center for a physical. Even though Dr. Green cleared me for full combat duty, he was on my butt about my weight. He gave me a stern warning that if I didn't follow his instructions to the letter, he would recommend forced retirement. I received written orders to report to Dr. Nicholson once a week for an evaluation of my progress." Jackson turned to look Frank in the eyes. "Bet you know how well I responded to an ultimatum."

"Yeah. Not well. What did you do?"

"I went to the local watering hole to blow off steam and got totally wasted. I started a drunken brawl with my West Point roommate." Jackson pointed at the large scar on his left forearm. "Chris threw a broken beer bottle. It cut the crap out of my arm. I don't even remember the trip to the hospital. When I woke up, Dr. Green said his staff sedated me after I tried to start another fight. The alcohol combined with the drugs gave me a huge hangover. It was too late to patch up our friendship. Chris left for his new duty assignment that morning. I don't drink because of what might happen if I drink too much."

Frank tapped his bottle on Jackson's chair. "You didn't have to tell me the story. You've come a long way to admit that to me."

"Yeah, I know. I thought I should explain."

"Are you ever going to patch things up with him?"

Jackson poked the fire with a sharp stick. Orange sparks flew into the air. "If I ever get the chance, yes. I started the fight. But given my current situation, who knows when that might be."

On the other side of the fire, Mikey yelled, "Dinner's ready. Everyone grab your plates."

First in line were Mangus and Sara. Jackson stood behind them. As he stepped up to the fire, Mikey plopped the steak on his plate. Juices oozed from the meat as Jackson stabbed a baked potato in the coals with his fork.

"Much better than last time, Mikey." Jackson balanced the plate on his right palm with his silverware gripped in his other hand.

"Yes, sir." Mikey tapped the meat fork on the grate. "Kept a close eye on it tonight."

Jackson returned to his chair and set the plate in his lap.

Frank sat beside him with his plate containing a much smaller steak and potato. "That steak has to weigh two pounds. The baked potato's the size of a softball."

Jackson turned to Frank, knife in hand. "Please leave me alone for a few minutes so I can eat in peace. I'm starving. We can talk about this later."

The sun sank lower and lower until the blood-red dot snuck below the horizon. Mikey pulled out S'mores. The roaring wood fire was perfect for roasting marshmallows.

"Mmm." Jackson stuffed his face with chocolate, gooey white marshmallows, and graham crackers.

Sara poked Jackson in the shoulder. "You have chipmunk cheeks, honey." She brought up her camera. "Smile." *Click*, and a flashbulb went off.

Jackson rolled his eyes. He licked the chocolate residue off his lips. Harry handed him little JJ. He settled into the chair with his godson nestled protectively in his arms.

"Oh, that one's even better." Sara pointed her camera at them. "Hold him up so I can get your faces together." *Click*.

"Aunt Sara, you're blinding me!"

Bill tossed a paper ball in the fire. "Ty, remember when the colonel launched the food tray across his cell like a two-year-old?"

Ty tipped up his beer bottle. "Which time? There were so many. We had to wash potatoes out of his hair every week."

"Yeah. It was like scraping cement off his head. How about the day..."

Frank listened to the embarrassing stories, watching Jackson's reaction to them. Jackson didn't seem to mind, even laughing at a few of them with his friends.

At 2145 hours, Harry stood in front of Jackson. "Sorry, buddy. We need to get little JJ into his crib."

"Okay. Easy. He's asleep. Don't wake him." Jackson gently placed his godson in Harry's waiting arms.

Sara and Mangus stood. She looped her arm around Mangus' extended elbow. "You kids enjoy yourselves. We're going to bed."

Jackson kissed her cheek. "Have fun. I heard strange noises coming from the house last night."

"You're a brat." Sara pointed at him. "I want grandchildren one of these days."

"Isn't that what you were doing last night, Aunt Sara?"

"Hush, young man or you're grounded." Sara winked then walked with Mangus to the house.

Ty and Bill gathered the leftover food and beer.

"Where are you guys going?" Jackson looked at his watch. "It's only 2200 hours."

Bill fished his car keys out of his pocket. "To get the house presentable for Sunday dinner with our girlfriends."

"Bet it looks like a pigsty."

"Nag, nag, nag. You sound like an old woman. See you on Monday."

Bill jerked Ty's arm. Both men walked toward the driveway, each with a sack under their arm.

Mikey ran to catch up. "Can I catch a ride? The colonel has company."

Bill held out his hand. "Sure, for a price. You can help us clean up for an hour."

"I don't have a choice with no wheels." Mikey slapped Bill's palm. "Deal."

"What happened to loyalty, guys?" Jackson skipped a rock next to Ty's retreating feet.

Ty grinned over his shoulder. "Not when it comes to women, sir."

"Hmph!" Jackson placed his hands on the back of Frank and Chief's chairs and leaned between them. "Do you guys want to stay here or call it a night?"

"I'm going inside, boss." Chief rubbed his throat.

"Go gargle salt water to get your voice back unless you want Frank to help." Jackson grabbed the bucket next to the bunkhouse wall and dumped water on the fire to put it out.

Chief stacked the chairs against the wall. "No. I can take care of it. Don't need your doctor to help me."

Frank started to ask Chief a question, then Jackson, holding a 30-30 lever-action Winchester rifle, spun him around by the shoulder. "You coming?"

"Checking on the foal?" Frank fell in step with him.

"Yep. I need to make sure he's okay for the night." Jackson whistled along the well-worn dirt path. A bounce to each step. He went inside the small barn and propped the rifle against the wall.

Lady's ears twitched with his footsteps. She nuzzled Jackson's chest as he petted her. In return, he fed her a handful of peppermints. Lady crunched then returned to her hay. Her foal squealed when she moved, milk dribbling from his mouth.

"Chief's right." Frank shook his finger at Jackson. "You're going to spoil that colt."

Jackson set his foot on the bottom rail of Lady's stall. "Got a question for you."

Frank copied his stance. "Sure."

"What have you heard, not what the Army's telling the press?"

"They don't know where you went, and it has them stumped." Frank braced his elbows on the top rail. "The rumor circulating around CID is you're working as assassins for the highest bidder. They're trying to pin a few international murders on you, but the descriptions don't match."

Jackson stuck a piece of straw in his mouth. "We know that's not true. Anything else?"

"Yeah. An APB went out on Christmas Eve, requesting law enforcement agencies check medical facilities for a sick individual matching your description. When I pointed it out to my superiors, they told me to drop the issue if I knew what was good for me."

Lady's head jerked up when Jackson banged the rail with his toe. "Hammond calls me a liar when I couldn't hold my head up. The Army announces I faked everything. They tell the police to look for a sick man. It's hypocrisy. I would've died in that crappy cell. I have no way to prove it."

Frank leaned against the rail sideways. "Dr. Rose sent me your records and test results. He kept great notes and took pictures. If it ever comes to that, I can prove how close you came to dying."

"I've had this same discussion with Curtis. I'll tell you the same thing. If the Army ever catches me, I won't go quietly. It took a lot of hard work to get this far in my recovery. I don't want to die, but I can't go through that pain again. I'll find a way out. You won't like the second option."

"No, I don't like it, but I do understand. I hope it never comes to that. If it does, I'll get you out. Even if I have to go all the way to the President."

"I thought you should know. I owe you that much."

Frank gripped Jackson's shoulder. "Thanks. It takes a lot to earn your trust."

Jackson pointed at the mare and foal. "Let's go. They're good for the night." He picked up his rifle, followed Frank outside, then closed and locked the barn door.

CHAPTER 21

2300 Hours
June 30, 1973
Double M Ranch
Beaver Creek, MT

As Frank and Jackson walked into the bunkhouse, Chief met them on the other side of the threshold. "Everything okay with the new momma?"

"Yeah, they're fine." Jackson leaned his rifle against the doorjamb then headed to the coffee pot.

Frank grabbed his bag from the closet and tossed it on the bunk across the aisle from Jackson's.

Chief placed a small rotating fan on the table next to Frank's bunk.

"What's with the fan?" Frank asked.

"It gets stuffy in here at night." Chief plugged the cord into a socket. "The fan keeps you cool and muffles the sounds of the animals. You'll love hearing the wolves howl in the early morning hours. It takes some getting used to. The colonel keeps his 30-30 next to the door in case one tries to climb in through the half-open windows."

"Thanks. Why'd they leave us alone earlier?"

Chief pulled off his shirt. Sweat gleamed on his hairless tanned chest. The American Bald Eagle in flight tattoo Frank read about in the ABP was impressive as it covered Chief's entire right shoulder and pectoral.

"They don't like the fire. The colonel's picked a few off prowling around the main living area. They steer clear of us. That's why the barn doors are locked at night. Don't be alarmed if he jumps up and grabs his rifle." Chief pointed at the window. "Somethin' might be trying to get in."

Jackson set his stained white coffee mug on the table next to his bunk. He pulled off his boots and jeans then put on a faded pair of Army-issue gray workout shorts. Probably from a surplus store. But it showed Jackson's continuing loyalty, even betrayed, to the Army and his country.

Frank changed into the same shorts, except his were newly issued and never worn. He worked out when he had the time in his civilian running attire. It was much more comfortable.

Jackson leaned back into the pillows on his bunk and picked up a paperback book.

Frank sat across from him on the next bunk. "What're you reading?"

Jackson eyed his friend over the novel. *"Smoky the Cowhorse.* Uncle Manny had it in the house. Never read it but saw the movie. They showed it at my firebase in '68. Everyone was rooting for the horse at the end. I guess it served a purpose by getting everyone's mind off the war."

Never heard of it. At the 95th, we got mostly old movies one step above silent films and awful B-rate monster stuff...except for MASH. "There was a movie? Was it any good?"

"The book's better than the movie, and the movie was good." Jackson took a sip of coffee.

Frank pointed at the mug. "Doesn't that keep you awake?" *That much caffeine would keep me bouncing off the wall for days.*

"Nah, just used to it." Jackson grabbed a chocolate bar from his table, nibbling on it as he read his book.

Frank looked at the picture on the wall behind Jackson. He was still amazed at how much Jackson resembled his father. Except for the age difference, they could be identical twins.

"Like the picture? That's my dad and me in Korea," Jackson said, lowering his book to catch Frank's eyes.

"Yeah, I can tell. He's the one wearing eagles. You're his younger mirror image with corporal stripes. Was that taken on a Marine base? The Marine Corps flag is behind you."

"Yep. I visited Dad on a one-day pass right before he died."

Frank picked up a framed photograph of a man in a Marine uniform, a woman in a blue dress, and two young boys in black suits on Jackson's table. "Is this your family? Your mother was a beautiful woman."

"I was ten years old in that picture. It was taken after Dad received the Medal of Honor for his bravery at the battle of Okinawa." Jackson's face lit up with a huge smile. "That's my older brother, Jim, next to me. I agree, Mom was beautiful."

"How did your mother die?"

"She was the head nurse of an Army MASH unit in Korea. Her jeep ran over a landmine after delivering supplies to an aid station. Killed her and the driver instantly. She died the same day as Dad," Jackson said in a sad tone.

Frank thought he saw a tear slip unceremoniously down Jackson's cheek. *Oh God, she was a nurse in a war zone like the ones I served with. One of those sacrificing special angels. Should I ask about Cathy? See if he knows her. No, with her a nurse, it's not a good time.* "Sorry to bring it up." Frank ran a finger along the glass. "You can see your love for each other in the photo."

Jackson took the picture and returned it to the table. "It's okay. I keep it next to my bed to remember the happy times."

"That tells me a lot." *I miss my parents too. We're both alone. It sucks.*

Harry strolled into the building, a small green duffle bag slung over his shoulder.

Jackson eyeballed him. "Thought you were staying with your wife?"

"I haven't seen you in over nine months." Harry walked to Jackson's bunk with a cheeky grin. "You were so out of it the last time your sorry ass didn't even know I was in the room. You're my best friend. I'm worried about you. Gabby understands."

Jackson dog-eared a page corner, closed his book, and laid it on his table. "You're here for the same reason as Frank, to make sure everything's okay. Right?"

Frank nodded but kept his mouth shut. He wanted to watch Jackson's response to Harry.

"Yeah." Harry rubbed his chin. "Pretty much."

"I'm fine, Harry," Jackson insisted.

"I can tell. You're back to your old self. I have to reassure myself for my peace of mind, okay. Wanna see my foot?"

"What foot, the left or the right one?" Jackson held up his finger. "Oh, you mean the plastic one."

"Funny." Harry tossed his bag on the bunk next to Jackson. He changed into a pair of red shorts and a white t-shirt, then removed his prosthetic foot and waved it in the air.

Coffee poured from Jackson's nose. "Your stump looks better than my back."

Harry grinned. "You're right. At least I can cover mine up, you goofball."

"I can too. With a shirt." Jackson flexed his right arm. "No bare-chested posing at the beach for me, showing off my beautiful muscles. You can hop around on one foot and drive the women wild with your fur-covered chest, Mr. Woolly Bear."

"Chicken legs!" Harry flapped his arms like wings. "Bok, bok, bokok!"

"Aren't you the funny one tonight." Jackson shook his head.

Harry pointed at Jackson's mug. "Got any more of that coffee?"

"Yeah, plenty. The cups are in the cabinet. Are you going to put that foot on or hop over there and back? The coffee won't stay in the cup. It'll spill all over my clean floor. I just mopped it."

"Brat." Harry strapped on his foot.

As Harry walked back, Frank watched him carefully.

Jackson beat him to it by saying what Frank was thinking. "No limp?"

Harry set his coffee cup on his table. "Nope. Been working on that in rehab. Got it licked."

"Noticed. I wish I could've been there for you."

"I know. We could've helped each other."

"Yeah, things would've gone better if I had you to lean on for support." Jackson swung his legs off his bunk and stood.

Harry threw his arms around Jackson in a tight hug. Jackson wrapped his arms around Harry. Time stood still until Harry backed away first.

Frank knew being this close again in semi-privacy meant a lot to both men. He looked over at Chief, who was smiling from ear to ear. "You're quiet," he whispered.

"Not my place to join in," Chief whispered back, returning to his *Popular Mechanics* magazine.

Jackson fiddled with the St. John's medal around his neck. "I missed you so much."

"Same here. I was so worried. Dr. Howard called me after he talked to Dr. Rose. I wanted to see you. I couldn't take the chance with CID following us and tapping our phones."

"Figured they had you under surveillance." Jackson sat on his bunk. "Why'd they stop?"

Harry plopped down on his bunk. "Gabby asked the lawyer at the paper for help. He filed a cease and desist order in federal court since the Army kept infringing on our fourth amendment rights. After the order went into effect, we received a written apology from the Secretary of the Army. Since I lost my foot, they didn't want the bad press. Good idea going through my doctor at the VA to keep me informed on your progress."

Jackson cocked his head in confusion. "Wasn't my idea."

Frank sat next to Harry. "It was mine. I figured you should know."

"Thanks so much for saving his life." Harry held out his hand.

Frank took it in a tight grip then felt something hard and cold between their palms. He released Harry's hand and held up a silver chain. Dangling on the end was a St. Michael's medal. "What's this?"

"A token of my friendship. JJ gave us ones like it after the camp. Since you joined our little club, I had one engraved with your name."

Jackson smiled. "Nice touch. I agree with you."

I'm a member of the family now. "Thank you." *It means more than you'll ever know. I hate being alone.* Frank flipped the chain around his neck. "I just did my job. It still floors me that someone can break the unbreakable rules and override a doctor's recommendation, who, by regulation, can't be overridden. That's not supposed to happen."

Harry crossed his arms over his chest. "Well, it did. JJ almost died because of it."

"I'll keep harping on the subject with my superiors until I get an answer as to why." Frank tucked the medal under his t-shirt.

Jackson sighed. "Let's drop this conversation. There's nothing we can do about it anyway."

"True," Harry admitted.

"Do me a favor, Harry?"

"Anything? Name it." Harry grinned as Jackson pulled electric hair clippers from the shelf above his bunk. "Do you want it the same as always?"

"Yep. Why change now? I've had the same haircut since I was nine years old."

"Just like your dad. Okay, one Marine regulation high and tight coming up." Harry plugged the clippers into the wall socket.

Jackson grabbed a folding chair and a towel from the hamper. He placed the chair in front of Harry and sat with the towel around his neck.

Frank watched the interactions closely. Their humor was infectious. He felt happier being around them. This was much better than being in his apartment.

Harry gripped Jackson's shoulder. "You've gone gray."

Jackson vehemently shook his head. "No, I haven't. My hair's still blond."

Frank agreed with Harry. Jackson's hair was definitely a dark steel gray. But why spoil the fun.

"Yeah, grayish blond." Harry chuckled. "Too much stress from almost dying twice in a year."

"I'll agree with the dying part. Not the color of my hair."

"Okay, it's blond. Only in your mind," Harry muttered under his breath.

"I heard that," Jackson replied cheekily.

"Heard what? You're hallucinating. Maybe you're still having mental problems. I didn't hear anything." Harry turned on the clippers.

"Right. Only in my mind and your dreams, woolly bear."

Harry jerked up the clippers and burst out laughing.

"Why'd you stop?"

"Didn't want to cut a bald streak across your head."

Frank couldn't hold back his laughter, leaning back on his bunk and holding onto his stomach. These two were hilarious. They should sell tickets to their act as a comedy show. He'd love to see Jackson with a bald streak in the middle of his head.

"Oh…okay. Get control of yourself and finish." Jackson clapped his hands. "Chop, chop."

"Hush up, or I'll make you look funny." Harry hit the on/off switch several times.

Jackson shut up as Harry buzzed the top of his head.

"Done. Check it," Harry said, wiping the blades with a towel.

Jackson ran a hand across his head. The sides were nearly shaved with a quarter-inch of hair on top. "Perfect."

"Was there any doubt? Are you ready for bed, or do you wanna stay up for a while longer?"

Jackson pulled down the quilt on his bunk. "Consider lights out called. I have a lot of work to do tomorrow. You get to be a lazy ass."

"Funny." Harry nodded. "You're right. I get to watch you work."

Harry and Frank laughed as they lay down on their bunks. Chief remained so quiet during the shenanigans Frank forgot about him. He'd already turned off his bedside light and retired for the night with his blanket over his head.

"Shut off the coffee pot, JJ, since most of it's in your stomach." Harry pulled his blanket over his head.

"Whatever." Jackson flipped the switch on the coffee pot then turned off the lights. Darkness shrouded the room in shadows. A few seconds later, he yelled, "Ouch!"

Frank threw off his blanket and started to get out of bed to grab his medical bag under his bunk. He'd heard the crunch. It sounded like Jackson just broke a toe. "Are you okay, Jackson?"

"Yeah, go to sleep," Jackson muttered painfully under his breath.

I bet that toe looks like a black balloon in the morning. Frank retrieved his blanket. He considered how Jackson's foot might benefit from him taping the broken toe to the toe next to it. Tired of being poked by doctors, Jackson probably wouldn't tell him, even if it was broken. Why not get some sleep and see if Jackson limps in the morning?

CHAPTER 22

July 1, 1973
Double M Ranch
Beaver Creek, MT

At 0510 hours, Frank heard a strange noise. It sounded like a small engine revving at high speed. He looked over at Jackson's made-up empty bunk so military-tight you could bounce a quarter off the quilt. It even had tucked-in hospital corners. "Where'd he go?" *I hope he didn't have a nightmare and sneak out. Green Berets are famous for that under the cover of darkness.*

Harry sat up, rubbing his eyes. "I was thinking the same thing."

"What's that sound? It's coming from the other room."

Frank and Harry got up and opened the old foreman's room door. A few feet away under a window was a sweaty Jackson in shorts, a t-shirt, and sneakers running full out on an electric treadmill. They walked around him, observing his technique.

Frank noticed Jackson wasn't limping. *Guess he didn't break a toe. I bet it's bruised, swollen, and painful.*

"Your running style's a lot smoother since you've gained weight. In 'Nam, it was choppy and slow." Harry glanced at his watch. "How far and how fast?"

Jackson panted with each quick, long stride. "Six miles in thirty minutes."

"A five-minute mile. Excellent."

"Yeah, I thought so. Haven't done a five-minute mile since I was on the high school track team and training all the time."

Finished with his run, Jackson hopped off the treadmill, grabbed a towel, and dried the sweat from his face and head. He sat on the weight bench. "One of you wanna spot me?"

The first to move, Harry stood behind the suspended bar with four black twenty-five-pound Olympic bumper weight plates on each side. "What did you start with?"

Frank scribbled notes in his black notebook. This was unexpected. He could only bench press about one-fifty at the base gym. But he really didn't push himself hard either. All he needed to do was pass the Army physical fitness test, not ace it.

"Just the empty bar," Jackson replied. He grabbed the bar, pushed it above his face, and brought it down to his chest.

"Take it easy. There's two hundred pounds on the bar. It weighs more than you do."

"Harry, can it! Your job is to keep me from dropping it on my neck. I don't think Frank wants to do an emergency tracheostomy with my knife and his pen."

Frank didn't want to think about doing that in this dust-filled room. Considering they were on a cattle ranch with who knows what ground into the wood plank floor, he wouldn't even attempt it except in an absolute emergency. He watched Jackson's herculean effort as he grunted through four sets of ten bench presses.

Then Jackson stood and removed fifty pounds from the bar. He pushed it over his head and settled it across his shoulders.

Harry stood next to him. "Be careful, JJ."

"Harry, I'm trying to concentrate. Make sure I don't topple over. I've got this."

Jackson squatted four sets of ten with 150 pounds on the bar.

Frank's eyes widened. "That's impressive for someone who six months ago could barely walk and had skinny sticks for legs."

Jackson ignored him and did fifty arm curls.

Harry flexed his arm. "Look at his biceps. They look like bowling balls."

Frank flexed his right arm then quit in embarrassment, dropping his hand back to his notebook. His bicep looked nothing like Jackson's, more like a puny teenager's.

Finished with that exercise, Jackson wrapped his hands and pulled on the boxing gloves. Circling the eighty-pound well-used black Everlast heavy bag with duct tape wrapped around the center, he used lateral movement to set up his punches. He balanced on his toes, transferring weight from one foot to the other—using his legs to generate powerful punches at different ranges. Elbows in and hands up while moving. Ready to react as if facing an opponent.

Wow! Frank logged everything in his notebook. As a former boxer in high school, Frank knew this was an excellent way to remove stress, as a physically exhausting, aggressive activity, demanding total concentration. It also allowed Jackson to pound out his frustrations in a constructive manner instead of a destructive one.

But well on his way to recovery, Jackson was perfecting his boxing and punching technique, along with his power and overall coordination, which were now excellent, sharply honed, and a contributing factor to his fitness level. Frank had to discuss this method with his psychiatrist friend. Jackson's transformation was amazing. He might even write a paper for a medical journal about Jackson's recovery and the horse's role in it. Of course, with a *nom de guerre* to keep Jackson safe.

Chief came in and grabbed a pair of focus mitts.

Jackson bobbed and weaved as he moved around Chief, who raised or lowered a pad for him to hit. Chief punched, making Jackson evade, pursue, and cut angles. Sharpening his boxing skills further. Each four-minute round timed with the wall clock. Five in total with a minute rest in between.

Jackson pulled off the gloves and switched to a black speed bag. Frank watched Jackson start slowly in a right-right-left-left rhythmic circular motion with his wrapped fists, repeating it, going faster and faster until the bag became a blur. His hand-eye coordination seemed nearly perfect. And last, Jackson did three hundred crunches on the floor.

Frank winced watching that, but he didn't have a muscular abdomen like Jackson either. While not fat, he didn't have an athletic body. He looked like a tall, lanky teenager with old eyes from the hazards of duty in a war zone. Jackson's eyes still held that same aged war zone look in the depths.

Chief handed Jackson a red plastic cup. Frank glanced over at the liquid inside. It was pink, thick, and smelled berryish. Protein drink? That explained the muscle growth and strength gains.

Jackson grimaced, wiping sweat from his forehead with a towel. "Strawberry's not any better than the chocolate." He gulped down the contents and headed into the main living quarters, showing his disgust by smacking his lips. "I need coffee to wash the aftertaste out of my mouth."

Protein drink. That crap tastes terrible. Frank scribbled that in his notebook then joined Harry in the doorway as Jackson poured black liquid from the coffee pot into his mug. *How can he drink that nasty stuff?*

"You do that every morning?" Harry fiddled with the laces of a boxing glove. "You look more like a boxer than a cowboy."

Jackson smiled as he pulled a set of clean clothes out of the community dresser. "Yep. Worked up to it the last few months."

"No wonder you look so good. I'm impressed." Harry looked at Frank, who nodded vigorously. "And the doc is too."

You got that right. Frank leaned against the jamb, wondering what Jackson would do next. Surely he was done with his workout now. That was more work in less than two hours than Frank did at the base gym in an entire week.

"Thanks. I'm headed to the shower unless someone wants to go first. My first stop is the foaling barn to check on Lady, then take care of Bandit if you want to come along."

"Not me. I'm hightailing it to the guesthouse before Gabby divorces me. I'll catch you at breakfast. You're right. You need a shower, my stinky friend."

"But it's a good, honest stink. Candy ass."

Harry's lip bulged out in a hurt look, but he couldn't hold it. He threw the boxing glove at Jackson. It missed and skidded across the floor. Harry grabbed his bag and left the bunkhouse.

Frank pointed at the bathroom. "I'll only be a few minutes if you can wait?"

"Sure. Go ahead." Jackson held up his mug. "I'll drink coffee while you drain the hot water tank."

"You and your coffee." *Yuk.* "Be out in a few." Frank grabbed his clothes from his messy bunk. He took a quick shower, shaved, and dressed.

Jackson looked at his watch when Frank exited the bathroom.

What's that mean? Frank poured himself a cup of coffee. *Was he timing me? Why? It's not like I took forever. I was done in fifteen minutes.*

After grabbing a fresh towel from the wall rack, Jackson disappeared into the bathroom.

Frank poured himself a cup of coffee then added enough dry creamer and sugar to dilute and flavor the coffee. He couldn't drink Jackson's ultra-strong brew any other way.

As he brought the cup to his mouth, Jackson exited the bathroom. He dumped his dirty clothes in the hamper, put on his cowboy hat, grabbed his rifle, and left the bunkhouse.

Ten minutes. I couldn't even finish my coffee. Frank ran to catch up. He eyed the 30-30 lever-action Winchester Jackson had propped on his shoulder. "Why are you carrying the rifle?"

"The wolves are around at dawn. I bring it with me to the barn."

"The wolves are that bad?" *Never seen a live wolf. Only pictures of them in Natural Geographic or on TV. Hope we see one but far, far away.*

"Sometimes." Jackson chuckled. "Compliments of the US Government."

"Huh?" *What's he mean by that?*

"The Forest Service transplanted a bunch at Yellowstone a few years ago. Except they don't stay in Yellowstone. They're more trouble than the mountain lions. They run in packs, find their own territory, and take down our livestock. It's a problem with no predators other than us with rifles to keep them thinned out. You heard them howling last night, right?"

I did, but Jackson didn't even move except to breathe. Frank stared at him. "I thought you were asleep."

"I was. I woke up when I heard the noise. They were far away, so I went back to sleep."

"How'd you get familiar so quickly with ranch life?"

Jackson pointed at the barn with his rifle muzzle. "Aunt Sara wanted to stop moving from base to base with their kids. Uncle Manny wanted a cattle ranch. A manager ran the place until he retired. Uncle Manny took his leaves while his kids were out of school. Dad and I trailered my horse from Pendleton here every summer until we retired him. Uncle Manny made sure I had a horse to ride after that. I spent many an hour in these pastures tending the cattle. This was my go-to place during breaks from West Point and on leave until I married Carolyn. She liked JFK. He liked the Green Berets. She came looking for one and hooked me. It was only a few months before my first deployment to 'Nam. Bad choice and an even worse mistake on my part. That's a whole other story for another time, and not one I want to talk about."

"That makes sense. Where'd you sleep?"

"The bunkhouse. It gave me more independence from Aunt Sara's prying eyes. She could always tell when Jim and I were up to something. It was more like camping out."

Hmmm. Now Frank knew why Jackson felt so comfortable here. He grew up on the ranch. "Which bunk?"

"The same one I'm occupying now. The ones at the end give you more room and the wall space to hang things." Jackson rolled his eyes. "Bet you thought I wanted it for the corner to sit in."

He anticipated my next question. "Yeah, I did. Mikey told me you were still pretty out of it when you guys arrived."

"I was, but I always sleep in that bunk."

Frank stopped Jackson with a hand on his arm. "Do they know?" It explained their confusion on why Jackson insisted to the point of near panic on a specific bunk.

Jackson shook his head. "No, it's never come up." He started walking toward their destination on the well-worn path. "They probably wondered how I know the ranch so well."

"I don't know about them, but I did." *Scratch that question off my list.*

"Stop, Frank. There are fresh scratches on the door."

Frank did as ordered. He didn't want to become an early morning breakfast for a snarling wolf.

Jackson brought the rifle to his shoulder with his finger on the trigger. He eased around the corner and returned. "Good, they're gone." He unlocked the door and went inside. "You okay, girl?"

Lady shook her head over the stall door with a loud snort.

Frank cocked his head. "What's that mean?"

"She's hungry." Jackson stuck his palm under her nose. He offered her peppermints that way. Lady chewed the treats as he opened the turnout door at the back of the stall. She trotted into the pasture with her foal close on her heels.

Jackson pitched a load of dirty straw into the wheelbarrow then leaned on the pitchfork. "You can always help out."

Frank draped his upper body over the stall door. "That's okay. I'll watch you work. I have no idea what you're doing. I'd make a fool out of myself if I slipped in manure."

"Thanks a lot," Jackson huffed. "Mikey's more help than you."

With half of his chores completed, Jackson headed to the main barn. Even before they went inside, Bandit's forceful whinny echoed through the door. Jackson hung his hat on a nail near the tack room.

Bandit bobbed his head over the stall door and stomped his front feet.

"Guess you're hungry too, huh?" Jackson fed the horse a handful of peppermints.

Bandit jerked his head up. Before Jackson could get out of the way, Bandit's head landed on Jackson's. Slobber dripped on Jackson's head and ran down his neck.

Frank leaned against the wall and laughed.

Jackson wiped off the candy goo with a towel. "Glad you think this is funny."

Unable to talk, Frank laughed even harder. It was hilarious.

Full of spunk, Bandit bucked, bit, kicked up his rear feet, nibbled on Jackson's hair, and reared. To muck the stall, Jackson opened the turnout door. He flapped his arms to force the horse into the pasture.

Later, bringing him inside was a lot more manageable. Bandit just walked up to his full feed bucket and shoved his hungry mouth in it. The distraction gave Jackson enough time to groom him until his coat glistened such a glowing bright red Frank could only compare it to the cherry-red Chevy Corvette he wanted as a teenager but couldn't afford.

When Jackson turned Bandit out into the pasture, the hard-headed horse neighed and stomped his front feet like a five-year-old child throwing a tantrum. He reared, bucked, then trotted to the fence and whinnied.

"Didn't you just get enough of my attention?" Jackson fed him peppermints to quiet him down. Then he glanced at his watch and grabbed Frank by the arm. "Let's go. Aunt Sara's as much a Marine as Uncle Manny. She doesn't understand the concept of being late to any family function. Breakfast is a family function." He double-timed to the house with Frank at his side.

Frank looked back at the barn. "Why'd you put Bandit in the pasture instead of his stall?"

"Since this is your first time on a ranch, I'll give you a pointer. Horses crap a lot. I'm coming back after breakfast to saddle him. Why make more work for myself this afternoon?"

"Good point. Now I know how much work it is to take care of a horse. I can tell he made a difference in your recovery. You're right, he's more like a dog than a horse. He shoved his head into your chest first thing. When he plopped his head on yours, that was funny." *I'm sure I sprained something laughing so hard.*

"He does things like that all the time. That damn horse would grab my hat if I didn't take it off. He tore up my first one pulling it from my head and shaking it like a toy."

Frank pointed at Jackson's shirt. "He slobbered all over you."

Jackson brushed at the hardened spots. "Yeah, Bandit does that when he shakes his head. It was on purpose if you didn't notice."

I did, but it's funnier to act totally ignorant and watch his expression.

Harry and Gabby were at the table with their son drinking a bottle in his mother's arms.

Jackson kissed the baby's forehead. "I love you." He returned from the kitchen with a coffee cup and sat next to Harry.

Harry sniffed the air. "You smell better."

Jackson elbowed his friend in the ribs. "Feels like jello."

Harry returned the favor. "Ouch!" He rubbed his elbow. "Is that a concrete wall under your shirt? Where's the doctor? I need a cast."

"There goes the unit drama queen." Jackson put two fingers behind Harry's head like rabbit ears.

Gabby rolled her eyes as she held her son. "Better you than me, Jackson. I'm ready for a break. My sides hurt constantly."

Chief's eyes crinkled at the corners as he tried not to laugh.

Mangus shook his head.

Frank leaned back in his chair. "Leave me out of this." *But I love watching.*

Sara tittered like a schoolgirl in the doorway. "I'm glad Harry's back in your life. He makes you whole."

"Let me help you, Aunt Sara." Jackson stood, took the two serving platters from her, and placed them on the table.

"Thank you. You're such a gentleman." Sara sat in her chair next to Mangus.

Jackson sat in his chair, then pulled four pancakes onto his plate and filled a bowl with eggs.

Frank picked up a mason jar. "What's with the honey? I've never seen anyone pour honey on pancakes before. Is that a ranch thing?"

Jackson paused with the bite halfway to his mouth. "Ever since the POW camp, store-bought syrup upsets my stomach. I use honey instead."

"Another one of your quirks. I'll add it to my notes."

"Whatever." Jackson pulled another stack of pancakes onto his plate.

Frank scratched his head. "How much are you going to eat?"

"Make up your mind. When I first met you, it was *you're too skinny.* Now you're questioning my eating habits."

"No, I love it. I'll note that too."

Jackson rolled his eyes. "Doctors."

Yep. Always for my special patients. Frank watched Jackson carry his empty plate to the kitchen and return with the newspaper. He thought Jackson ate too fast. It was probably an internal, unconscious overreaction to being starved nearly to death in the POW camp.

Jackson read until Frank finished his meal, folded the paper then picked up his rifle and hat next to the door.

Outside the house, Frank hit Jackson with his best command stare. He knew it paled in comparison to the ones Jackson used on him. "What is it with you two?"

"What do you mean…us two?"

"You and Harry. You keep ribbing the crap out of each other."

"Oh, that." Jackson nonchalantly flipped the rifle over his shoulder. "We've done that since Special Forces training. Harry pulled pranks in the barracks. I always joined him. I joke around with the guys, and, yes, I did it in 'Nam. Never on duty. On duty, I was as serious as a heart attack. The men hated me because I didn't give them any slack. All bets were off when the day was over. It relieved the pressure for all of us. Especially me after the camp. I started a lot of it." He raised an eyebrow. "Is there a problem?"

"No. It's nice to see how close you are to your friends to say the things you do to make each other laugh. In the hospital, I only saw a man who felt betrayed by the Army." *I love seeing him so happy.*

"True. It's nice to laugh again without remembering all the pain."

At the barn, Jackson saddled a black and white pinto named Duke and handed the reins to Frank. Bandit stood still as Jackson put on the bridle, cinched up the saddle, and placed his rifle in the scabbard. With his horse ready to go, Jackson strapped on his chaps, pulled on his riding gloves, and secured his hunting knife to his belt.

Frank patted his foot. "Where's your canteen? It's ninety degrees outside. Didn't you learn your lesson about dehydration?"

"Yeah. No more enemas." Jackson grabbed two round, cloth-covered canteens from the tack room. He filled them in the sink, handed one to Frank, and hung the other one on his saddle horn.

"We can go now," Frank said.

Jackson led Bandit to the road. He stood waiting for Frank to catch up. The second Duke's hooves touched the gravel, Jackson slipped his left foot in the stirrup and in one fluid motion, mounted his horse.

Frank took a little longer. He hopped, jumped, and stretched to climb onto Duke. A pained grimace crossed his face as he swung his right leg over the saddle. This really hurt. It stretched his thighs and crotch to a breaking point. *I should've washed these new blue jeans first. They're stiff.*

"Hurry up, slowpoke. We're burning daylight. I have a lot of ground to cover." Jackson sidestepped Bandit in a large circle around Duke, showing off.

"Oh, hush up. I'm a doctor, not a cowboy. I may be out of my element on the back of a horse. But I'm a tenacious bulldog, prideful and stubborn. I will follow you around all day. No way am I backing out of your tour." Frank spurred his horse forward behind Jackson. "Ouch! The saddle is rubbing my ass and balls. What have I gotten myself into?" *Shit! It's going to be a long day.* Before the day was over, he'd need an infusion of morphine to numb the flames in the lower half of his body. But well worth it to spend time with his friend.

Jackson kicked open the latch on the north pasture gate from his horse and rode across the field.

Frank struggled to keep up. He held onto the horn to stay in the saddle as he bounced around like a ball. And those hurt as well.

An hour after they left the barn, Jackson opened the west pasture gate. He turned to Frank behind him. "I hope we don't find any newborn calves downed by the wolves. I found one yesterday. It was messy. Parts were scattered everywhere. They like babies because they're defenseless."

Frank cringed, feeling a shiver run down his spine. "That's horrible." *And disgusting. What would they do to us?*

Even though they didn't find any calves, a young steer wasn't so lucky.

Jackson pointed at the half-eaten carcass, covered in flies. "That's what the wolves do. It costs the ranch every time we lose a cow. They're averaging about forty dollars per every one hundred pounds this year. This guy was about nine hundred pounds. He would've pushed twelve hundred when he was ready for market. Do the math. That's four to five hundred dollars lost right here. Between the wolves and mountain lions, we lose about a dozen head a year. That's about a six-thousand-dollar loss on average."

"Now I understand how the wolves are a problem." *And we're smaller than a cow. What would they do to us? Stupid question. Kill us then eat us.*

To emphasize his point, Jackson patted his rifle scabbard. "If a pack can take down a nine-hundred-pound steer, think of what they can do if they catch you in the open without a gun. Bad news."

Frank pulled back on the reins when Duke stepped forward. "Whoa, boy. What are you going to do with the body?"

"When we head in, I'll send a ranch hand out here with the tractor. The only way to keep the flies and scavengers away from the house is to bury it in the pasture."

Frank shuddered. Luckily they were upwind of the carcass. He knew that awful smell from his time at the 95th Evac. While most of the soldiers transported to the hospital were alive, dying, or freshly dead. There were those few times the hospital was a transfer point for those found a few days or weeks later. Even the rubber-lined, zippered body bags didn't stop the nauseatingly pungent death stench of a decomposing body from drifting across the compound. You could never forget that smell. It was recognizable anywhere.

The shadows grew shorter as the sun climbed overhead while Jackson checked the horses in the south pasture. With them all accounted for, he checked the fence lines for breaks. All Frank did was sit on his horse and follow him around. He had no idea how to mend a barbed-wire fence. The rusted crap reminded him of the concertina wire that surrounded the 95th Evac.

At each stop, Jackson pointed out various locations. The clearing where he saw his first bear. His secret fishing pond. The log fort he built with Jim. The creek where they found the arrowheads in his collection.

Frank was amazed at the richness of Jackson's childhood experiences. With his father working as a surgeon at the local hospital and on-call for two others, they didn't take many vacations. Most of Frank's summers were spent at the local pool or playing with his friends. On those few trips his family did, they didn't go far. His father always wanted to be within driving distance of the hospitals if they needed him. It made him angry the Army brass wanted to railroad Jackson into the grave on trumped-up charges. Jackson had so much more to give to society and his country as a man and a soldier.

"Where are we going?" Frank asked as he rode beside Jackson as they headed toward a stand of trees in the south pasture.

"You'll see." Jackson pulled his horse up next to a large oak tree with a weathered wooden sign nailed to the trunk.

Frank looked at the name engraved in the wood. Taco – Born 1940 - Died 1960. "Who's Taco?"

"A quarter horse my dad bought me after he returned from World War II. I won most of my riding competitions with him. He bowed a tendon while I was in high school, so we retired him, and he lived the rest of his life here." Jackson patted the sign. "Hey, buddy. I'm here for my weekly visit."

Frank lifted himself in his stirrups to ease the pressure on his balls. "How big is this ranch?"

"About ten thousand acres of rolling hills. I bet it feels huge on the back of a horse."

Frank rubbed between his legs. *Shit, this really hurts.*

As the midday sun passed thirty-eight degrees toward the western horizon, around 1430 hours, Jackson and Frank approached the main house along the fence line. A passing truck backfired. A bay horse near the barn reared. The rider, one of the Double M ranch hands, flipped backward out of the saddle.

The rider got up, dusting himself off with his hands as the horse bolted, running straight for the open main gate and the highway.

Jackson spurred Bandit into a full gallop, leaving a trail of scattered dirt and gravel in their wake. As they flew along the gravel road, Jackson flipped the rope loop in a circle over his head several times. It left his hand and landed around the neck of the running horse. The noose tightened then the horse slowed, allowing Bandit to catch up. They came to a stop together. Jackson turned Bandit with the panting horse walking behind them.

Frank sat on Duke with his mouth wide open. It was amazing. He'd only seen things like this in the movies or TV. This gave him a new appreciation of Jackson's skill and how hard he worked to get his life back in order or some semblance of it.

Jackson pulled back on the reins next to Frank. "Whoa, boy." Bandit stopped. Jackson handed the rope to one of the ranch hands. "Like the show, Frank?"

"Sure did. You're a natural. If you hadn't gone into the Army, you would've wound up a cowboy on this ranch working for your godfather."

"Maybe or after the Olympics, I would've joined FEI and made a name for myself on the professional jumping and dressage circuit. But we'll never know." Jackson hung the coiled rope Larry gave him on his saddle horn. "I have to check the east pasture. You coming along, Frank?"

Frank slid off Duke and handed the reins to a waiting ranch hand. He couldn't take the pain any longer. His balls, thighs, and butt were a five-alarm fire, and he needed a painkiller to put out the flames.

"Guess not." Jackson rode off.

After dinner that evening, they all sat in the living room, drinking coffee and discussing current events. Except for Frank—he soaked his highly medicated, saddle sore body in a warm bathtub.

"Something wrong, Frank?" Jackson faked a limp across the living room.

Frank, in his pajamas, glared at Jackson from the recliner with his feet propped up and an ice pack between his legs. "You think this is funny, don't you?"

"Yes, since you're the doctor, and I'm not the one doing the limping."

"Rub it in, funny guy."

"Sure. How about going back out with me tomorrow?" Jackson poked Frank in the shoulder. "You'll be so numb you won't feel a thing."

Frank groaned, trying to shift himself into a more comfortable position and not finding one. "Ouch…Ouch…And I got myself into this by coming here…hey, Jackson."

Jackson turned from the bookshelf with a paperback book in his hand. "Yeah, need something, gimpy?"

"Very funny." *I'll never live this down.* "Would you mind getting me a beer?"

"Sure." Jackson paused for a moment with a serious look. "Anything else?"

"No, just the beer." *Maybe it'll help dull this pain. The aspirin with codeine isn't working.*

CHAPTER 23

1900 Hours
July 4, 1973
Double M Ranch
Beaver Creek, MT

Frank threw his empty beer bottle into a nearby trash can and grabbed another from the ice chest on one of the red, white, and blue bunted folding picnic tables. General Malone didn't cut corners on the ranch's holiday BBQ. He bought expensive beer and lots of it. The meal…fire-grilled steaks and hamburgers, courtesy of one of the ranch steers. They were tender, juicy, and delicious. Not like bland store-bought beef, dressed up with a slathering of steak sauce.

The ranch hands with their families brought homemade sides of baked beans, coleslaw, potato salad, and bags of chips. Besides the beer were pitchers of lemonade, cherry Kool-Aid, and iced tea. Sara Malone added ice-cold watermelon and homemade ice cream. It had been a long time since Frank had either of those two foods. Not since his childhood.

People stood around talking and munching. The trash cans filled up quickly with used paper plates, bowls, plastic utensils, and cups.

Frank settled into a lawn chair off to one side of the crowd.

To Frank's amazement, Jackson ate enough food for three people, something he loved seeing. His friend had moved on with his life. Another thing Frank loved, since most of the men working here were war veterans, General Malone banned all fireworks. He didn't want a repeat of last year, hiding under his lawn chair instead of sitting in it.

Frank drank a long draught from his bottle, relaxing in his chair watching the children playing games on the grass – horseshoes, corn hole, croquet, ring toss, red light/green light, and tag. Every once in a while, Jackson played a game with them then disappeared, helping Sara keep the food and drinks going and clean up the mess.

Jackson came up from behind and placed a hand on Frank's arm. "Can I talk to you for a moment?"

Frank straightened at the serious tone in Jackson's voice. "Sure."

"In private." Jackson nodded at the bunkhouse.

"Okay." Frank stood, taking a swig from his bottle. *Must be important. Maybe he had a flashback and wants to talk about it.* He followed Jackson into the bunkhouse.

Jackson shut the door and leaned on the dresser. "Are you okay, Frank?"

Frank drained the rest of the bottle and chucked it in the trash can. "Yeah, why do you ask? You're the one who's had a few problems."

"Are you sure?" Jackson retrieved the beer bottle from the trash and set it on the dresser.

"Yeah." Frank stared at the bottle. *Where's he going with this?* "Why?"

"Because I've watched you drink more beer than Harry, Chief, and Bill combined for the last few days. Chief can drink most people under the table. I did some brilliant juggling to get him out of the base drunk tank a few times in 'Nam."

"I'm fine," Frank insisted.

"Again, are you sure? Frank, don't pour yourself into a bottle like I almost did."

Frank paused, counting the number of beers he'd consumed since arriving at the ranch. Forty. He had to admit, eight a day was way more than his usual three to four. And Jackson noticed. Now he was getting lectured about it. "You have my assurances. I'm okay."

"Uh-huh. Do you drink alone, Frank?" Jackson asked.

"Ahh…yes. I'm older than most of the staff at the hospital. I don't have any—"

"Friends. I know the feeling. But it's not just that, and you know it."

"You mean Vietnam."

"Yes. I told you what happened when I got drunk at Gunslinger's Bar at Cam Ranh Bay and alienated my oldest friend. Did Dr. Rose tell you everything about what happened the night before we left for San Diego?"

Frank shook his head. "I have no idea. He caught you drinking in the living room."

"It was more than just that." Jackson took a deep breath and cleared his throat. "Curtis forgot to give me a sedative. So I wanted to test myself to see if my nightmares were gone and failed. I had one and grabbed a bottle of Jack Daniels from the wet bar to forget. I drank so much I thought I heard my dead parents talking to me. I kept seeing dead men and horrendous battles from Vietnam. The POW camp and what they did to me. Do you know what made me stop drinking that night?"

"A flashback?"

Jackson nodded. "Yeah. A bad one. Seeing in full living color the time I found someone I knew from selection training after he blew his brains out with his service pistol after being charged for conduct unbecoming by JAG. He got drunk on duty, and men died. I capped the bottle and poured the rest of the whiskey in my glass down the drain. When I turned around, Curtis was standing in the doorway watching me. You know what he said when I asked him how long he'd been there?"

Frank smiled. "Something prophetic?"

"Kinda. 'Long enough to watch you debate with yourself. I'm relieved you made the right decision.' I was so fucking plastered. We spent the rest of the night in the kitchen talking over coffee while I ate a peanut butter sandwich to settle my stomach and sober up."

"I'm glad you made the right decision. That could have led you down a road you'd never come back from." *And dead within a few weeks due to his recent bout with near organ failure. No way could his traumatized liver take the overload.*

"Exactly." Jackson held up the empty beer bottle. "Are you going down that same road?"

Frank opened his mouth then closed it. Was he going down that road and didn't realize it? The CIA guy, Cain, said the same thing. Called him a stick in the mud with no life other than his career. That couldn't be true. Could it? And that awful recurring nightmare about losing his legs.

"Frank, drinking alone in your apartment could be your way of escaping from Vietnam. The pain. The memories. To hide from the world of so many condemning eyes. Like so many of us who were there. Are you self-medicating? And about to become an alcoholic? I know you've got to be lonely with no one to talk to about what happened to you in Vietnam. You know I understand. I'm still trying to find myself too. Jason once told me, 'You need to find a way to cope with what happened to you in a healthy way. Not a self-destructive one.' That's what I did by focusing on taking care of my horse. And a lot of talking. You need to find your way too."

Frank thought for a moment. That kid still haunted him. So much so he imagined him while taking care of Jackson on that C-130 over the Pacific Ocean. And that recurring nightmare ate at his resolve. It came so often now, even last night. He had to get it off his chest. "Do you want to hear a story?"

Jackson smiled. "Yes." He motioned for Frank to sit on the couch, started a pot of coffee, and sat next to him. "When you're ready, I'm a great listener."

Angel Giacomo

I never thought I'd be the one spilling my guts to him. Isn't life ironic? Who knew Jackson would be the one helping me cope with my nightmares. Not the other way around. He needed to do this. "One day, a kid who looked about fourteen was brought into the OR at the 85th Evac…"

CHAPTER 24

0700 Hours
July 9, 1973
Blanchfield Army Hospital
Ft. Campbell, KY

While Frank waited for the elevator in the hospital lobby on the first floor, he wondered who would meet him at his office. His commanding officer or security. Maybe no one if he got away with his deception. It all depended on whether anyone, namely CID, FBI, or the CIA, had checked into his family history during his absence.

Nothing other than his parents' names were documented in his Army records. Most of his close relatives were dead. So if they did, they hit a hellacious dead end. He switched his briefcase back and forth between his hands until the elevator car arrived. Both hands were sweaty. Would someone be there when the doors opened?

Jackson was safe since Frank's travel arrangements were through the Marine Corps in General Malone's name. But the Army might try to catch him in a lie as to his destination, even though he never gave one.

The doors opened to an empty car. After taking a deep breath, he went inside, punched the *three* button, and the elevator car slowly ascended. Now what?

Frank exited the elevator on the third floor to a vacant hallway. He wondered if he was still in 301 or had they moved him back to 312. Or had his stuff been boxed up and placed in storage awaiting his arrest by the base MPs? That would be the first clue.

He stopped at 301. Next to the door, the brass plaque with his name and rank and his key unlocked the door. He breathed a sigh of relief and went inside. The room looked exactly as he left it. His desk was neat with a slight coating of dust on the empty blotter. All of his pictures, awards, and certificates were still on the walls. His white lab coat hung on the rack in the corner. He placed his briefcase on the desk.

"Dr. Howard," said Dr. Gaston's voice behind him.

Frank turned to face Gaston, standing in the doorway. "Sir."

"How's your brother?"

He sounds sincere. They didn't check. Caught by surprise at the question, he improvised. "Better, sir. The surgery went well. He's home

168

now with his wife…Sally and their three kids. They'll call me if anything happens."

"So you don't anticipate a surprise return trip anytime soon?"

"No, sir." *Unless Jackson falls off his damn horse or has a relapse. Or I do. Only a beer on special occasions now. I'll spend more time out of my apartment than in it. Including attending the Alcoholics Anonymous meeting at the VFW hall and spending more time at the gym. I look like a damn couch potato. Jackson was right. I was headed toward alcoholism. Not anymore. It took a veteran recovering from his problems to help me see mine. Who knew it would be that…calming. We had a good give and take. He learned about my nightmares, and I learned about some of his. That POW camp commander screwed Jackson up good. And the Army made it worse. I wouldn't want to fight that hard to regain some normalcy in my life.*

"Good. Are you ready to get back to work?"

"Yes, sir." Frank pulled off his class A uniform jacket, hung it on the rack, grabbed his white lab coat, and put it on. He was ready. "What's first, sir?"

Gaston pointed at the hall. "A soldier came into the emergency room about an hour ago after slamming his right middle finger in the breech block of a 155 Howitzer. His buddies found the finger and wrapped it in ice. I know you just got here. Do you feel up to a few hours in surgery sewing it back on?"

Frank smiled. He would type up his medical report on Jackson in the privacy of his apartment. "Lead on, sir. I sure am. Let's go look at the x-rays." *Sounds like a challenge. I'm ready for it.*

As they left the office together, Gaston handed Frank a folded piece of white paper.

"What's this?" Frank asked, wondering if he should read it now.

Gaston smiled. "A copy of my letter as your immediate superior officer to the upcoming Lieutenant Colonel's promotion board recommending you for advancement. You're way too good of a surgeon to keep toiling around as a major. I want you to take my spot here when I retire next year."

Guess he's totally convinced I don't know anything about Jackson. I'll take it. More rank, more pay, and more authority. Frank tucked the letter into his lab coat pocket. Even though he was curious about what Gaston wrote, he'd read it later. He had a job to do.

1800 Hours
July 9, 1973
Del Ray Apartments
Apartment 214
Oak Grove, KY

Frank took off his uniform and hung it in the closet. He was tired but a good kind of tired after saving the young man's finger. He'd see the soldier again tomorrow during rounds. After a check for infection, he'd sign his patient's hospital release papers and send him back to his barracks. As long as he followed Frank's post-surgical orders to the letter and took his antibiotics, he should regain full use of his finger with time and rehab.

This was unlike his time at the 95th Evac, where once the patient left the compound, Frank never knew what happened. Did they live or die? Go on to a normal life? Get married? Have children? Did they wind up on the streets homeless or drug addicts? It was better not to think about it.

To make use of his time while his frozen Salisbury Steak, corn, mashed potatoes, and brownie TV dinner heated in the oven, Frank sat at his table and opened his black notebook. He needed to transcribe his notes about Jackson's recovery into a legible document. His penmanship was horrible.

Next, he needed to start his paper on Jackson's inventive methods and write an official medical report to go with the others in his secret hidey-hole. He'd already documented Jackson's physical and mental injuries at the Army's hand. That way, he would be ready for the day when Jackson was finally cleared. And that bastard Hammond got his, both legally and Frank's fist to his bulbous red nose.

After the timer went off, Frank retrieved his dinner and sat at the table. As he ate and read through his notes, he realized something. Here he was about to write about Jackson's incredible recovery against the odds, but the joke was truly on him. Jackson, a broken man whose fate once rested in Frank's hands, had managed to fix Frank himself. Frank hadn't known how much the horrors of Vietnam had shattered his soul until Jackson confronted him with it.

Pushing aside his empty tin tray, Frank turned on his table lamp and started writing. He didn't realize the time until he looked at the digital clock glowing red on the end table next to his recliner. 2215 hours. He needed to get some sleep.

Closing his notebook, Frank smiled. Tomorrow will be another day of surgeries and rounds, but no more war. No more chewed-up bodies. No more endless suffering. No shellings or gunfire. He could relax with his mind clear and spirit revived. Now he could go back to work and focus on what he does best: being a damn good surgeon.

Ironically, Jackson turned into Frank's guardian angel by pointing out his drinking. Then Jackson doubled down by giving Frank an ear to listen and a shoulder to lean on. Jackson turned him around. That's what true friendship and brotherhood are all about, salvation.

Made in the USA
Columbia, SC
25 October 2022

70016364R00096